QUEST
for the
MAGIC KEYS

Quest for the Magic Keys

ISBN 978-0-9888173-1-9

Printed in the United States of America

Visit www.spencernelson.art
spencer@spencernelson.art

With love to my adult children:
Cimarron and Shane
who for years gently pressured me
to finish this book.

Humpty Dumpty
Sat on a Wall
Humpty Dumpty
Had a Great Fall
All the King's Horses
and All the King's Men
Could Not Put Humpty
Together Again*

*English nursery rhyme, probably put to
verse in the late 1700s. It was made famous
in Lewis Carroll's 1872 classic, *Through
the Looking-Glass*, where Humpty was first
described as an egg.

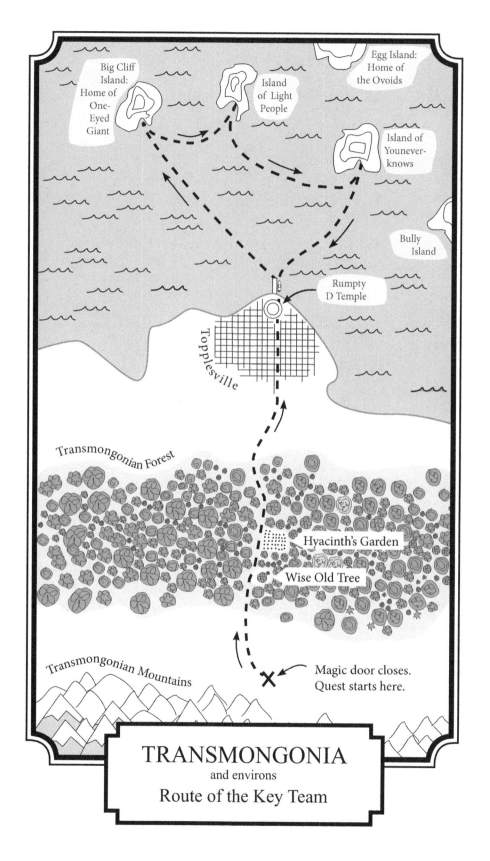

Chapter 1

Cassandra and Shawn

t started as a typical Saturday in Boulder, Colorado, in early June. The clear blue Colorado sky hosted a bright midmorning sun. There was nothing in the pleasant air to indicate that on this day, two seemingly ordinary young people would face great danger and have their lives changed forever.

* * *

Thirteen-year-old Cassandra Solskin—most people called her Cassie— sat with her sketchbook and drawing tools at a patio table behind her Boulder home. An enormous nearby cottonwood tree provided shade. Drawing a unicorn, she found inspiration from a book with pictures of fairies, elves, dragons, various mythical beasts, and, of course, unicorns.

Mom was at a teachers' meeting; Dad was running errands and would be back soon.

Cassie's brother, eleven-year-old Shawn, polished his basketball skills with the aid of a hoop attached to the garage in front.

It was Cassie's turn to create art in back and Shawn's turn to practice basketball in front. At other times, Shawn would be the artistic creator at the patio table while Cassie shot hoops on the driveway.

Both Cassie and Shawn were skilled in the realm of athletics, and each had considerable talent for creating artwork. However, while it might reasonably be assumed they would share their interests, they purposely avoided occupying a creative space at the same time or playing a sport together. Doing so, in their minds, would be collaborating with the enemy.

* * *

Shawn dribbled the ball and occasionally tossed it toward the hoop fastened above the garage door. "Shawn has the ball," he said to an imaginary television audience. "He's dribbling toward the hoop...Oops! Blocked! Still has the ball...see how he fakes out his opponents...what talent! If he's going to win this game, he had better score... seconds left...shoots... bank shot...misses! Three seconds left...another try...it's...in! The crowd goes wild!"

The would-be basketball champ stood still for a moment holding the basketball. A slight smirk of victory appeared on his face for sinking that last shot with just a few fictional seconds remaining.

He walked along the side of the house, peeked around the back corner, and confirmed to himself that his sister was focused on her task—too focused to notice him. He mentally noted her location, returned to the front of the house, and placed himself directly opposite where he calculated Cassie would be on the other side.

He studied the roof. "Missile ready," he said to himself. "Three...two... one...launch!" He threw the ball onto the roof, nearly over the top, and it rolled back. "Oh, missile failure," he said. "Try again."

Taking his time and with considerable concentration, he tossed the ball once more onto the roof with more force. This time it made it over the top and rolled down the other side. He scampered as quickly as he could to the back of the house, but he was not fast enough to see if his projectile would land on the intended target.

It did.

The ball crashed onto Cassie's table with a thud. She issued a shriek likely to be heard throughout the neighborhood. The outcry reached Shawn's ears for sure—much to his delight. Cassie's fear faded in a second, but her anger lingered. "Ohhh, that *brat*," she muttered between her clenched teeth.

Shawn casually walked onto the patio. He faked meekness as he approached his sister. "Oh gee," he said, "it looks like I overshot. Did it land on...did it scare you? Gosh, I'm so sorry." He avoided smiling, which took some effort as he was quite proud of himself.

He picked up the basketball. "Well, I better get back to—"

Cassie grabbed the ball. "Oh, look!" she said. "Big Sister has taken the ball right out of Little Brat's hands! She dodges...she weaves...she fakes... she goes after Little Brat." Cassie pushed the ball at Shawn repeatedly, causing him to back away, holding up his arms to protect himself. "What's the girl up to?" Cassie asked. "What's that she's saying? She's had it with Little Brat? And...what's that? She's going to do *what* to Creepy Little Brat?" She kept pushing the ball at Shawn—sometimes an inch from his face, sometimes an inch from his chest. He flinched with each thrust. She didn't hit Shawn with the ball; she just threatened to.

Her little brother continued backing up.

"Come on," Shawn said. "Stop! I said I'm sorry."

"Oh," Cassie said. "Did you hear that? He's sorry! Oh! And where have we heard *that* before? Well, we—"

Shawn backed into a cylindrical plaster pedestal, about half his height, on top of which rested a decorated clay pot full of flowers. He inadvertently knocked the pedestal over, breaking it in half. The flowerpot fell with it, crashed to the ground, and split into a dozen pieces. Dirt and flowers were scattered across the patio.

Shawn tripped and fell backward on top of the pedestal. Cassie froze in place. She frowned, momentarily fearful Shawn might be injured.

"Are you OK?" she asked as he lay still and groaned for a short while.

"No!" Shawn said. He rolled over onto his hands and knees, rose to his feet, and dusted himself off. His pain was minor, but he grimaced and twisted his body as though it was major.

Cassie came close to apologizing, but that would have let her brother off the hook.

"Now look what you've done," said Shawn as he surveyed the damage.

Cassie's sympathy vanished. "Me?" she said. "You're the one who did that!"

"No, you made me!" said Shawn as he surveyed the damage. "You know you did. And boy, when Dad gets home—you will be *so* busted!"

"No," said Cassie, "*you* will be busted, you little brat. *You* knocked over the flowers. *You* made me get mad in the first place."

She turned and threw the basketball high into the enormous cottonwood tree in their backyard. It came to rest in branches well beyond the reach of either sibling.

"Hey! What did you do that for?" said Shawn. "You're such a…such a—"

Just then, something caught Shawn's eye.

"Look!" he said. "The branches are moving. And the leaves are moving too. Just a little bit, but they're moving…like there's some kind of breeze or something. Am I seeing things?"

"It's not your imagination," said Cassie as she joined her brother in staring at the tree's canopy. "You're right," she said. "It's like there's a breeze, but the wind isn't blowing. Not even slightly."

"Do you think tossing the basketball up there did that?"

"No," said Cassie. "See? Now the whole tree is shaking. The ball wouldn't have done that for sure."

"Weird," said Shawn.

"I know, right?"

"Shhh!" whispered Shawn. He looked around in all directions. "I hear something. Sounds like bells or something."

"Kind of like wind chimes," said Cassie, her voice as low as Shawn's. "Except we don't have wind chimes."

"And the wind's not blowing anyway," said Shawn.

The musical tinkling grew louder.

"It sounds like it's coming from the tree," said Cassie. They both walked into the shadow of the cottonwood. "No, it's not the tree," she said. "It's like, near the tree. Does it seem that way to you?"

"Yeah," said Shawn. "But there's nothing there."

As if to challenge Shawn's observation, a white mist appeared in the air where the mysterious sound seemed to originate. The vapor, barely visible at first, soon became a dense cloud as it revolved with increasing speed, accompanied by the intensifying *tinkle-tinkle* sound. The kids cautiously stepped back a couple of paces from the whirlwind. A mass of thick brown dust replaced the fog and continued spinning. A quiet *whooshhhhhhhh*, like a calm breeze, could be heard. The dust cloud coalesced into gravel-sized pieces that, in turn, formed brick-sized chunks. The spinning ceased as the expanding fragments joined each other and, with a *crunch-clack-crunch*, solidified into—

a doorway.

The wind-chime music faded to silence.

"Oh my gosh!" said Cassie and Shawn together.

The unopened door and the sturdy thick frame surrounding it consisted of dark brown wood decorated with elaborate carvings of flowers, leaves, vines, and abstract shapes that had no meaning.

The kids slowly—very slowly—approached the doorway in silence.

Shawn slowly—very slowly—reached for the door's glistening brass knob.

"Shawn," cautioned Cassie, "don't—"

Shawn paused with his fingers an inch from the knob. He and his sister stood motionless. Fear was in the air.

The knob turned as if on its own, and, accompanied by a *creeeek*, the door began to open slowly.

The kids gasped at the sight before their eyes.

Chapter 2

Grayson

 assie and Shawn quickly retreated from the door. It finally opened to reveal a young man on its far side with a hand on that side's doorknob.

The visitor was a little taller than Cassie, who herself was of average height for a thirteen-year-old girl. (Shawn, being eleven, was about a half-head shorter than his sister.) The visitor appeared to be a shade older than Cassie as well. He wore simple clothing consisting of a light-weight, long-sleeved brown shirt over loose brown slacks. A thick, dark brown belt wrapped around his waist. His shoes, featuring buckles and curled-up toes, added to his elf-like appearance. He had a round hat—a *beanie*—perched on his head. Red and blue stripes radiated out from a white furry ball on the beanie's top. While the visitor's overall attire made him appear out of place as if from another time, his goofy hat—not to mention his pointed ears—made him appear *especially* out of place.

A meadow—*not* Cassie and Shawn's backyard—could be seen behind him through the doorway. A path led from the opening across the lush green grass. Unlike the usual dirt path one would expect to see while hiking in the Colorado high country, it consisted of rust-red cobblestones bordered on each side with bright white flowers. Cassie and Shawn were familiar with the trails in the mountains of Colorado. This was not Colorado.

The young man smiled sheepishly, nodded, and walked through the doorway onto Cassie and Shawn's backyard. As he did so, he seemed unaware that the air surrounding him in the portal rippled as if it were a curtain of transparent liquid. He looked around, taking in a world that was as new to him as his world was to Cassie and Shawn. "Wow!" he quietly muttered to himself.

The kids warily backed away as the visitor approached them. Sensing their apprehension, he removed his beanie and held it in his hands—a gesture that made the siblings feel slightly more at ease. They stared at him, mouths ajar. "Oh, I'm sorry," he said. "Did I startle you? I didn't mean to."

"Uh…" said Shawn. "Who are you? And what, uh…"

The kids allowed him to move closer.

"Excuse me," the young man said. "I should have introduced myself. I'm Grayson. Humblebee. Grayson Humblebee."

"Are you…are you, like, *real*?" asked Cassie.

"Well, if I am not, that would be a problem. Yes. Very real, indeed."

"Are you human?" asked Shawn.

"Yes, it is safe to say I am human."

"But you don't *look* human," said Cassie. "You're more like an elf. I mean, like, you have pointy ears. Humans don't have pointy ears. Only elves do."

"That may be true in your world, but in my world, all us humans have ears like mine."

"And you are way too big for an elf," said Shawn. "I mean, like, elves are tiny."

"Well, there you go," said Grayson.

"OK, you *are* human," acknowledged Cassie.

"A real person," said Shawn.

"A real person with pointy ears," said Cassie.

"Whew!" said Grayson. "Glad we got that settled."

"It's still kind of weird, though," said Shawn. "I don't mean, like, *you* are weird. Well, maybe you are—a little—but it's weird that you just showed up—"

"Out of thin air," said Cassie.

"Yeah," agreed Shawn.

"Perhaps I should explain," said Grayson. "You see, I've come here… well, I was *told* to come here…to your world…to find two people—"

"Is that your cat?" asked Shawn, interrupting Grayson. Despite the presence of an odd-looking teenager with pointed ears who appeared through a magical door that popped up out of nowhere, Shawn's attention had abruptly shifted to a cat standing in the other world's path. The creature appealed to the boy in some mysterious way he could not understand.

"Shawn!" scolded Cassie with her hands on her hips. "You interrupted Grayson."

"Sorry," said Shawn. "It's just that there's something about the cat."

Grayson, apparently not bothered by Shawn's interruption, turned and saw the feline. "Oh my goodness!" he exclaimed. "No, it's not mine. It seems to have followed me."

The cat approached the door, looked at Shawn, and meowed. "Hi, kitty," said Shawn.

The cat moved a few feet away from the door, farther into Grayson's world, then turned and looked at Shawn and meowed again, as if inviting the youth to follow. Its expressive, emerald green eyes had a near-hypnotic appeal.

Shawn cautiously put his hand through the door's opening. Ripples of air, like wavelets of water, spread outward from his hand though he felt nothing. He looked at Grayson for approval. "Can I...?"

"Perhaps, but don't go too far," said Grayson. "And come right back."

Shawn stepped through the doorway, unaware of the disturbances he generated in the opening's curtain of air. He walked up to the cat, bent down, gently scratched it behind its ears, and stroked its head. "Nice kitty," he said.

The cat purred.

Cassie, being Cassie, did not bother to ask Grayson for permission and walked through the doorway, wrinkling the opening's air curtain herself. She walked up to Shawn, who stood up from petting the cat.

The cat's fur consisted of black and white shapes in the form of swirls.

"Kind of a strange-looking cat," said Cassie. "I've never seen one like that before."

"Me either," said Shawn. "It is kind of weird."

The cat issued what might be taken as a quiet, sorrowful meow.

"Maybe cats like this are normal," said Cassie, "in...um...wherever we are."

"Probably," said Shawn. "Anyway, weird or not, I think it's cute."

"Yeah," said Cassie, "I'll have to agree. I could get used to it."

The cat meowed pleasantly.

Cassie reached down and petted the cat. "You have really pretty eyes, kitty," she said. "And I hope we didn't hurt your feelings by saying you're weird and stuff."

Another pleasant purr could be heard.

With a gentle smile on his face, Grayson quietly muttered "Hmph!" to himself, rolled his eyes, then stepped through the doorway (air ripples again). He joined the kids and allowed them time to survey this very unfamiliar landscape.

Cassie and Shawn became aware of the new environment. Their eyes widened; this magical place clearly enchanted them.

Grayson smiled and surveyed the surroundings himself. Although his world was not new to him, he took time to appreciate it anew through Cassie's and Shawn's eyes.

For a moment, Grayson seemed lost in thought. Then, as though aware of Cassie and Shawn for the first time, he frowned. "Oh my goodness!" he said. "I just realized…you're young."

"So?" asked Cassie and Shawn together.

"I need to find adults, not children," said Grayson. "I…I shouldn't have let you…I don't think you should be here. We better get you back to your world—"

Suddenly the door slammed shut.

* * *

"Uh-oh!" said Grayson.

Cracks began to appear in the doorway—both the door and the frame. The cracks widened, and the portal split into large chunks of wood that drifted apart and, suspended in midair, began to circle each other. Like a movie of the structure's first appearance running in reverse, the chunks broke further apart into thousands of tiny bits that in turn became nothing but dust, spinning around ever faster, as if part of a small tornado. Then, accompanied by a whooshing noise and the same wind chime music, the dust vanished. Not a hint of the doorway remained.

A cool breeze briefly rustled the grass near Grayson, Shawn, Cassie, and the cat. They stood motionless, quietly gazing at the spot where the doorway once stood.

Grayson broke the silence. In a soft, quivering voice, he said, "I didn't think the door would disappear. Now we're in trouble."

Chapter 3

Curse of the Good or Evil Witch

h my gosh!" said Cassie, cupping her hands to her mouth.

"What happened? Where are we?" asked Shawn.

"You're in…um…*Transmongonia*," said Grayson.

"Transma…Transma…Transmongonia? What's Transmongonia?" demanded Cassie.

"It's a place. A country."

"Never heard of it."

"Well, no, you wouldn't. It's…in another world."

"Another *world*?" asked Cassie. "What do you mean, 'another world'?"

"A world that is not…um…*your* world."

"*Our* world? You mean, like, Shawn's and my world?"

"Yes. Your world is a different *place* than my world," said Grayson.

Cassie sneered. "A different *place*?"

"Well," said Grayson, "a different *place* wouldn't be quite right, but—"

"Another planet?" interrupted Shawn.

"You could say that, I guess," said Grayson. "Transmongonia is on the planet *Thur*."

"There is no planet Thur," said Cassie. "Not in our solar system."

"Is it in our galaxy?" asked Shawn.

"No," said Grayson.

"*Another* galaxy?" asked Shawn.

"No, not really," said Grayson. "Not in the way you mean it."

"Another *universe*!" exclaimed Cassie.

"Well…yes…sort of," said Grayson. "I mean, well, it's not completely *another* universe separate from your universe. I mean, it's like, connected to your universe—your world—in some way. And when I say 'your world,' I don't mean like, your planet although it's kind of like your planet."

"So," said Cassie. "You're from another *universe*?

"Well, sort of, yes," said Grayson. "But not entirely. It is connected to your universe."

"Connected?" asked Shawn. "How?"

"I don't know. It just is. I mean, like, I entered your world through that door, so it's *connected* somehow."

"Oh, you're really narrowing it down for us," said Cassie in a sarcastic, mocking tone. "It's so obvious: another place, or universe, sort of, that's not exactly another universe, connected to our world somehow through some crazy door that appears out of nowhere. And when you say 'your world,' you don't just mean Earth, you mean something else besides a planet called 'Thur,' and you can't explain what that something else is, but you do know we're *connected*, but you don't know how. It's all so clear…plain as day."

Grayson lowered his head. "Sorry," he said, almost in a whisper.

A few awkward seconds passed.

Shawn's face puckered, his lips trembled, and his eyes welled with tears. "I want to go home," he whimpered.

"Me too," said Cassie in a demanding tone, as though she was commanding Grayson to return her and her brother to Boulder. A wrinkled brow and tears in her eyes revealed her fear.

Cassie and Shawn's brief enchantment with Transmongonia had vanished along with the magical doorway.

A few more seconds passed as Cassie contemplated her and her brother's situation. Her body stiffened. She held her arms straight down and clenched her fists—a stance she often took when confronting Shawn. "I don't think we're going home, are we, *Grayson*," she said with a deep, angry, tense, now quivering voice. "I mean, we're stuck here forever, aren't we, *Grayson*." She emphasized Grayson's name with considerable harshness. Her tears intensified.

"You've kidnapped us," said Shawn, also with an angry tone.

"No, not at all," said Grayson. "I didn't mean for you to be here. I didn't think the doorway would disappear. I intended to bring back some *grown-ups* from your world, not children. And the adults were to come *only* if they were aware of—I mean if they *wanted* to come, if they volunteered. I am sorry. So sorry."

Cassie and Shawn became aware of Grayson wiping at tears of his own. His failed attempt to hide his vulnerability by turning his head to the side melted both Cassie's and Shawn's hearts. Their anger turned to sympathy as they realized that Grayson truly regretted taking them away from their home.

Cassie relaxed. "Aware of what?" she asked, wiping away her tears. "If the adults volunteered for what?"

Grayson paused and gathered his thoughts. "I was assigned to recover the Magic Keys, and I was told to go to your world to find two people 'brave enough and smart enough' to help me, but—"

"We're brave and smart," interrupted Shawn.

"Oh, I am sure you are, but you're both children, *kids*, like me, and the quest may be dangerous. Your parents would never let you join me, and I wouldn't even ask them. I need *older* people who know beforehand what they are in for and who *agree* to come. So it would be quite wrong of me to ask you to be part of this mission."

Cassie and Shawn frowned at the idea of being thought of as mere unqualified children.

"However, with the door gone," continued Grayson, "it...it looks like I have no choice. But of course you are brave and smart."

"You're only saying that to be nice," said Shawn.

"Will we see our mom and dad again?" asked Cassie.

"I think so, yes. I'm sure the Good or Evil Witch won't keep you here forever. I believe her better nature, her good side, will prevail, and she'll return you to your world at the very same time you left it—after we've recovered the Magic Keys, that is."

"The Good *or* Evil Witch?" asked Shawn.

"Yes. It is hard to tell if she is genuinely good or genuinely evil. She loves to cast spells and curses, and they make us suffer. They cause pain. And yet, when we overcome whatever challenge she puts before us, we grow, we learn, and we seem to come out better for our experience. So, is she *evil* for causing all that pain, or is she *good* for teaching us lessons? We can't decide, so we call her the Good or Evil Witch.

"It was her order," continued Grayson, "that I should go to your world and find someone to help—"

"Ohmygosh!" Cassie suddenly interrupted.

(Perhaps it should be noted here that while a good grammarian might insist that 'Oh my gosh!' consists of three separate words, Cassie, in her excitement, often compressed the phrase into a single word: *Ohmygosh!*)

"Look!" said Cassie as she pointed at what appeared to be three horses on a distant rise in the shade of a lone tree. The animals had spotted the new arrivals and commenced galloping toward them. "Ohmygosh!" she screamed again. Cassie and Shawn huddled behind Grayson as best they could. Grayson faced the creatures and held out his arms to protect his new charges—as if that would do any good. Shawn crouched with fear behind one of Grayson's arms; Cassie crouched behind the other.

The cat sought shelter behind Grayson.

The beasts picked up speed and ran at full gallop, making whinnying sounds as they did so. A sparkle of golden light glinted off the tops of their foreheads.

Cassie and Shawn whimpered and clenched their teeth.

Grayson, who recognized the creatures' true intent, said in a calm voice, "Don't be afraid. They won't hurt us."

The animals came to an abrupt stop a yard from the adolescents—and the cat.

Cassie and Shawn's fear lessened, but they did not relax. "Ohmygosh!" squealed Cassie again. "They're unicorns! Ohmygosh!" She bounced up and down with delight.

The unicorns, pure white with a single gold horn on each of their heads, moved closer to the now-smiling companions. "They wish to greet the new visitors," said Grayson, who, together with Cassie and Shawn, petted the unicorns on their cheeks and sides of their necks. The unicorns also bent down so the cat could touch the tips of their noses with its paw. The horned creatures snorted, whinnied, then scampered back in the direction from which they came.

"I've never seen a unicorn before," said Cassie. "I mean, like, a *real* one."

"Me neither," said Shawn.

"Glad you had the opportunity," said Grayson. "Now, I think we had better get going."

"Going? Going where?" asked Cassie.

"Topplesville," said Grayson, "the capital of Transmongonia. It's on the other side of the forest. Not far."

He put his beanie back on and the group proceeded to walk along the path toward the forest. The cat led the way.

Shawn and Cassie chose not to comment on Grayson's odd-looking, colorful beanie, assuming it must be considered stylish in his world.

"You were talking about Magic Keys and the Good or Evil Witch and coming to our world and stuff," said Shawn.

"Yes," said Grayson. "The Magic Keys—they're said to be magic any-way—unlock a chest that holds the secrets to the three ultimate powers required to be king of Transmongonia. The chest is under guard at the Rumpty D Temple, in possession of The Great Rumpty D himself. The temple is in Topplesville. That's why we're going there."

"Who's The Great Rumpty D?" asked Shawn.

"He is the ruler—the current ruler—of Transmongonia. If he gains knowledge of the three powers, he will have the right to wear the crown—the right to be king."

"But if he's, like, the ruler, couldn't he be the king right now if he wants to be?"

"That is certainly his wish, but he can't be king—not now at any rate."

"Who says?"

"Well, the crown, for one. It refuses to stay on his head."

"What do you mean, 'refuses to stay'?" asked Cassie.

"Just that," answered Grayson. "When the crown is placed on Rumpty D's head, it pops right off."

"Seriously?" asked Cassie.

"Yes, seriously," answered Grayson. "And, you know, one cannot be a king if the crown itself does not wish to cooperate."

"Oh, of course," said Cassie sarcastically. "Everyone knows that."

"Does the crown talk?" asked Shawn.

"No. It's just a crown."

"And when you say 'ultimate powers,'" asked Cassie, "what does 'ultimate' mean?"

"In this case, 'ultimate' means most important, most powerful. The Great Rumpty D *must* possess them if he is to be king. And if he is king, he will be very powerful indeed. He'll have more powers than he does now."

"So, where are the keys?" asked Cassie.

"I don't know. The witch placed them at locations we are to learn about later. It will be up to us to recover them."

"I'm confused," said Shawn. "If this Rumpty D wants the keys so bad, why can't he just get them himself?"

Grayson laughed, "He couldn't even if he wanted to. When you meet him, you'll understand."

"Why do *we* have to help you?" asked Cassie.

"Excellent question. All I know is that on the witch's orders, I *must* be helped by two people from your world—"

"'Brave enough and smart enough,'" interrupted Shawn.

"Yes," said Grayson. "*Why* from your world, I do not know."

"Do you think she wanted *us* in particular, I mean, me and Cassie?" asked Shawn.

"I don't see why she would. But she could have, I guess. She didn't *say* I should find adults only. I just assumed that. The witch's ways are sometimes puzzling."

"But if Rumpty D is the ruler," said Shawn, "he should be able to order whoever he wants to get the keys."

"Not even The Great Rumpty D can alter a curse by the Good or Evil Witch," said Grayson. "And the witch designated me, unfortunately, to do the job—with you, of course."

"Do you know Rumpty?" asked Shawn. "Does he know you?"

"I do know him. And yes, I am afraid he knows me."

"You must be pretty important; I mean, like, friends with the head guy!"

"'Important' is not a word I would use to describe myself. Far from it. And we are certainly not friends."

Chapter 4

Ayeli

Shawn looked down at the cat, who was now walking beside him. "So, this isn't your cat?" he asked.

"No," said Grayson, "I don't know who it belongs to—or even if it belongs to anyone. I don't recall seeing it before."

"You wouldn't know its name then."

"No." He bent over and examined the cat from various angles, front and back. "Why don't *you* name her?" he said.

"It's a *her*?" asked Shawn.

"Indeed."

"How do you know?"

Grayson blushed. "Um…" he muttered. He hesitated a bit, then said, "The sound of her meows. She meows in a very lady-like way. Very feminine. Gentle."

"Huh!" said Shawn. "I didn't know that about cats."

Cassie smiled to herself.

"OK," said Shawn. "How about we name her just plain Cat or… Catso!"

"I think that sounds like a boy cat's name," said Cassie. "Catsa would be more like a girl cat's name. What do you think, Grayson?"

"You're probably right," said Grayson, "but let's explore more options for a name—a name with deeper meaning, perhaps."

A few quiet seconds passed as visitors and host alike furrowed their brows and pursed their lips in deep thought.

Cassie broke the silence: "Ailuros!" she said with a touch of excitement in her voice.

"Huh?" said Shawn.

"Ailuros," repeated Cassie. "She's the queen of cats in Greek mythology. I read about her in my mythology book."

"Al…Alyu…" said Shawn, attempting to pronounce the name.

"Ailuros," said Cassie. "*Ay-yel-you-rous*. Say it fast: *Ayelurous!*"

Shawn frowned. "Too complicated."

"I think Ailuros is an excellent name," said Grayson, "very appropriate indeed."

Shawn lowered his head with a still more pronounced frown. He seemed to be pouting.

"But I agree with you, Shawn," said Grayson. "It is a bit of a mouthful."

Shawn looked up; his frown faded to neutral.

"How about we call her Ally for short," said Cassie.

"That should work," said Grayson. "Any other ideas?"

"Ayeli!" suggested Shawn confidently.

"Excellent," said Grayson. "Retains the essence of Ailuros but is easy to pronounce. Smart lad!"

"I hate to agree with my brother," said Cassie. "Not that he's smart—he isn't—but yeah, Ayeli is a good name."

At this, Shawn raised his head high and grinned (or perhaps we should say *smirked*).

"So," said Grayson, "Ayeli it is. Ayeli the Cat!"

"Yay!" said Cassie and Shawn in unison. Shawn's brief look of superiority had melted into a more respectful, less obnoxious expression.

Ayeli meowed, perhaps approving her new name.

"Maybe Ayeli can come with us on our mission," said Shawn. "Be part of our team."

"Perhaps," said Grayson, "if she's willing."

"If we're going to be a team," said Cassie, "we should have a name, like...the Magic Key Team...or Key Finders...or, what do you think, Grayson?"

"I trust your judgment to come up with a good name."

"Key Bringer Backer Team?" suggested Cassie.

"Imaginative," said Grayson.

"Or maybe just plain Key Team," said Shawn.

"That's not bad," said Cassie. "Grayson?"

"Works for me," said Grayson.

Thus, Cassie, Shawn, Grayson, and Ayeli would be known as the Key Team.

"Well, my goodness," said Grayson, "I just realized I don't know *your* names."

"I'm Cassandra," said Cassie. "People usually call me Cassie."

"I'm Shawn," said Shawn. "People usually call me Shawn." He added a fake laugh: "Ha-ha."

"Shawn Ha Ha?"

"No," said Shawn. "See, like, *Cassie* is short for *Cassandra,* and she says, 'people usually call me Cassie,' and so I say, 'I'm Shawn, people usually call me Shawn,' and then I say, 'ha-ha,' so people will know I'm being funny, 'cause my name's already short. So, it's supposed to be like, a joke, sort of."

"I see," said Grayson. "It is funny, yes."

"You don't want to know what I usually call him," said Cassie.

"No, I suppose I don't," said Grayson.

"And your last names?" asked Grayson.

"Solskin," said Shawn.

"It means sunshine in Danish," said Cassie.

"I see," said Grayson, "'Danish' being a language in your world?"

"Yes."

The Key Team entered the forest. "We'll soon be passing through the Garden of the Flower Queen," said Grayson. "But before that, there's someone you'll enjoy meeting."

Chapter 5

A Wise Old Tree

The forest was dark, with lush green trees overhanging the flower-lined path. A tree, lacking the height of those around it, grew in a small clearing not far from the forest entrance. Rough chunks of bark coated its thick trunk. Gnarly branches spread in all directions. Next to it stood a large, powerfully built man, at least a head taller than Grayson. His clothing appeared to be a uniform made of black leather. Silver buttons and decorations adorned his vest. The garment was open, showing off his bare tattoo-covered chest, and it was sleeveless, displaying his bulging tattoo-covered muscles. Tall black boots covered his calves. His head, propped on a thick neck, was bald. Most scary were his yellow eyes, with pupils appearing as tiny black specks. His eyes' yellow hue was especially creepy against the chalk-white color of his skin. He fixed the visitors with an angry, suspicious glare and held an ax with both of his oversized hands. He clearly was not someone to be messed with.

"We'll enjoy meeting *this* guy?" Cassie whispered to Grayson.

"No," Grayson whispered back. "Not him."

With a hint of fear in her voice, Cassie said to the man, "Who... who are *you*?"

"Me Dumlock," said the man in a deep, unpleasant, growly voice. In Shawn and Cassie's world, he would correctly be called a thug.

"He's an *axman*," said a deep voice that seemed to be coming from the tree. In fact, it *was* the tree that spoke! The tree's bark reshaped itself into a mouth and old, weathered eyes.

The axman raised his weapon a bit and glared at the tree.

"If you want to get technical," said the tree, "he is Dumlock, Axman by the Garden in the Forest for the Special Guards." Dumlock, soothed by the long and official-sounding title, grunted, displayed a smug expression of satisfaction, and lowered his weapon.

"We just call him Dumlock the Garden Axman for short," said the tree. "And in case you are wondering, there *is* a garden a short way down the path. I've heard it's beautiful. You'll like it, I'm sure."

"Oh my gosh!" said Cassie to the tree. "You...you're a *tree*! I mean, like, you can *talk* and everything."

"You've noticed."

"This is one of our Wise Old Trees," said Grayson.

"You flatter me, Master Grayson," said the tree.

Ayeli rubbed against the base of the tree with a purr, then scampered up its trunk to a thick branch where she settled herself slightly above and behind the head of Dumlock. The axman gave her a frowning glance then re-focused his attention on the tree and the new visitors.

"He is, in fact, *quite* wise," said Grayson, referring to the tree. "He and the other wise trees have counseled the citizens of

Transmongonia for centuries. I personally have been comforted many times by their sage advice. They have also provided reliable news about the latest goings-on in Transmongonia—until recently."

"Until recently?" asked Shawn.

"Yes," said Grayson. "Since The Great Rumpty D came to power, the Wise Old Trees have been…ah…controlled."

Dumlock moved toward Grayson with his weapon raised.

"…for the benefit of the citizens," clarified Grayson, realizing he ought not to imply ill intent on the part of The Great Rumpty D.

The axman lowered his ax and returned to his position near the tree.

Ayeli, from her perch on the tree's branch, hissed as she swiped her outstretched paw with claws extended in the direction of Dumlock's nearby head. She couldn't reach him—nor is it likely she intended to—but her gesture brought a smile to the human team members' faces. With his back to Ayeli, the axman could not see the cat's gesture but having heard her hiss and observed the kids' smiles, he swiftly turned to the feline. Before the ruffian could detect her insult, however, Ayeli assumed the pose of a cute, innocent, wide-eyed kitty. The axman again focused on the visitors.

"The Wise Old Trees are controlled?" Cassie asked the tree. "By the Great Whatever?"

"Indeed," said the tree. "The Great Rumpty D does not want Transmongonians receiving untrue news, especially false news about him. So, in his unfailing wisdom, our revered leader has posted ax men such as this gentleman to protect us from divulging news that would cast our august ruler in a bad light. Any news that would make Mister D look bad would, of course, be untrue."

"There must be *some* bad news about him that's true," said Shawn.

"No," said the tree. "The Great Rumpty D, demonstrating his superior insight and intelligence, has made it clear that any unfavorable news about him is untrue news."

"Can there be *bad* news that's true?" asked Cassie. "Not about him, necessarily, but about anyone?"

"Certainly," said the tree. "Bad news relating to the Crown Prince is true news."

"The Crown Prince?" asked Cassie.

"Yes. You see, until recently, Transmongonia was ruled by a king—King Edwin. We old trees knew him well. He was much beloved by the people and by us."

"Grandfather," cried a sapling that grew by the tree. The youngster, with smooth bark and thin branches, was about as tall as Shawn and much shorter than the old tree. He looked up at his elder. "Be careful, Grandfather," he pleaded. "Don't say too much. Please!"

As if to reinforce the sapling's wish, Dumlock raised his ax and stepped closer to the old tree, threatening to deal it a deadly blow.

The old tree looked down at the sapling, smiled, and said, "Don't worry, Jeune Arbre, I'll watch my tongue." Then, he resumed talking to Cassie and Shawn: "The Crown Prince *could* have become king on his father's disappearance, but rather than accepting his responsibilities, he went into hiding. Perhaps the burden would be too much for him.

"I should add that we *assume* King Edwin died; his body was never found.

"So," continued the tree, "absent a new king, The Great Rumpty D came to power and in his monumental wisdom decreed that the people of Transmongonia are not to speak of the Crown Prince; in fact, they must not even *know* him or, if they think they know him, not recognize him."

"That's dumb," said Shawn. "How can you make somebody not know somebody?"

"It's the law."

"It's a silly law," said Cassie.

The axman stepped toward Cassie and Shawn and glared at them with his ax slightly raised. The kids backed away, their eyes wide with fear.

"I think it's a *great* law," said Grayson, correcting Cassie with no conviction in his voice. He looked intently at both siblings and nodded his head up and down in an exaggerated manner. "Perhaps, considering the circumstances, you'll both agree after all?"

Cassie and Shawn understood Grayson's hint and, realizing the peril in which they had placed themselves, grudgingly nodded their heads in agreement.

Dumlock returned to his position. The children's fear lessened, though it did not vanish.

Ayeli cheered them up with a repeat of her hissing-pretending-to-swipe-at-the-axman routine, only to resume being the picture of pure cuteness before the brute had a chance to catch her defiant act.

"Obviously," said the tree, "anything good said about the Crown Prince would be untrue news."

"Obviously," said Cassie in her trademark sarcastic tone.

The tree, perhaps suspecting that Cassie knew he was spouting nonsense, smiled briefly. "If the prince got wind of nice things being said about him," he said, "he might be encouraged to come out from hiding and become king, and that would be disastrous for the Great Rump—I mean, the people."

"How so?" asked Shawn.

"Oh my!" said the tree. "A calamity! Why, the prince might…for example…ah…free the *dissenters*."

Dumlock frowned, turned toward the tree, and raised his weapon.

"The dissenters?" asked Cassie.

"Yes. Our ruler has them held as prisoners in the temple dungeons. The dissenters are very dangerous people!"

The axman relaxed and once again resumed his position facing the three visitors and the tree.

"Dangerous?" asked Cassie.

"Oh my, yes! The dissenters have had the nerve to disagree with The Great Rumpty D's wise rule—can you imagine that? And they don't just simply and quietly disagree; they voice their disagreements *out loud,* for all to hear! If the Crown Prince were king, he would set the dissenters free because he is too kind. And then they could say whatever they want. *Anyone* could say whatever is on their mind without fear of punishment. And we can't have that, can we, most splendid Axman by the Garden in the Forest for the Special Guards?"

Axman Dumlock agreed by shaking his head and issuing a throaty grunt. "Mmm," he muttered, "Dissenters bad, dangerous."

"I'm confused," Cassie said to the tree. "If you're so wise like Grayson says, how come you're standing up for The Great Rumpty D, who sounds like a real creep, and how come you're saying bad things about the Crown Prince, who sounds like a pretty good guy?"

"Yeah," said Shawn.

Ayeli meowed as if in agreement.

The tree placed arm-like limbs on each side of his trunk, looked at the sky, looked conspicuously at Dumlock, looked back at the kids, and said nothing. Cassie and Shawn were beginning to realize that the tree had to speak gibberish to avoid the axman's wrath.

"You said this guard is protecting you," said Shawn. "What's he protecting you from?"

"Me," said the tree.

"From you?"

"Indeed. This most splendid axman here is one of The Great Rumpty D's Special Guards. The great and exalted ruler has assigned him the task of protecting me from saying things I shouldn't."

"Like, bad news about Rumpty D and good news about the Crown Prince—untrue news?" said Shawn.

"Precisely," said the tree. "Much of the untrue news relates to the situation involving the Crown Prince, who is the king to be, or at least the king *meant* to be. I am not to discuss these matters in any detail."

"I bet *you* know where the Crown Prince is hiding," said Shawn.

"If there *is* a Crown Prince, I would certainly know," said the tree. "Perhaps I should have mentioned that the Crown Prince may not exist."

"Wait, what do you mean, 'may not exist'?" asked Shawn. "Didn't you just say—" Cassie nudged her brother and nodded her head toward the axman. The tree winked at Shawn, who then looked at the glowering Special Guard. "Oh, I understand," said Shawn. "*If* there is a Crown Prince, would you know him if you saw him?"

"Probably, yes."

"But if you tell us, you'll be in big trouble?"

"Huge trouble, yes."

"Do you know about the Magic Keys?" asked Shawn.

"I do."

"And like, what those 'ultimate powers' are?"

The tree paused and then said, "Let us say that I have my suspicions."

"So, what are they?"

"Grandfather!" said the sapling.

The tree smiled at his grandson, nodded, and turned back to Shawn. "I believe the answer to your question is to be found in the quest you are about to undertake."

"You seem to know a lot of stuff that The Great Rumpty D doesn't want anybody else to know," said Cassie. "So, when you say he's 'protecting' you, he's really protecting himself...*from* you."

The axman glared at Cassie. She glared at him. He stepped toward her, ax raised. Ayeli growled loudly and fiercely. The Special Guard stopped in his tracks, turned toward Ayeli, and this time witnessed a not-so-cuddly, not-so-innocent cat baring sharp teeth with hair raised and threatening claws.

The guard raised his ax high with the clear intent of terminating Ayeli, but she managed to hop onto higher branches well out of harm's way.

The scowling Axman silently returned to his post.

The tree continued his lecture. "The Great Rumpty D," he said, "believes we old trees are a danger to the state, to Transmongonia. We have been around for a very long time, and our roots run deep. We have too much knowledge about The Great Rumpty D and the Crown—"

"Grandfather, please!" interrupted the sapling.

The tree acknowledged his grandson's pleading and changed the subject—sort of. "The people trust us to be honest," he said, "to let them know the truth they need to know."

Dumlock made another threatening gesture.

"Of course," said the tree, "only The Great Rumpty D, in all his astonishing and magnificent insight, knows what the people need to know."

The axman relaxed.

"And so, The Great Rumpty D, in his inspired, glorious, and wondrous wisdom, has instructed gentlemen such as this axman to chop us down if we go too far.

"In that regard," continued the tree with an eye on the guard, "I should emphasize that The Great Rumpty D—the most honest and humble Rumpty D—insists that all this fuss about the Crown Prince becoming king is just rumors, falsehoods spread by the enemies of Rumpty D, fake stories designed to put our splendid and majestic ruler in a bad light. The Great Rumpty D wants to guard us—I mean *protect* us—from saying bad things, untrue things, based on false rumors. It is to our benefit, you see."

"No, I don't see," said Cassie.

"Me neither," said Shawn.

The tree again placed limbs on the sides of his trunk, looked up at the sky, and said nothing.

"You're putting us on," said Cassie.

"What?" said the tree, as if offended. "Putting you on? Not being honest with you? I am shocked—shocked!—that you could even *suggest* such a thing."

Cassie, finally having understood that the tree was playing a game with her and her brother, decided to participate in his act, using only words she, Grayson, and the tree would comprehend. She thought for a moment, studied the guard, and then said, "Mister Tree, when you say all this stuff about The Great Rumpty D being so wise, and that bad news about him is untrue news and stuff—are you obfuscating?"

"What, me?" said the tree, "Obfuscating?" He paused, thought about what she said, then laughed. "Why, yes, indeed!" he said, "How kind of you to say so."

Cassie had learned in her English class that to obfuscate meant to hide the truth.

"It sounds like The Great Rumpty D," said Cassie, "is quite maleficent."

She also learned that a maleficent person was up to no good—*evil*, perhaps.

"Yes! He is maleficent! Maleficent indeed!" said the tree, who was enjoying this exchange. "It's nice to know I have given you such a positive impression of our cherished and beloved ruler."

Grayson chuckled to himself.

Ayeli meowed in a way that sounded like a chuckle as well.

Cassie correctly guessed that the axman would not understand words with more than two syllables. As if to confirm her opinion, the guard's face wrinkled in confusion while she and the tree were conversing. The thug continually shifted his glare from Cassie to Grayson, to the tree, to a grinning Shawn, then back again to Cassie. He held up his ax and seemed somewhat angry but had no idea what to do. Finally, he looked at Grayson for an explanation.

"Cassie complimented the tree," said Grayson, "for his honesty and insight."

Dumlock, mostly silent up until now, grunted and nodded. "Great Rumpty D good," he said with a deep, rough voice. "Crown Prince bad. Untrue news about Great Rumpty D a lie!"

"Excellent!" said the tree. "Well put, my good friend!"

"Great Rumpty D mal...mal..." uttered the axman.

"Maleficent," said Cassie. "Yes, The Great Rumpty D must be truly maleficent. I am so looking forward to meeting him."

Dumlock grinned, thinking, perhaps, that *maleficent* was the same as *magnificent* when, in fact, Rumpty was likely a villain. The Special Guard grunted and lowered his weapon.

"Mister Tree, we do understand what you've been saying," said Grayson as he gave a wink to Shawn and Cassie. "We certainly don't want you spreading vicious rumors about The Great and Exalted Rumpty D. It's so wonderfully pernicious of him to keep you muzzled like this." He nodded at the axman, who again grudgingly nodded back in half-agreement and complete ignorance. The axman's one arched eyebrow indicated a slight bit of suspicion, but his small mind did not fully discern that both the Wise Old Tree and Grayson were not only insulting him but insulting The Great Rumpty D as well.

"You have enabled me to be honest in a satirical manner," said The Wise Old Tree to his visitors, "and have honored my true nature. For that, I thank you."

"You have a cool grandfather," Shawn said to Jeune.

"I know," said the sapling. "I hope to be like him someday."

"A noble goal," said Grayson.

To the Wise Old Tree, Shawn said, "I think we better get going. We don't want to bug you anymore, do we, Cassie."

"No," said Cassie, "we don't want to get you into trouble."

"You're not 'bugging' me," said the tree, "whatever that means, but you're not a bother at all. I do enjoy speaking with young people. And I agree that you had best be on your way. You have quite a journey ahead of you." He paused, then said, "That's why you're here, you know. To help young Grayson uncover the truth, for the sake of all Transmongonians, to—"

"Grandfather!" pleaded Jeune.

His brief flirtation with being agreeable having once again vanished, the axman stepped between the tree and the Key Team and uttered a low-level growl.

"Well," said the tree, peering from behind the axman, "perhaps I should say goodbye."

Ayeli jumped down from the tree's branches and joined her companions.

"Goodbye, Wise Old Tree," said the humans together.

"Goodbye, Dumlock," said Shawn as he waved at the axman.

The guard grunted and hesitantly waved back. He still managed to retain his sour expression, however.

The Team started down the path. Ayeli hesitated, padded back to the tree, rubbed against his trunk, gave one last hiss at the axman, then re-joined her teammates.

Once out of earshot of the axman, Shawn said, "I bet I know what *pernicious* means."

"And that would be—" said Grayson.

"Cruel."

"Astute lad," said Grayson. "The Great Rumpty D is exceptionally cruel to keep the Wise Old Trees silent."

"It was clever of you, Cassie," said Grayson, "to draw the tree out as you did, to get him to show his true feelings without putting him in danger. You allowed him to maintain his self-respect as well.

"And I must say," he added, "you have quite the impressive vocabulary."

"My sister's smart," said Shawn before he had a chance to realize he was paying her a compliment.

"As I suspect you are as well," said Grayson.

"He is," said Cassie, unaware that she, in turn, complimented her brother.

"But Shawn," said Grayson, "I am surprised you would suggest to Jeune that his grandfather is cold."

"What?" said Shawn. "I didn't—no! I said he was *cool*."

Cassie and Shawn chuckled at Grayson's misunderstanding.

"If people are cool," said Cassie, "it means they are like nice, smart, fun to be with."

"Ah," said Grayson, smiling. "Cool!"

"You've got it," said Cassie.

A few minutes passed.

"I have a feeling," said Shawn to Grayson, "that you don't think much of The Great Rumpty D."

Grayson stepped closer to Shawn and said, almost in a whisper, "I am not one of his greatest fans."

After a pause, Shawn said, "I didn't want to say anything, but couldn't Rumpty D just have the Wise Old Trees chopped down if he's afraid they'll say too much?"

"That would be a problem," said Grayson. "The Wise Old Trees are very much admired and loved by nearly all Transmongonians. If The Great Rumpty D were to destroy even one, the people might be so angry they would lose their fear and rise up against him. They *might*, I say."

"The tree we talked to seemed really nice," said Cassie. "He must be sad that he's not allowed to be himself. I mean, like, he has a bunch of interesting things to say. I feel sorry for him."

"He has my sympathy as well," said Grayson. "But at least we cheered him up a bit. I think he's a little happier now."

"The tree," said Shawn, "mentioned something about the 'situation with the Crown Prince.' So, like, what's the *situation*?"

"It's complicated," said Grayson. "Let's enjoy the garden."

Chapter 6

Hyacinth

The foursome continued down the forest trail and shortly arrived at a garden that could occupy a city block in Shawn and Cassie's world. Standing side-by-side in the path and blocking the Key Team's way were two Special Guards poised defiantly with arms folded across their chests. They were barely distinguishable from the axman with their tattoos, tall muscular bodies, black leather uniforms, boots up to their knees, white-as-snow complexions, and scary yellow eyes. Rather than carrying axes, however, they had swords attached to thick belts.

"Oh dear," said Grayson.

"What'r' these?" said the first guard with a deep, gravelly voice.

"Young people," said Grayson, as he placed his hands on Cassie's and Shawn's shoulders.

"No kiddin'," said the first guard. "We can see they's young. Tell us these ain't the people yous was supposed ta bring back from the other woyld."

"They are," said Grayson. "Kids, meet Glert and Smert. They are Special Guards for The Great Rumpty D."

"I'm Glert," said the first guard as he pointed to himself. Then, pointing at the second guard, he said, "This 'ere's Smert."

"A pleasure to meet you, sirs," said Cassie.

"Can't say the same," said Glert.

"Me neither," said Smert, his voice also deep and raspy.

"Who are yous?" asked Glert.

"I'm Cassandra. Most people call me Cassie."

"I'm Shawn. Most people call me Shawn."

"The kid's try'n ta be funny," said Smert.

"Not funny," said Glert.

"What's wrong with yer ears?" asked Smert.

"Our ears are fine," snapped Cassie. "What's wrong with—"

She stopped herself mid-sentence, realizing it is not wise to insult over-sized, sword-carrying thugs.

"So, Humblebee," said Smert, "The Great Rumpty D, he's gonna be really mad when he sees yous brought back kids like yerself when yous was supposed ta bring back grown-ups. He'll have you thrown into the dungeons for sure. Maybe worse."

"It wasn't his fault," said Shawn.

"We came through the door on our own," said Cassie.

"Then it slammed shut," said Shawn.

"All by itself," said Cassie.

"Grayson didn't want us to come through it," said Shawn.

"Tell that to The Great Rumpty D," said Glert.

To the guards, Grayson said, "What brings you gentlemen here?"

"Ta guard yous," said Glert. "An' ta keep yer friends 'ere from hearin' bad things about our beloved ruler."

"Like untrue bad news?" asked Shawn.

"Yeah," said Smert. "An' untrue *good news* about that Crown Prince, who don't even exist."

"An' ta make sure ya Grayson Humblebee 'ere don't pull no funny stuff," said Glert to Shawn. He pointed his thumb in the direction of the path. "Now, let's get goin'."

The Key Team, with the guards following, continued down the path. They were soon in the midst of a garden populated with a rich display of flowers—daisies, petunias, marigolds, chrysanthemums, and more. The flowers glowed with all the colors of the rainbow.

"Our parents would really like these," said Cassie to Grayson. "Especially our dad. He loves flowers."

"Too bad yous will prob'ly never see yer parents again," said Smert.

With wrinkled brows, pouting lips, and tears ready to appear in their eyes, the kids looked to Grayson. He shook his head and gave a dismissive back and forth motion with his hand as if to say, 'not true—don't pay attention.' Grayson's young guests relaxed; slight smiles appeared on their faces.

One of the plants by the path attracted Shawn. It had grown to his waist's height and supported a grapefruit-sized ball covered with what appeared to be long strands of bright red hair.

"That's a porcupine weed," said Grayson.

"Stroke its head," said Glert, smiling as he nudged the side of Smert with his elbow. "It'll give ya magical powers."

Shawn proceeded to stroke the plant without considering why it was likened to a porcupine.

"Shawn, don't—" cautioned Grayson with alarm in his voice.

His warning was too late. Interspersed and hidden among the weed's soft strands of hair were dozens of long sharp needles. When Shawn moved his hand across the ball, three of the needles thrust themselves into his palm. "Ow!" he screamed as he quickly jumped away from the weed.

"Ow! Ow! Ow!" he cried as he extracted the offending needles and squeezed his hand in an effort to subdue the pain.

"Oh dear," said Grayson.

Glert and Smert laughed with great pleasure.

Cassie came close to laughing at Shawn's predicament as well, but when she realized his pain was quite severe, she winced as if experiencing the pain herself. "Oh, Shawn," she said sympathetically. She raised a hand to put on his shoulder to comfort him but held back, lest her gesture be perceived as a sign of affection.

Ayeli the Cat rubbed against Shawn's leg.

"Ow-ow-ow-ow," the boy quietly moaned. Red streaks spread outward from the wound. His hand began to swell. A red burning infection spread onto his wrist and proceeded up his arm.

At that moment, a cloud of white mist appeared in the garden near the visitors. Sprinkled with star-like sparkles of light, it swirled around and around—not unlike the twirling fog Cassie and Shawn encountered earlier in their backyard.

A gentle, melodic sound like a pretty chorus of small bells accompanied the mist's debut. Then, a bright violet glow appeared in its center and, as the mist faded away, the glow gave way to a stunningly beautiful young woman. Her smooth, dark, coffee-with-cream skin was unblemished. Shiny black hair flowed over her shoulders. She wore a lavender gown with a gold braided rope around her waist, and her head bore a crown of multicolored flowers. Her emerald green eyes, similar in color to those of Ayeli's, radiated intelligence and kindness.

Glert and Smert ceased their laughter.

The woman floated over to Shawn and hovered just above the ground. "Oh, you poor dear," she said as she held his hand and examined it.

She narrowed her eyes as she frowned momentarily at Glert and Smert.

She then turned toward the garden and motioned toward a tall, leafy plant not far away. One of its thick leaves detached itself from the plant, floated over to her, and landed in her outstretched hand. She held the leaf over Shawn's upturned palm. His entire arm had become swollen and red, and it appeared he might faint. "This is healing nectar," she said. "It will help—and don't worry, it won't hurt a bit." She squeezed three golden honey-like drops from the leaf onto the three wounds. Within seconds, a healthy pink tint spread over the rest of Shawn's hand, onto his wrist, and finally up the length of his arm. His fingers, hand, and arm returned to their normal size and color.

Best of all, the pain vanished.

The woman held Shawn's injured hand warmly in both of hers. "I am so sorry this happened," she said. "I am Hyacinth."

"She's Queen of the Flowers—the *Flower Queen*," said Grayson as he sheepishly removed his weird beanie and tucked it under his belt. His introduction brought a smile to her face.

"Hi," Shawn said to the queen. "Thanks for making me, like, better and all."

"You are most welcome. And you are…?"

"Shawn. Shawn Solskin."

Queen Hyacinth turned to Cassie. "And…?"

"Cassandra Solskin," said Cassie, who offered a slight, appropriate bow.

"Cassandra and Shawn," said the queen. "Lovely names. *Strong* names for ones chosen to be in our world. I am so pleased and honored to meet you."

"They's 'ere ta get the keys," said Glert.

"I know that," said Hyacinth sternly. "And you, Glert and Smert—yes, I know your names—shame on you for rejoicing at the pain of this young man. But then, you *are* from Bully Island. I suppose you can't help it."

The two guards issued low-level growls but did nothing more—for the time being.

"You're very pretty," said Cassie to Hyacinth.

"Why, thank you."

"And those flowers around your head. They're pretty too," said Cassie.

"Thanks once more," said the queen.

"Are they, like, your *crown*?" asked Cassie.

The queen smiled. "They are," she said. "Would you like a crown of your own, dear?"

"I...sure...I mean, like, I'm not a queen or anything."

"But you are a princess," said Hyacinth.

A broad smile flashed across Cassie's face.

The queen turned to Shawn. "And you, my young friend, are a prince."

A deep red blush accompanied Shawn's smile.

Hyacinth turned toward the garden and made a broad sweeping gesture with her hand. A dozen flowers with short stems rose from the garden and gathered near her in midair. She turned back to Cassie and moved her hand in a circular motion above the teenaged visitor. Following the queen's direction, the flowers weaved themselves together to form a beautiful crown that landed lightly on Cassie's head.

"Oh, how do I look?" asked Cassie.

"Marvelous," said Grayson.

"Cool," said Shawn. "I guess."

To Grayson, the queen said, "You have assembled quite an impressive team, Master Humblebee."

"Well, I didn't quite *assemble* them," said Grayson, "but I do agree that Cassie and Shawn are most impressive."

"And Ayeli," said Shawn.

"And Ayeli," said Grayson.

"We're the Key Team," said Cassie.

"The Key Team—for what is surely a most important mission," said the queen.

"Most important," said Grayson.

"Hey!" said Glert. He drew his sword, held it threateningly, and walked a couple of paces toward Hyacinth. Looking at both the queen and Grayson, he said, "Yous two better watch what yous say, about any *missions* an' stuff."

Hyacinth showed no fear.

Although Grayson might have felt intimidated, he didn't show it as he stepped between Glert and the queen and faced the guard. "We are well aware of the rules," he said. "You can put away your sword." Up until now, he had not spoken so firmly.

Ayeli issued a brief, quiet meow.

Glert looked down at Ayeli. "What's dis?" he said.

"A cat," said Shawn. "Her name is Ayeli."

"I can see it's a cat," said Glert. (One might sense that Glert and Smert were only a tad smarter than the Ax Man.)

"Don't like cats," said Glert. "Dis world don't need no cats. Gonna get rid'a one right now." He raised his sword high in preparation to end Ayeli's existence. But before executing the feline, he scanned the anguished faces of the Key Team members and Hyacinth with a sinister smile indicating foul pleasure.

"Don't!" cried Shawn.

"Leave the cat alone," demanded Hyacinth. "Harm it, and you will be very, *very* sorry."

"Oh yeah, who says?"

"*I* say, as the sister of the Good or Evil Witch. You should know that the witch takes a very dim view of any who would harm a beautiful and innocent creature such as this." She picked up Ayeli and cuddled her in her arms. Ayeli purred while glaring at the Special Guard.

"Yeah, well, the witch ain't here," said Glert. "She's vanished."

"I wouldn't be so sure of that," said Hyacinth as she held Ayeli lovingly to her cheek. Ayeli's purr grew loud enough for all to hear.

"The witch *isn't* here," said Shawn, whose smart-alecky nature sometimes led him down a dangerous path.

Glert turned toward the defiant youth and glared. "What? I just said that!"

"No, you said, 'the witch *ain't* here,'" said Shawn. "That's bad grammar. Your grammar needs work."

"Don't you correct me, kid," said Glert as he approached Shawn with his sword still drawn. "Dis world don't need none a yous brats neither."

Shawn's cockiness turned to dread as he backed up from his tormentor. Grayson's courage once again became evident as he stepped between Glert and the boy. He held the palm of his hand up, facing the guard, motioning the guard not to come closer.

"Sir," he said, "might I remind you that Cassie and Shawn are here to help me recover the Magic Keys—by order of The Great Rumpty D as well as the Good or Evil Witch. Doing violence of any sort to members of our Key Team might bring down the wrath of both the ruler *and* the witch in a most unpleasant way."

"He's right, Glert," said Smert. "Better put away yer weapon."

"Humph!" muttered Glert. He sheathed his sword and pouted.

Shawn placed his fists on his hips and smirked.

Cassie and Hyacinth smiled.

Ayeli meowed.

* * *

A short, ordinary tree—not to be confused with the wise and talking kind—stood in the garden. Beautifully crafted ornaments of silver, colored glass, and gold adorned its branches. It could easily have been a Christmas tree in Shawn and Cassie's world. Hyacinth gently placed Ayeli on the ground, floated to the tree, surveyed the ornaments, and selected a small, shiny gold vial. She plucked another leaf from the healing nectar tree and drifted back to the Team. She handed the vial to Grayson. It was a small narrow container with a hinged lid on top. She opened the lid, held the leaf over the vial's opening, filled it with a few ounces of nectar, and closed it.

"Grayson, dear," she said, "I fear you might be needing this on your quest. Please take it and use it wisely." The vial was attached to a delicate gold necklace. The queen draped it around Grayson's neck. "Now, you must be on your way."

"Aww," said Shawn. "I kind of like it here."

"Me too," said Cassie.

"And I enjoy having you," said the queen, "but you do have that important mission to which you must attend."

"I agree," said Grayson.

The Key Team proceeded down the path, and the Special Guards followed.

Chapter 7

The Great Rumpty D

The Key Team, followed closely by Glert and Smert, soon entered a village. "Welcome to Topplesville," said Grayson. The team and the guards walked along a narrow cobblestone street lined with small shops, all of which appeared old-fashioned with hand-painted signs hanging over their entrances.

"I don't see any cars," said Cassie.

"Cars?" asked Grayson.

"Yes. You know what cars are, right?"

"No, I am afraid not."

"I don't see any lights either," said Shawn. "I mean like, *electric* lights. Do you know what electricity is?"

"Electricity?"

"Never mind," said Shawn.

Topplesville inhabitants, many carrying cloth shopping bags, walked about. There were men and women, boys and girls. As in

Cassie and Shawn's world, they appeared to come from various cultures with skin colors ranging from light to very dark. Brightly hued shirts and blouses decorated with flowers and abstract shapes adorned nearly everyone. Their clothing was much more appealing than Grayson's modest, dull, brownish attire. Although some Topplesvillians donned hats, none of the hats were as odd-looking as Grayson's beanie—still tucked under his belt.

A boy approached, stared at Shawn, and said, "You have funny ears."

"No," said Shawn, "you have funny—"

Shawn interrupted himself, realizing that, as with Grayson, the boy and all the other residents had pointed ears. Shawn's ears were indeed unusual in this world. He reached up with his right hand and touched the top of one of his ears as if to check its roundedness.

As the Key Team continued their walk, villagers smiled and gave a slight bow to Grayson. He smiled and bowed to them in return.

"The people here seem to know you," whispered Cassie to Grayson. "And I think they like you. They bow to you as if you're some kind of nobility or something. Are you?"

Grayson quietly chuckled. "Oh no," he said. "They're just … polite." The kids didn't entirely buy Grayson's modesty but they didn't challenge him.

On seeing Shawn and Cassie, some of the citizens pointed, smiled hesitantly, cocked their heads in curiosity, and whispered to each other while continuing to watch the youngsters.

"I can't tell if they like us or not," said Shawn.

"They don't know you," said Grayson. "You're new to them. You're a curiosity, especially the way you're dressed and with your ears the way they are."

"That's funny," said Cassie. "Our clothes and our ears make *us* look peculiar?"

"Afraid so."

Indeed, Cassie and Shawn, with their T-shirts, jeans, and sneakers—not to mention rounded ears—definitely stood out.

If any of the villagers approached too closely, a stern look from Glert and Smert kept them at their distance.

"Ohmygosh, look!" shouted Cassie, pointing at a corral where a dozen unicorns pranced about. The young visitor hopped up and down in pure delight. "Unicorns! Ohmygosh! Ohmygosh! Ohmygosh!"

"Cool," said Shawn. He acted more restrained than his sister, though, in fact, he was pretty excited as well.

Grayson allowed Cassie and Shawn to make a beeline for the corral (as if he could have prevented them). A young man, a little older than Cassie and about Grayson's age, stood just outside the corral's fence, feeding the unicorns by hand from a basket of edibles. His broad-brimmed hat was similar to those worn by American cowboys.

"Ah, Grayson Humblebee," he said to the Team's leader.

Grayson smiled and shook the wrangler's hand. "These are my new friends," said Grayson, "Cassandra and Shawn."

The wrangler nodded politely and smiled. "I'm Spenerton," he said. He shook hands with Shawn and tipped his hat to Cassie. Although his attention shifted back and forth between the new arrivals, he mainly focused on Cassie. "You're not from these parts, are you?" he asked.

"No. How can you tell?" asked Cassie.

"Well, not meaning to be impolite, but uh…"

"Our ears?" asked Shawn.

"To be honest…"

"They's funny ears," said Smert, who, along with Glert, had been keeping a close watch.

Spenerton, who up until now had done his best to ignore the guards, gave Smert a barely detectable sneer; a more pronounced look of contempt would have put him in trouble.

"Cassie and Shawn are from far away," said Grayson.

"Oh. I see," said the unicorn wrangler. Of course, he didn't see but did not want to further push the matter with Grayson, whom he clearly respected.

"Are you giving the unicorns candy?" asked Shawn.

"Oh no, I wouldn't do that." He held up the basket. "You don't know what these are? Fruit. Wherlops and zingtons. Very nutritious." He motioned his head toward the unicorns. "Want to feed them?" He handed Cassie a piece of fruit that was shaped flat, like a pancake, with red and white swirls around the center.

She showed it to Grayson. "Reminds me of your cap," she said.

"Not certain I like the comparison," said Grayson.

"It's a wherlop," said the wrangler. He handed Shawn a piece of fruit that had a shape approaching that of a pear with blue and violet markings. "This is a zington."

Cassie and Shawn cautiously offered the fruit to the unicorns, two of whom accepted the gifts and gently snorted and nodded their heads up and down as if to say thank you. Each of the youngsters patted the unicorns' foreheads, taking care to avoid the horns. The creatures backed up and allowed other unicorns to take their places so that they, too, might be petted and fed.

"They like you," said the young wrangler to Cassie and Shawn, both of whom smiled at the compliment.

All the unicorns, like those encountered previously, were snow white with golden horns. Cassie and Shawn quickly sensed their gentle and friendly natures.

Ayeli the Cat jumped onto the top of a post that was part of the corral's fence, and when the unicorns neared her, she reached out with her paw and touched one on its nose. The recipient of Ayeli's gesture backed off so the other unicorns could have their noses touched by the gentle feline as well.

"Ayeli has a way with unicorns," said Cassie.

"It's almost like she's talking with them," said Shawn.

"Are unicorns unusual in your world?" asked Grayson.

"Ohmygosh, yes!" said Cassie with barely contained excitement.

"And they are not real," said Shawn. "I mean, not in *our* world. We read about them and see pictures of them in books. My sister likes that sort of stuff."

Ayeli turned toward her companions, meowed, jumped down from the post, and trotted away from the corral. She looked back at her quest associates and meowed once again.

"I believe Ayeli is reminding us that we have an appointment with The Great Rumpty D," said Grayson. "She seems in a hurry."

"Aw," said Cassie. "Can't we stay? Just a little while?"

"Afraid not," said Grayson. "We do have a big day ahead of us. Sorry." His voice was gentle yet firm.

* * *

The Key Team came to a large open area covered with lush green grass like a well-manicured city park. It had no trees. A wide circular mound rose in its center. On top of the hill stood an enormous, magnificent structure—a temple that reminded Cassie of Greek temples illustrated in an ancient mythology textbook. It was round with two dozen white marble columns, each three stories tall, spaced evenly along the outside edge. Small cannons pointing outward, away from the building, occupied spaces between the columns. The columns supported a massive white sparkling dome that covered an area half the size of a football field. Chiseled along the side of the dome were the words, **RUMPTY D TEMPLE**. The lettering was substantial enough to be seen from anywhere in Topplesville.

With Ayeli leading the way, Grayson escorted Cassie and Shawn up a path that led to the temple. From the temple's base, they could see the Transmongonian Sea and the faint, gray outlines of islands on the horizon. Glert and Smert, continuing to follow behind, had been subdued since Grayson and Queen Hyacinth pointed out their obligations to The Great Rumpty D and the witch.

Dozens of Transmongonians, dwarfed by the grand building's size, milled about on its vast marble floor. Among them were many soldiers, smartly dressed in brightly colored red and blue uniforms.

Two Special Guards, who looked very much like Glert and Smert, met the Key Team at the edge of the temple. "Cassie and Shawn," said Grayson, "I'd like you to meet Morfo and Flippo, two distinguished and very special guards."

"Hello," said Cassie.

"Hi," said Shawn.

The voices of the siblings and their facial expressions displayed a hint of forced friendliness. Their previous experience with Glert, Smert, and the Garden axman had instilled in them a negative bias toward the Special Guards.

Morfo and Flippo grunted. Without saying a word, they left Glert and Smert behind and escorted the Team toward the center of the room. "Oh," said Grayson, "I forgot to tell you: don't comment on The Great Rumpty D's appearance."

"Why would we?" asked Shawn.

"Uh, well," said Grayson, "he looks like—"

Morfo and Flippo each narrowed their eyes, scowled at Grayson, and slowly shook their heads. Grayson took their hint: "Never mind," he said to Shawn. "You'll see."

The Key Team and the guards approached a circular stage rising a yard off the floor. Steps around its circumference enabled easy access. More than a half-dozen nasty-looking Special Guards paced about on the stage. All appeared nearly identical to the guards Cassie and Shawn had recently met on their journey; they could be distinguished from each other only by the variety of tattoos on their bare arms and chests. Each was at least a head taller than Grayson. All wore black leather uniforms with open vests, had muscular builds, white skin, and bald heads supported by thick necks. All viewed their world through tiny black pupils in solid yellow eyes. Nearly all had swords mounted on their sides and bore perpetual scowls as they continually eyed citizens and soldiers on the main floor for suspicious activity.

A familiar-looking tree resided in a stone container near the stage's center. The tree displayed few human-like features, so the kids were barely aware of it, nor did it occur to them to ask why an ax-carrying guard was positioned close by.

No, it was not the tree or even the guards that captured Cassie and Shawn's attention; instead, their eyes were drawn to the *creature* sitting atop a massive, round, six-foot-tall platform—a dais—located at the center of the stage. An ornate gold and silver throne atop the dais supported the *being* that did not look like any human or animal Shawn and Cassie had ever seen. What it did look like was…an *egg*!

Yes, The Great Rumpty D's body had an egg's oval shape. And, it was quite large for an egg—about the same height as Grayson and much wider.

Between the throne's already plush red velvet cushion and Rumpty D's bottom was a fancy, oversized, violet pillow with yellow tassels on each corner. It must have been his very own personal pillow as it did not match the throne itself. Wherever it came from, it prevented the ruler from rolling over. His spindly legs could not reach the floor. Cassie and Shawn wondered how he could stand upright, let alone walk more than a few feet. His arms, extending from his sides, were as thin as his legs, utterly lacking in muscle. He had a mouth, nose, and ears on his egg-white head (if you could call it a head). His creepy eyes consisted of small black dots for pupils surrounded by white eyeballs surrounded in turn by dark shadows.

He wore a black uniform befitting a military general, royalty, or—more appropriately—a *dictator*. Attached to his chest (if you could call it a chest) were multiple ribbons, a medal, brass stars, and a striped silk-like sash.

A well-polished gold crown occupied—or rather was *forced* to occupy—the top of The Great Rumpty D's hairless head. A variety of jewels—sapphires, emeralds, rubies, pearls, and diamonds—were embedded in the crown.

A distinguished-looking gray-haired gentleman wearing clothing like that of 1700s British royalty (in Shawn and Cassie's world) stood erect behind The Great Rumpty D. His role was that of Royal Crownkeeper. (Technically speaking, he should *not* have been designated *Royal* since he did not serve an actual king, but The Great Rumpty D, dismissive of propriety, insisted on using the term.)

The crownkeeper's task was to keep the crown positioned correctly atop his boss's head—not an easy chore due to the crown's rebellious nature. The headpiece might stay put for a few seconds but then would quickly slide off Rumpty D, only to be stopped by the alert crownkeeper before it fell to the ground. Very often, especially when Rumpty D was agitated—and he was frequently agitated—the crown would simply pop straight up and be caught mid-air by the crownkeeper's white-gloved hands. Over and over, the crownkeeper would carefully reposition the crown.

If time permitted, he would slowly remove his hands and place them behind his back while the crown temporarily rested. Unfortunately, the crownkeeper could hold this dignified stance for no more than a few seconds before the crown misbehaved once again.

The ruler became aware of the Key Team when they arrived at the stage.

Looking down from atop the dais, he eyed Grayson. "Oh, it's you, Liddle Fumblebum," he said.

"Humblebee," corrected Grayson, almost in a whisper.

"Whatever," said Rumpty D. "Where's your beanie?"

"Oh, sorry, sir," said Grayson. He withdrew his beanie from his belt and placed it on his head.

"That's better," said The Great Rumpty D. "What are these?"

"Kids," said Grayson. "Young folks like me."

"I can see that," said Rumpty. "Are they—oh no, don't tell me: these *surely* are not the people you brought from the other world!"

"They are."

"You mean these…these…whatever, are the people the witch said should be 'brave enough and smart enough' to help you bring back the Magic Keys?" (He demonstrated contempt for the words 'brave enough and smart enough' by making an air quote gesture with his fingers.) "Those words, 'brave' or whatever, are the witch's words—not mine.

"Well, Dumblebum," he continued, "you're even more incompetent than I thought. You're sent to the other world to bring back grown-ups, and you bring back *these?*"

"Sir, I was not told to bring back grown-ups specifically. But I agree I should have—"

"SILENCE!" said Rumpty D. "Don't argue with me."

"Yes, sir." Although Grayson had stood fearless before Glert and Smert in the flower garden, his courage sadly failed to materialize in the presence of The Great Rumpty D.

"It wasn't his fault," said Cassie. "We went through the door on our own, and it shut behind us and—"

"SILENCE!" said Rumpty D. He peered down at Cassie. "Who are you?"

"Cassandra. Most people call me Cassie."

Rumpty furrowed his forehead, squinted his eyes, and sneered at the young lady. Whereas he viewed Grayson as though he were looking at days-old garbage, the nasty ruler observed Cassie as though contemplating rotting fish. "You're a *girl*," he said.

"That's observant of you," said Cassie.

"A girl!" snapped Rumpty. "Now the mission is doomed for sure. You're gonna sit down and cry at the first sign of danger. You're gonna mess it up for everybody."

"Oh my goodness!" said Cassie. "You're a *male chauvinist!* This is the first time I've met a real male chauvinist in person."

"A male chauv...chauv..." muttered Rumpty. Frowning, he turned slightly to get the crownkeeper's attention.

The old gentleman bent over and started to whisper in Rumpty's ear, but Cassie was ahead of him: "Excuse me, Mr. Crownkeeper," she said, "may I explain?" The crownkeeper politely nodded.

"A male chauvinist," said Cassie, "is a guy who thinks women are inferior to men."

To the crownkeeper, she said, "Sorry to interrupt you, sir."

"Not a problem, my dear," said the crownkeeper with a deep, pleasant voice.

"What?" said Rumpty, switching attention between Cassie and, as much as possible, the crownkeeper. "You think I regard women as inferior to men? Not true! No one has done more for women— and girls—than I have. I have passed more regulations in favor of ladies than anyone in Transmongonian history."

"Oh, really?" asked Cassie. "Can you name some?"

"Yes. Absolutely. Let me think."

Rumpty pursed his lips, looked up at the ceiling of the dome for a few seconds, then said, "I'll have you know I give a warm cup of gruel to *every* dissenter in the dungeons—men *and* women— regardless."

Both the crownkeeper and Ayeli issued a quiet cough.

"Of course," added the ruler, "the men do get a little more gruel. They need the nourishment."

"Oh," said Cassie, "that's magnanimous of you."

"I agree," said Rumpty. He paused a second, then said, "Magna-nana-whatever: that's a good thing, is it not, Crownkeeper?"

"It is, sir," said the crownkeeper.

"Describe more of your generous regulations," said Cassie.

"I don't have time," said Rumpty. "There are too many. Dozens and dozens. Good regulations. Wonderful regulations. *Fair* regulations. But it would take all day."

He turned to Shawn. "Who are you?" he said with a mild sneer.

"Shawn," said the young visitor, "most people call me Shawn. Ha-ha."

"Shawn Ha Ha? What kind of name is that?"

"The 'ha-ha' isn't part of my name, sir," said Shawn. "I say 'ha-ha' 'cause 'ha-ha' is, like, a laugh. See, my sister says 'Cassandra, most people call me Cassie' and so I say 'Shawn, most people call me Shawn,' and then I say 'ha-ha' because it's, like, a joke. It's funny. I think."

"Not funny," said Rumpty D. "I don't get it."

"See," said Shawn, "my name—"

"Don't bother," said the ruler.

After a short, awkward silence, Shawn said, "Sir, you look kinda like Humpty Dumpty. Are you—"

"What? WHAT?!" snapped Rumpty D. "How DARE you compare me to that arrogant little twerp!"

Rumpty's crown hopped a yard straight up from his head, only to be safely caught by the crownkeeper.

"Well," said Shawn, "you do sort of look like an egg, and your name rhymes with Humpty and—"

Rumpty D's normally egg-white face flushed red. "THERE IS NO HUMPER DUMPER OR WHATEVER! What was his name again?"

"Humpty Dumpty, sir."

"Right, well, this 'HUMPTY DUMPTY' DOESN'T EXIST. NEVER HEARD OF HIM! OR IF I DID HEAR OF HIM, HE'S SOME KIND OF LOWLIFE ON EGG ISLAND or whatever it's called."

His loud rant echoed throughout the temple, with words bouncing from the massive temple dome to the marble floor beneath and back again.

"I'm a little confused," said Shawn. "You say you never heard of him, but you also say he's a little twerp and a lowlife. How would you know that if you never heard of—"

"I SAID I NEVER HEARD OF HIM, BUT *IF* I DID HEAR OF HIM!"

"Really?"

"Yes! PAY ATTENTION!"

"Well, OK," said Shawn, "but you look like an egg, and your last name starts with 'D,' like in Dumpty, and your first name rhymes with 'Humpty,' so, you know, your name would be Rumpty Dump—"

"THE 'D' DOESN'T STAND FOR ANYTHING. IT'S JUST A 'D.' And STOP ARGUING WITH ME! I ought a have you arrested for treason."

"Sir?" said Cassie.

"WHAT?" snapped Rumpty.

"My brother didn't mean to upset you. He's not familiar with your customs. He didn't know you had an issue with, um—"

"There is NO ISSUE!" shouted the agitated ruler. "NO ISSUE! I have NO ISSUE with HUMPTY DUMPTY or whatever his name is. NO ISSUE AT ALL. Besides, the creep doesn't exist. All rumors! Fake rumors! Whoever said I was his cousin is a liar! A LIAR! How could I be related to some SPOILED NOBODY THAT'S NEVER BEEN BORN WHO THINKS HE'S SOMEBODY?"

"I'm sorry I upset you," said Shawn meekly, then whispered to himself, "I guess."

"WHAT?" shouted Rumpty D. "I heard that. You *guess* you're sorry? You *guess*? Guards! Take the impudent brat to the dungeons. Teach him his manners."

Ayeli hissed.

Two Special Guards took Shawn by his arms.

"Uh, sir?" said Grayson to Rumpty.

"Did I ask you to speak, Thirdlewop?" snarled the ruler.

"No, sir, you didn't. But Shawn is here to help me recover the Magic Keys if you recall."

"So?"

"Remember that according to the Good or Evil Witch's curse, Shawn and Cassie *must* go with me in search of the Magic Keys. And Shawn can't do that if he's kept in the dungeons."

"Oh yeah, the witch," interrupted Rumpty. "Her and her curses. Never mind, guards. Let the brat go."

The guards released their young captive.

"Thank you, sir," said Grayson, Shawn, and Cassie together.

Rumpty calmed down. The normal egg-white color in his face returned. He eyed Cassie's crown of flowers and scrunched his face. "Where did you get that thing on your head?"

"It's a flower crown," said Cassie, "from Queen Hyacinth. Do you like it?"

"No. Ugly. The so-called Flower Queen—rules over *flowers*, of all things. Scrawny flowers! And she calls herself a queen. Hmph! Probably made your so-called 'crown' from weeds she was going to throw away before you came along."

"I think it's quite pretty," said Grayson.

"SILENCE!" said Rumpty D. "What *you* think, Humbledorp, is irrelevant."

"Hyacinth is a really nice lady," said Shawn.

"That's right," said Cassie. "And she's beautiful and smart too… way smarter than, uh…"

Rumpty D glared at her.

"Never mind," she said.

Rumpty D studied the newcomers. "Funny looking ears," he said.

"Actually," said Grayson, "they're quite normal for—"

"SILENCE!" said Rumpty D. "If I want your opinion, I'll ask for it."

"Is 'The Great Rumpty D' your formal name?" asked Cassie.

"What? You don't know?" said Rumpty. "I am much more than that. I am known far and wide as The Great and Exalted, Magnificent and All-powerful, Benevolent and Kind, Magisterial and August, Holder of All Knowledge, Master of Sciences and the Arts, Brilliant, Courageous, Fantastic, Wise, Generous, Merciful Ruler of Transmongonia and Future King of Transmongonia, Beloved by All, and I must say, Modest and Humble Genius, Rumpty D.

"But," he added, "most people just call me 'The Great Rumpty D'…ha-ha. Get it? The Great Rumpty D. *Ha-ha.*"

Shawn and Cassie showed fake smiles through gritted teeth. "Yes, very funny, sir," they said together.

"All those words, holder of knowledge and stuff," asked Cassie, "do they really make up your full name?"

"Yes, of course. Didn't Thumperdumper tell you?"

"His name is Grayson Humblebee," said Cassie. "He did say you are called The Great Rumpty D."

"At least the doofus got that right," said Rumpty.

The ruler glared at Shawn and said, "To answer your question, the *D* is just a *D*. It sounds like 'dee.' Nothing more. You got that, Shern or whatever?"

"Shawn," said Shawn. "Yes, sir."

Rumpty turned to Grayson. "What I want to know, Grayser-bumper, is how can three incompetent brats—you and these, these whatevers—how're ya gonna get the keys? The answer is: You can't. This quest is going to be a disaster."

"Sir?" asked a deep voice coming from the tree near the dais the kids saw earlier. A rough but well-defined mouth and nose, as well as eyes and ears, took shape on the tree's thick, rough, gnarled trunk. With its comparatively short height, it very much resembled the Wise Old Tree the Key Team had met near the Flower Queen's magical garden.

Cassie and Shawn waved at the tree. The tree gave a quick, cautionary side glance at the nearby *Temple* Axman, then smiled just a bit and hesitantly waved back with one of his branches.

As with the Garden Axman guarding the first Wise Old Tree, the Temple Axman's job was to give the tree a whack lest it say the wrong thing. *This* guard did not, however, appear to be paying much attention to his charge. He yawned and stretched while observing Cassie and Shawn with mild curiosity. His relaxed nature did not conform at all to that of the other guards, who were rigid, ill-mannered, and ill-tempered at best. He did wear tattoos as did the others but while the others' tattoos were characterized by skulls, knives, snakes, and other symbols of nastiness, the Axman's portrayed flowers, a heart, and other symbols of gentleness.

The kids waved at the axman. He nodded and returned a hint of a smile.

"I think that guard might be kind of nice," whispered Cassie.

"Yeah," whispered Shawn. "Being nice might get him into trouble, though. I hope not."

"Sir?" repeated the Wise Old Tree.

"What?" demanded Rumpty D.

"Even if mere children have been selected to recover the keys," said the tree, "it will be the wish of the Good or Evil Witch to proceed with the mission."

"Hmph!" grunted Rumpty. "You're probably right. Okay, tree, go over the details of the curse again. There's too much to remember."

"Great and Exalted Ruler," said the tree while winking at the human Team members, "according to the terms of the Good or Evil Witch's curse, when the Magic Keys—of which there are three—are recovered and brought here, three ultimate powers will be revealed. The throne will come to rest on the head of the one who holds those powers, the one destined to be king of Transmongonia—"

"That would be me," interrupted Rumpty D.

The Wise Old Tree rolled his eyes and gave a quiet sigh. Cassie and Shawn noticed the non-conforming axman rolling his eyes as well.

"The Good or Evil Witch," continued the tree, "has entrusted one key to Cyril, the one-eyed giant who resides on Bigcliff Island; the second key to Valdoc, king of Voids on the Island of Light People; and the third to the cave monster who recently appeared on the Island of Youneverknows. It is essential to understand that the giant, the Voids, and the cave monster will offer significant resistance—*deadly* resistance—to surrendering their keys.

"As for how young Humblebee was chosen to lead a team to recover the keys: the Good or Evil Witch placed folded pieces of paper with a name on each into a hat. If you recall, your Gloryness, you generously volunteered to be blindfolded and draw a name, with the understanding that whoever's name you drew would be the Key Team leader. And the name drawn was—"

"What's-his-face—Grokey Humfel whatever," interrupted Rumpty D.

"Grayson Humblebee. Yes, sir," said the tree. "Now it was decreed—"

"That name drawing thing was rigged," interrupted Rumpty. "Look around you. Look at all these handsome Special Guards. Any of them could easily get the keys: brave, gallant lads—"

"Lads?" interrupted Cassie. "What about lasses? Girls? Don't you—"

"SILENCE!" said Rumpty D. "As I was saying, any one of my guards would be a great choice, a fantastic choice. But no! The witch chose—and yes, I say she *chose*—this, this nothing, this nobody, this meek little…Groser Stumble or whatever…to go on the most dangerous mission ever."

Rumpty paused, wrinkled his brow, lowered his eyes, and pursed his lips as though meditating on how unfair the world is to him.

"May I continue?" said the tree, disturbing the brief tranquility.

"Oh!" said Rumpty as if awakened from a trance. "Yes, yes. Go on."

"The Good or Evil Witch," said the tree, "decreed that Master Humblebee would need to go to the other world to find two people brave enough and smart enough to help him recover the keys—"

"Did she say kids? Brats?"

"No, sir. Just two people. I assumed she intended that they be grown-ups, and I know Grayson wished to recruit *only* adults. He stated at the outset that he would never put children at risk."

"Well, he failed," said Rumpty D. "Truth is, Thumble-thump can't even find—he's so incompetent, so incompetent—sad!—can't even find good *adult* people in the other world. So, what does he do? He brings back little brats that can't do diddly squat."

"Hey!" said Cassie. "That's not fair."

"SILENCE!" said Rumpty D.

Rumpty stared at Cassie and Shawn. "Aha!" he said, "It's so obvious: little Dumperthump didn't *want* to find adults! That's it! He's afraid to talk to adults, let alone ask them for a favor. So, what does he do? He lures these poor, sweet, innocent children into our world—kids he can control. What a coward! Pathetic!"

"Not true!" said Shawn. "Grayson is not a coward! He tried to make us go back, but the door closed before we—"

"SILENCE!" said Rumpty D. "Now he's got you to lie for him. Sad! Anyway, keep quiet."

Dozens of Transmongonians, interested in the goings-on, had started to gather around the stage. Rumpty D addressed his growing audience as well as those immediately near him. "You know *why* the witch rigged the drawing?" he said, "Because she doesn't *want* the keys recovered." He stopped talking for a moment and looked around. "Where *is* the so-called witch, by the way? Probably snuck back to the Island of Witches and Wizards. Hooked up with some wizard or something. Anyway, no, she doesn't want the keys recovered. 'Good or evil,' my backside. Just plain evil, I say. And she doesn't want me to be king either, believe me, despite all the good I would do for you beautiful people. Sad! She's probably jealous."

Ayeli hissed.

"One other thing," said the tree.

"What?" asked Rumpty D impatiently in a tone that suggested he did not wish to be bothered with more information.

"It concerns the Crown Prince," said the tree.

"Irrelevant," said Rumpty D.

"Well, sir," said the tree, "as you know, and as everyone knows, the prince is in hiding."

"So?"

"The terms of the curse—they're quite clear about this—state that if the prince comes out of hiding, *he* will have the right to the throne. *He* will be king—assuming he displays kingly qualities, of course, and it is *he* who will hold the ultimate powers."

Ayeli meowed affirmatively.

"Won't happen," said The Great Rumpty D. "The crown is mine!"

At that, the crown once more leapt a yard off Rumpty D's head. The crownkeeper caught it in midair, returned it to the dictator's head with great effort, and held it tightly with considerable strength as it shook and wiggled in an attempt to break free.

"Crownkeeper!" snarled Rumpty D. "What's your problem?"

"It's the crown, sir," said the crownkeeper. "It's… um… *resisting*, sir. It doesn't seem to want to stay in its proper place."

"On my head, you mean."

"Yes, sir. It's never behaved this badly before."

"Well, make it stay put."

"I'm doing my best, sir."

"Goes to show you how important this mission is," said Rumpty D. "When the keys are recovered—and they had *better* be recovered—and the ultimate powers are revealed to me, my right to wear the crown will be confirmed. The crown will respect me so much, and it will have so much love for me, it will be happy to rest on my head!

"Now about this rumor of the 'Crown Prince' becoming king," continued the tyrant, "not a problem. I know the prince: snively runny-nose little coward. Afraid of rustling leaves. Couldn't rule over a colony of mice, let alone a great land like ours." The dictator turned toward Cassie and Shawn and said, "He's the son of the former king, in case you didn't know. The king died. Fortunately, I was here to take the king's place."

And to the gathering crowd, as well as to Cassie and Shawn, he said, "The prince lives in the shadow of his father. He knows he can't measure up. He thinks the king was wonderful."

"The king *was* wonderful," said Grayson quietly.

"SILENCE!" said Rumpty D. "You don't know that, Feemlefopper."

"It's Humblebee, sir!" said Grayson with just a hint of anger in his voice, then added, "Grayson Humblebee."

"Whatever," said Rumpty D. "Let me tell you, Geeky Humber or whatever: The king's rule was a disaster. A complete disaster! Sad! Well, he died. It happens. Sorry he died. But it's a good thing for Transmongonia because I alone am saving this great land and, when I become king, I alone will make Transmongonia even greater. Believe me!"

Ayeli hissed and twitched her tail back and forth.

Grayson's lips tightened. He said nothing.

"Mr. Rumpty, sir," said Shawn.

"Yes, what?"

"Can you spell?"

"Of course, I can spell. You think I'm an idiot?"

"Well, sir, how would you pronounce I-A-M-A-J-E-R-K?"

Grayson lowered his head so that his chuckle was not too noticeable. Cassie put her hand over her mouth to stifle a laugh.

Even Ayeli made a sound that could be interpreted as a suppressed snicker.

The Great Rumpty D again turned toward the crownkeeper, who, with furrowed brow, whispered a few words into the ruler's ear and returned to his place.

"I'm a *what*?" said Rumpty, glaring intently at Shawn. "Are you calling me a jer—guards! Take this brat to the dungeons. No! Give him thirty lashes, *then* take him to the dungeons!"

Suddenly, a loud *clickity-clack-clickity-clack* sound of hooves echoed throughout the temple. The dozen unicorns the Team encountered earlier walked onto the temple's marble floor. They approached Cassie and Shawn and nuzzled up to their newfound friends. The young Team members, including Grayson, smiled and stroked the creatures. One unicorn bent down so Ayeli could touch its nose with her paw. Spenerton, the unicorn wrangler, appeared just behind his charges, nearly out of breath. He looked up at The Great Rumpty D. "Sorry, sir," he said with a tremble in his voice. "They ran off when I took them for their walk. They seem to have taken a shine to our visitors."

"What?" said Rumpty D. "You can't control your horses?"

"Unicorns," corrected Cassie.

"Whatever," said Rumpty D. "Guards! Take these beasts to the dungeons."

"With all due respect, sir," said the wrangler. "You can't do that."

"Oh? And why is that?"

"Unicorns are a protected species, sir. The Good or Evil Witch—"

"The witch again," said Rumpty. "Her and her curses. Well, take these uni-whatevers away."

"Yes, sir." The wrangler ushered the unicorns out of the temple.

"Where were we?" said Rumpty D. "Oh right—the brat. How many lashes?"

"Three," said Shawn.

"Appreciate your honesty, kid," said Rumpty D.

Shawn smirked and folded his arms.

"Guards! Three lashes and to the dungeons with the brat."

"He's with me," said Grayson as he placed a hand on Shawn's shoulder.

Cassie placed a hand on Shawn's other shoulder. "Me too," she said.

"We're the Key Team," said Grayson with a firm voice.

"Yeah," agreed Cassie. "And we're going to the islands together. All of us."

"Or none of us," added Grayson.

Ayeli meowed in solidarity and rubbed against Grayson's leg.

Shawn turned his attention to the Wise Old Tree. "Mr. Tree?" he said.

"Yes, son?"

"Can Ayeli come?"

"Oh, yes, indeed. I suspect the witch would want such a noble creature to join your mission."

"Yay!" said Shawn and Cassie together.

Rumpty D pouted for a moment, then said, "All right, all right. We'll deal with the brat later. Guards! Get this, this 'Key Team' or whatever, get them out of here."

Morfo and Flippo, the two Special Guards who had met the Key Team at the temple entrance, nudged Grayson, Cassie, and Shawn toward the temple's ocean-side exit. The trio of humans and Ayeli disliked being pushed. They defiantly stood their ground and glared at the guards, who then looked to The Great Rumpty D for guidance. The dictator raised both arms slightly with hands outstretched, palms up. The guards took the gesture to mean *don't look at me for guidance*, and the two beefy men stepped back from the rebellious Team members.

"OK. Cassie, Shawn . . . and Ayeli," said Grayson, "Let us be off!"

Grayson guided the Key Team toward the edge of the building.

"Hey, Deedlewhopper!" said Rumpty D in a loud voice.

Grayson and his teammates paused for a second, then continued without looking back.

"GRAYSON HUMBLEBEE!" shouted The Great Rumpty D.

The Key Team members abruptly stopped, slowly turned, and looked at the tyrant.

"You and your little companions will probably die out there," said Rumpty D, "but if you don't, and you come back here without the keys, you'll die *here*. You got that?"

Grayson gave a gentle, restrained nod. He said nothing. Then he, the kids, and Ayeli turned back toward the ocean and continued walking.

Before they reached the edge of the temple, a tall soldier with a commanding presence approached them.

"Captain Mackenzie," said Grayson with a respectful bow of his head. "It is good to see you."

"Master Humblebee, sir," said the soldier. "I want you to know we're with you. Best of luck."

"Thank you, Captain. I'm sure that means a great deal to all of us."

Ayeli seemed to agree with a pleasant meow.

Chapter 8

The One-Eyed Giant

The Key Team walked from the temple down a pathway leading to a dock extending far out over the water. A dozen dolphins frolicked about the dock where a boat was moored. The craft was nearly as long and as wide as a school bus, with a small cabin in its center. Grayson effortlessly stepped over the boat's side railing and onto its deck. The craft rocked as he did so, but Grayson didn't seem concerned—he had apparently been at sea before. Cassie and Shawn, with the Team leader's help, gingerly stepped onto the boat. It rocked again, and it took some effort for the kids to keep their balance. They had *not* been at sea before!

Still, each smiled. This was going to be fun!

Ayeli stood at the dock's edge and watched Grayson proceed to untie the boat from its *mooring*.

"Grayson?" asked Shawn. "What about Ayeli?"

"Hmm," answered Grayson. "What do you think?"

"I'm worried," said Shawn. "I know the Wise Old Tree at the temple said she could come—*should* come—but I'm afraid she could get hurt or something."

"You may very well be right," said Grayson.

"And if she gets hurt, it will be our fault," said Cassie.

"Perhaps," said Grayson.

"I think we should leave her here," said Shawn. "I mean, for her own good."

"I can't say I disagree," said Grayson.

The boat, now unmoored, started to drift away. Ayeli, still on the dock, swayed side to side.

"Oh, Ayeli," said Cassie, "we'll miss you!"

"Yeah," said Shawn

Ayeli meowed a long, sad, plaintive meow.

"Aww," said Grayson, Cassie, and Shawn in unison.

The boat had drifted too far for any ordinary cat, any *sensible* cat, to jump over the water and onto the craft. Ayeli crouched and slightly lifted one paw and then the other as if preparing to jump. She seemed determined to disregard the danger.

Realizing Ayeli's intent, Shawn said, "Don't jump, Ayeli! It's too far!"

"You can't make it!" said Cassie.

But Ayeli, being a cat, and furthermore, being *Ayeli*, ignored their pleas. With an impressive leap, she all but *flew* from the dock onto the boat's side railing and then onto its deck.

The human Team members cheered. In their hearts, they had wanted her to join them. Now there was no way they were going to put her back on the dock.

"All for one and one for all," said Grayson.

The boat continued to drift.

"Uh, Grayson?" said Shawn.

"Yes, Shawn?"

"Um, how are we going to get where we're going?" Shawn observed that while the boat had a mast, the sail was not deployed. "I mean, shouldn't we put up the sail or something?"

"And even if we put up the sail, there's no wind," said Cassie. "We're not going to row, are we? It would take us, like, forever."

"No, we are not going to row," said Grayson with a chuckle.

"Does this boat have a motor?" asked Cassie.

"A motor?" said Grayson. "I don't quite know what a motor is, but no, I don't think so."

"I know." said Shawn, "Magic! You're gonna make this boat go by magic, cast a spell or something."

"Good heavens, no." said Grayson, "I'm not a wizard. Hold on, you'll see…"

Grayson tossed six pairs of harnesses—twelve harnesses in all—into the water. They were attached to a single large rope that in turn was secured to the front of the boat—its bow. The harnesses were spaced a little more than a dolphin-length apart from each other. Each consisted of a large collar into which a dolphin could easily fit.

The twelve dolphins (properly called a pod) had stopped their playing and were watching Grayson. Their bodies trembled with anticipation when they saw him preparing the harnesses. "Dolphins!" he said to them, "We must go to Bigcliff Island, home of the One-Eyed Giant." In a haphazard flurry and with a great splashing of water, the dolphins swam to the dozen harnesses and slipped into them. Within seconds, they were ready. Still trembling with excitement, they turned toward Grayson and awaited his command.

But Grayson first needed to caution his shipmates: "Lady and gentleman," he said to Cassie and Shawn, "you had best take a seat." He motioned to the wide front-facing bench near the bow.

Grayson turned toward the dolphins. Bracing himself and firmly holding the waist-high front railing with one hand, he pointed with his other hand at an island far in the distance. "To the Island of the Big Cliff," he shouted to the dolphins, "GO!"

The dolphins faced the open sea and bolted forward, causing the boat to lurch with them. Cassie and Shawn, who had been politely sitting upright on the bench, were thrown back by the sudden acceleration. They squealed in delight as if on a roller coaster.

Within seconds, the boat was speedily heading toward Bigcliff Island. The team of dolphins reminded Cassie and Shawn of huskies pulling a sled over deep snow. The harnesses were designed to enable the creatures to continually dive under and out of the water, as dolphins love to do.

The boat gently bounced over mild ocean waves: *whump-whump-whump!* Cassie and Shawn stood up from the bench and checked out the craft. They walked cautiously around the cabin to the back—the stern. They leaned on the stern's railing and could see Topplesville receding in the distance. The great white dome of Rumpty Temple seemed to diminish in size along with Topplesville itself. The siblings were impressed by the bubbly trail left in the boat's wake as the craft cut through the water. Small, gentle waves generated by the vessel spread ever outward.

Cassie and Shawn returned to the bench near the bow.

With the boat up to speed, Grayson could relax. Leaning with his back against the front railing, he observed his young friends as they enjoyed the feel of the wind on their faces and the light mist of ocean spray churned up by the dolphins. This brought a smile to the Team leader's face.

A few minutes passed. Grayson's attention focused on Cassie, then Shawn, then Cassie again.

"I know what you're thinking," said Cassie.

"Oh? And what would that be?"

"We don't look like brother and sister," said Shawn.

Cassie's olive skin and long, shiny black hair made her complexion appear similar to that of Hyacinth the Flower Queen. The hazel color of her eyes seemed to shift between brown and green. Shawn's complexion was fair, with freckles decorating his face. His medium-length hair was bright red, his eyes sparkling blue.

"Well, I—" said Grayson.

"We're adopted," interrupted Shawn.

"My biological parents are from Mexico and Canada," said Cassie. "I'm mixed-race."

"Mine are from Ireland," said Shawn. "I look Irish, don't I?"

"I wouldn't know," said Grayson. "I am not familiar with Ireland."

"Of course you wouldn't be," said Cassie.

"Your parents," said Grayson, "the ones who adopted you, are very fortunate."

"You think so?" asked Shawn. "Why?"

"They got two great, beautiful kids," said Grayson. "What luck!"

"Aww!" said Cassie and Shawn together.

"But we're the lucky ones," said Cassie. "It's our parents that are great—the ones who adopted and raised us, I mean."

"Yeah," said Shawn. "We feel like they are our *real* parents."

"It's nice that you see them that way," said Grayson.

A few minutes passed.

"Speaking of parents," said Cassie, "what do your mom and dad have to say about your going on this quest? I mean, like, it's dangerous. I should think they would do everything they can to keep you from going—despite what Rumpty D or even the Good or Evil Witch wants."

Grayson frowned, his face shadowed with sadness. "Yes," he said, "it would be Mom and Dad's wish for me to stay home, and yes, they would do everything in their power to keep me safe. And yes, they certainly would stand up to The Great Rumpty D."

"So like, why don't they?" asked Cassie.

"I am afraid they are…gone," said Grayson

"Gone? Where did they go?"

Grayson's voice quivered. It was difficult for him to speak. "They were lost at sea. Their empty boat was found washed ashore about three months ago, severely damaged. It is assumed they perished."

"Oh, Grayson," said Cassie. "I am so sorry to hear that."

"Me too," said Shawn.

Ayeli issued a sad meow.

"Mom and Dad were very accomplished sailors," said Grayson. "And good people. Very good people. Smart, wise, gentle, and kind. They should not have died. It's not right."

A long silence ensued while Cassie and Shawn contemplated Grayson's loss, each reflecting on how fortunate they were to have parents who were alive and healthy.

"This sure is a nice boat," said Cassie, changing the subject.

Grayson's mood lifted. "I agree," he said with a smile.

"Is it yours?" asked Shawn.

"Don't I wish! But no, it belongs to Transmongonia. It's called *The People's Boat*."

Grayson's beanie was suddenly blown off and landed on the bench between Cassie and Shawn, who were sitting apart at each end.

"Oh my goodness!" said the Team Leader.

The kids laughed. Cassie picked up the hat and handed it to Grayson. "Careful!" she said. "We don't want you to lose your amazing hat."

"True," answered Grayson. "Wouldn't that be a shame?"

"I have a feeling you're not serious," said Cassie.

"What? Me?" said Grayson as he fidgeted with the head covering. "Lose my precious and beloved beanie?"

"Do you really like it?" asked Shawn.

Grayson looked to his left and to his right, pretending to be sure nobody other than the kids could hear him. He leaned toward them, held a hand beside his mouth as if to whisper, and said in a low voice, "No, not really."

"Can I say something?" asked Cassie.

"Be my guest."

"I don't like it either," said Cassie, almost in a whisper.

"Me too," said Shawn. "I mean, like, I don't want to offend you or anything, but it's really kind of, uh…"

"Silly looking?" said Grayson.

"Yes," said Cassie and Shawn together.

Grayson nodded his head in agreement.

"Then why do you wear it?" asked Cassie.

"Orders of The Great Rumpty D."

"Really?" asked Cassie. "Why?"

"He gave me a choice. Wear it or be taken to the dungeons. Same with my boring outfit."

"Send you to the dungeons?" asked Cassie. "Why? What did you do?"

"I…ah…questioned his judgment," said Grayson.

"Judgment?"

"Yes. Rumpty made a disparaging remark about the former king."

"What did he say?" asked Shawn.

"He said the former king was incompetent."

"And you said…" pressed Cassie.

"Well, to be honest, Cassie, I lost my temper. I know I shouldn't have, but I did, and I said that the king was wonderful, that he was the best thing that ever happened to Transmongonia."

"And he's punishing you because of *that*?" said Shawn. "He *is* a jerk!"

"Wearing that foolish costume is a lot better than going to jail," said Cassie.

Grayson nodded in agreement.

"Rumpty D must really hate you," said Shawn.

"I wouldn't know," said Grayson. "I have no way of knowing what's in another's heart."

"Do you hate him?"

"No, I don't hate him."

"I hate my brother sometimes," said Cassie.

"And I hate my sister sometimes," said Shawn.

"It grieves me to hear you say that," said Grayson. "Hate is such a useless emotion. It accomplishes nothing."

Cassie and Shawn remained quiet. Each nodded their heads ever so slightly as if absorbing Grayson's words. Perhaps they agreed with him, but they were not about to let Grayson or each other know that.

"I have a surprise for you," said Grayson. "The animosity you have for each other will fade away. Someday, when you are older, you will discover that you have grown quite fond of each other."

"Eww, yuk!" said Shawn while making a face that suggested he had bit into a sour lemon.

"Never!" said Cassie as she defiantly shook her head.

"You sound like our parents," said Shawn.

"All adults say what you said," Cassie opined.

"Wise parents," said Grayson. "Wise adults."

"But you're not a parent *or* an adult," said Shawn. "So, what makes *you* so wise?"

"I don't claim to be wise," said Grayson, "but my parents certainly were, and they gave me wise advice. My mother, for example, said that she and her brother—my uncle—fought a lot, and furiously too, when they were young. They hated each other, or at least they felt they did. But as they grew up, their animosity faded away, and they became best friends.

"And she pointed out how all the adults we know get along very well, even though many were at odds when they were kids. That's what makes adults adults. So yeah, someday you will both learn to see the good in each other and accept each other's flaws. I know that for sure; I can see that you are both great kids even if you can't."

Cassie and Shawn folded their arms. "Hmph!" they muttered.

Cassie returned to the previous subject: "You know why Rumpty's making you wear your silly hat?" she asked. She waited for an answer that did not come and then said, "He wants to humiliate you. It's not just that you argued with him."

"It's so obvious he doesn't like you," said Shawn. "I mean, he doesn't like anybody, and he's mean to everybody, but he's *really* mean to you."

"There has to be a reason," said Cassie. "Maybe it's because you're nice. He just doesn't like nice people."

"You are kind to say that," said Grayson.

Cassie thought for a moment and said, "I know; he's *afraid* of you!"

Grayson laughed. "I doubt it," he said. "I am hardly a threat. Mister D would say I am like the Crown Prince, frightened by rustling leaves."

"You're not afraid of rustling leaves," assured Shawn.

Grayson smiled at the affirmation.

83

"I mean," said Shawn, "look how you stood up to creepy Rumpty when he insulted your king and when he said he was going to send me to the dungeons."

"And when you told him we're the Key Team, and we are all going together," added Cassie.

"But those are the only times you stood up to him," said Shawn. "He insults you so much, and you don't say anything."

"You stand up for others but not for yourself," said Cassie.

"Yeah," said Shawn. "We wish you would stand up more for yourself."

"But I guess Rumpty would throw you in the dungeons if you did," said Cassie.

"Very true," said Grayson.

"Still…" said Cassie.

She pondered Grayson's predicament for a while, and then said, "Grayson, is there something you're not telling us?"

"Perhaps," said Grayson.

Dodging the issue, he pretended to study the beanie from different angles. "But now to the important task at hand," he said. "What to do with this?"

"Toss it into the ocean," said Shawn.

"It will be an 'accident,'" said Cassie.

"Nice idea," said Grayson, "but the *dungeons*, remember?"

"Oh, yeah," said Cassie and Shawn together.

Grayson stuffed the hat under his belt. "Safer here," he said, "won't blow away."

* * *

In less than twenty minutes, the Key Team reached the One-Eyed Giant's Island—a flat-topped mountain rising out of the Transmongonian Sea. The dolphins conveyed the Team into a U-shaped cove formed by the mountain's slopes on either side of a sheer granite cliff as high as a skyscraper. The Team members—including Ayeli—looked up at the cliff's top far above them. "I can see why they call this Bigcliff Island," said Shawn.

Grayson tied their boat to a large dock jutting out from near the cliff's base. A rowboat was tethered there. About the same size as *The People's Boat*, the vessel was huge for a rowboat but a good fit for a giant.

The Key Team disembarked and walked fifty yards to the sloping mountainside beside the cliff. They discovered a dirt path wide enough for the Team members to walk side-by-side but adequate for only a single giant. The Team commenced hiking up the steep, hard-packed, zigzagging path, gaining elevation with each step. Tall, thick-trunked trees on either side of the trail supported an overhead canopy of densely clustered branches that nearly blotted out the sun.

"It sure is dark in here," said Shawn.

"Like a tunnel," agreed Grayson.

"Spooky," said Cassie.

The dark, ugly, twisted trees growing on both sides of the path did not seem at all friendly. They squirmed, creaked, and made deep growling sounds as the Team passed. Unlike the Wise Old Trees, these trees had no eyes or other features that might have given them human-like qualities. They certainly lacked the Wise Old Trees' intelligence and charm.

Many of the flowers lining the path were taller than the human Team members and bore yucky, dull, muddy green leaves. Grayish petals sprouted from their basketball-sized heads. The flowers slowly twisted to and fro and hissed at the Team as they walked by. Cassie wondered aloud how they managed this since they lacked visible mouths, eyes, or ears.

While the humans moved carefully up the path in fearful silence, Ayeli answered every flower's hiss and every tree's snarl with a hiss and raspy growl of her own.

After a quarter-hour of strenuous hiking, the Team reached the island's summit. Before them lay a sun-drenched meadow carpeted with lush green grass sprinkled with normal size brightly colored flowers that showed no antipathy toward the Team.

The distant trees were calm as well.

"Wow," said Cassie.

"This sure beats the awful trees and flowers we just passed," said Shawn. "I wonder why it's so different."

Grayson nodded in the direction of three white unicorns emerging from a cluster of trees and trotting toward the Team. "Maybe they have something to do with it," he said.

"Yay!" said Cassie.

"Grayson, they're not going to hurt us?" said Shawn, more as a statement than a question, although there was a slight tremble in his voice. He was still unnerved by the rude and frightening reception the Team had just received on the trail. "I mean, like, they're unicorns. Unicorns don't hurt people, do they?" he asked.

"Quite right," assured Grayson. "Nice as can be."

When the gentle beasts reached the visitors, Cassie displayed her usual glee and, together with Shawn and Grayson, petted the friendly creatures. As before, the unicorns bent down so Ayeli could touch their noses with her paw. She expressed an affectionate meow. The unicorns' golden horns sparkled in the sun.

The Team walked a few paces to the nearby top of the cliff. The human members peered over the edge with understandable trepidation. Ayeli was curious as well but displayed no fear of heights. The Team could see the cove a hundred yards below with the dock and the tethered boats that looked like small floating toys. The dolphins seemed to be miniatures lazily swimming about the watercrafts.

The Team resumed their quest. The path ahead cut across the meadow and weaved among rolling mounds whose heights reached no more than a dozen feet.

The cheerful mood created by the interlude with the unicorns gave way to a sense of foreboding as the Team approached a mansion-sized cottage. The massive front door—more than five times as tall as Shawn—was slightly ajar, and the Team cautiously entered through the narrow opening. They moved into the kitchen area where the sweet aroma of cooking food hung in the air and steam issued from a giant-sized pot on a mammoth wood-fired stove. With the stove's surface a dozen feet above them, the Team could only see the pot's edge and a spoon's handle.

A sudden creaking noise indicated that the front door was opening. The giant was returning. The intruders quickly hid as best they could behind a stack of logs set beside the stove. They briefly peeked and observed the giant, who appeared to be about two-and-a-half stories in height. His uncombed coarse black hair fell to his shoulders and was complemented by a scraggly beard. His simple, wrinkled clothes had a slept-in appearance. Contrary to what one might expect, he was a young man and not bad-looking despite his shabby aspect.

Most significantly, while Cassie and Shawn had assumed the giant would have a single large eye centered on his forehead, he had *two* eyes, with one covered by a black patch that gave him the look of a pirate.

A key was attached to a relatively small (for a giant) golden necklace that, in turn, was attached to a thick cord looped around the large man's neck. The key was too small to be of any use to a giant but would undoubtedly be of use to Grayson and his companions: with its ornate golden design, it was surely a Magic Key!

The giant placed some freshly picked carrots on a chopping block and began cutting them into pieces with a cleaver. He paused and sipped wine from a nearly empty quart-sized glass. He refilled it from a gallon-sized bottle sitting on the counter. He held still for a moment, looked up, and sniffed the air. With a deep baritone voice, he bellowed,

"Fee fi fo fum!

I smell the blood of a Transmongonian.

Be he—"

He hesitated, then said to himself in a quieter voice, "Now, how does that go? Oh, yes,

"...Be he alive or be he dead

I'll grind his bones to make my bread!"

He laughed and remarked to himself, "I've always wanted to say that.

"But wait!" he said, again to himself. "I *do* smell the blood of... *three* Transmongonians! Or are they *all* Transmongonians? No. Two are *not*...and...there's a fourth interloper, a creature of some sort."

He set down the cleaver.

He appeared to put effort into looking around for his prey. Within a few seconds, he spotted the Team huddling behind the logs. "Ah-ha!" he said as if surprised. He bent down and got on his knees for a closer look. "Well well, young Grayson Humblebee, I believe. I have been expecting you. You're just in time for dinner."

"Oh...um...thank you...I think," said Grayson, his voice trembling.

"That's a little joke, you know," said the giant. "Do you get it? 'Expecting you for dinner?'"

"Oh…oh my goodness!" said Grayson. "You're expecting us to *be* your dinner!"

"Very good," said the giant. Eying Cassie and Shawn, he said, "And what are these?"

"Ch-children," said Grayson.

"Oh, how delightful! I love children!" said the giant, clapping his hands together. "Preferably cooked in butter, with mushrooms, onions, a little pepper, lemon peel, and just a hint of salt. Mmm!

"And this?" he asked, reaching for Ayeli. He gingerly scooped up the feline and inspected her closely with his single eye. Looking more like a mouse in the giant's massive hand, Ayeli hissed in defiance. "Cats make for great appetizers, you know. They inspire a hunger for the main course."

Ayeli hissed again and bared her teeth.

"Nasty little thing," he said. "I love it when my food puts up a fuss—makes it even tastier." He cautiously lifted Ayeli with two fingers by the nape of her neck and held her near his open mouth, presumably ready to swallow her whole. The cat hissed and pawed frantically at the air.

"Hey!" shouted Shawn.

"What," said the giant, a little irritated as he placed Ayeli back on his hand.

"Don't you dare!" said Shawn.

"Don't I *dare*?" The giant laughed. "That's so adorable! Are you *threatening* me?"

"Well, yeah," stammered Shawn with a slightly more tempered voice.

The giant looked at Shawn and laughed again. "Oh, I am *so* frightened!" he said.

He again moved Ayeli to his open mouth while watching Cassie and Shawn for their response.

"Please don't! Please!" the youngsters squealed together.

"Hey," said the giant, "I'm just messin' with ya. You really didn't believe I—" He pointed at Ayeli with his free hand, then at his open mouth, then at Ayeli again. "How crude and primitive do you think I am? Eat your beloved pet—*raw*? No! I'll cook her first, of course." He held Ayeli once more by the nape of her neck, this time over the steaming pot. The cat hissed and pawed at the air even more frantically. "I think she'll add flavoring to the stew," he said. "Except she's so nasty, she may make the stew bitter.

"But not to worry; I'll just add honey."

"No! No! No!" Cassie and Shawn again begged.

"Oh, all right," said the giant. He placed Ayeli on a shelf on a wall opposite the counter and stove. While shelves for normal humans—and most Transmongonians—might be a foot wide at most, this shelf was nearly four feet wide. "You know what?" said the giant. "As much as I'd like to cook the cat right now—what's its name?"

"*Her* name is Ailuros. We call her Ayeli," said Cassie.

"Well," continued the giant, "I think I'll save 'her name is Ayeli' for desert…cook her in a little brandy, *a la flambé*. With honey, of course. Do you know what flambé means? It means—"

"I know what it means!" interrupted Cassie with considerable anger.

"Good for you," said the giant. "Smart girl. Anyway, *Ayeli a la flambé* would be nice."

He gathered up Grayson, Cassie, and Shawn and placed them on the same wide shelf as Ayeli.

"What does *a la flambé* mean," whispered Shawn to Cassie.

"Cooked with fire," answered Cassie.

Shawn's face twisted in disgust.

"Say!" the giant said to the Team. "I'm about finished preparing some unicorn stew. Would you care to join me?"

Cassie cupped her hands over her mouth. "Oh no," she said, "please tell me you didn't—"

"Didn't what?"

"Cook a...oh, how could you?"

"Cook a unicorn?"

"Yes!"

"Not hard: just skin it, chop it up, throw it in a pot with broth, add vegetables, onion, spices..." The giant leaned toward the boiling stew and waved some of its vapor into his face. "Smell that?" he said. "Doesn't that smell great! Unicorn stew—hard to beat."

"You're mean...and disgusting," said Cassie.

"Not at all," said the giant. He had another sip of wine. "But you know what would make the stew even better?"

No one answered—no one *dared* answer.

"Diced Grayson Humblebee," said the giant, "Imagine: unicorns and, for added flavor, this young gentleman here."

The giant took another sip of wine, removed Grayson from the shelf, and placed him on the cutting board. Holding the Team leader with one hand, he grabbed the cleaver.

"No!" cried Shawn.

Grayson, helpless, said nothing; he just clenched his teeth.

The giant raised the cleaver, ready to bring a quick stop to Grayson's quest for the Magic Keys.

"He won't be good for you," said Cassie.

The giant paused, cleaver in midair. "Oh?"

"No," said Cassie, "I mean, like, he's old, and he has a poor diet, and he's got all that gristle and stuff. And...and there's all that red meat; I mean, like, red meat's really bad for you...clogs your arteries, destroys your liver and stuff."

"That's what my wife says," said the giant, continuing to hold the cleaver over Grayson.

"Your wife?" asked Shawn.

"Yes," said the giant. He paused for a moment and then said, "Oh well..." He brought the cleaver swiftly down on the cutting board, just shy of Grayson's head, and returned the shaken teenager to the shelf.

"I'm *old*?" whispered Grayson to Cassie. "I'm *fourteen*!"

"I had to think fast," whispered Cassie.

The giant took a sip of wine. "My wife's a vegetarian," he said, "very strict about what she eats—*we* eat, that is. She's a health nut. Always on my case about what I consume. Makes me eat nutritious food, like these carrots. Now I feel bad about almost eating Master Humblebee. Not that I care for him—I don't—but today, I almost went omnivorous. You know what 'omnivorous' means, don't you? Means I would eat *anything* if I could, including people. Anyway, eating you young folks would upset my wife. Why did you have to bring her up, anyway?"

"We didn't," said Shawn. "You did."

"Here I was," said the giant, "all set to have a delicious meal of Humblebee-unicorn stew, made with Master Grayson as the main ingredient and two more children for added flavor—and a nice *kitty a la flambé* for dessert—and now I can't do that because I would think of my wife with every bite and I'd feel...*guilty*."

He glared at Cassie and Shawn. "Curses on you," he said.

"Sorry," said Cassie and Shawn together, secretly smiling at each other and at Grayson, who smiled back.

Ayeli meowed pleasantly.

"Then you're not going to eat the unicorn stew?" said Shawn. "I mean, your wife would be, like, really mad if you did."

"Furious!" added Cassie.

The giant finished the glass of wine and refilled it. "Yes, of course I'm going to eat the stew!" He paused for a moment and said, "Oh, all right...I left the unicorns out. It's unicorn stew without unicorns—unicorn stew *sans* unicorns if you will. Does that make you happy?"

"Yes," said Cassie and Shawn.

"Where is your wife?" asked Grayson.

"She left me."

"I'm sorry to hear that," said Grayson.

"Why did she leave?" asked Shawn.

"I became hard to live with...*harder* to live with," said the giant. "I've been sort of mean, well, *quite* mean, since the witch put this key around my neck and put that curse on me. I'd say nasty things to her—my wife, I mean. I'd lose my temper. I never touched her in anger, though, I'll say that."

"That's good," said Cassie. "What's her name? What's *your* name?"

"I'm Cyril. She's Krythelia." The giant removed the glass and bottle of wine and slid down onto the floor with his back against a cupboard door. He looked up at the Team high on the shelf opposite the cupboard and placed the wine beside him. He turned his face away and became lost in thought. Half-talking to the Key Team and half-talking to himself, he said, "She's a wonderful lady, Krythelia. Gentle. You should see her with the unicorns. They love her. And she's smart—read almost every book here." He swept his hands toward the shelves full of books in the adjoining room. "We read together every night. We have great talks. We—"

Cyril turned his attention to Cassie, who, together with her companions, was peering down at him. The expression on the giant's face changed from wistful yearning to outright anger. "Hey!" he said, glaring at the young Team member, "What is this, an interrogation? What goes on with my wife and me is none of your business!"

"Sorry, *Cyril*," said Cassie, "I'm just trying to—"

"Well, don't try!" he said.

"You don't have to be so nasty," said Cassie. "No wonder she left you."

Cyril stood up, wine glass in hand, and put his face close to Cassie and her companions. He glared at each, one by one with his single eye. "Yes, I *do* have to be nasty," he said. "Same with the flowers and plants on the side of this island. Did you notice they were dark and ugly and nasty when you walked up here?"

"They sure were," said Shawn.

"Well," said the giant. "There you are: the witch cursed this whole island—"

"Not everything," interrupted Shawn. "The meadow with the unicorns was nice and green, and the flowers were pretty too. And I don't think they minded us being there."

"Oh yeah?" said Cyril. "The witch probably didn't want to make it unpleasant for the unicorns. She has a soft spot for the little monsters."

"They're not monsters!" said Cassie.

"Hmpf," said Cyril, not responding to Cassie. "'Good *or* Evil Witch': some misguided souls think she's good at heart. *Evil*, I say!"

Ayeli let out a rather deep, prolonged meow.

"The path you took on the mountainside used to be beautiful," continued Cyril. "Flowers were colorful. The trees were nice. Now it's…it's—"

"Dark and ugly and nasty," said Shawn. "But you don't have to take it out on us."

"Yes, I *do* have to take it out on you. The curse. You just don't get it, do you."

All three non-cat members of the Team shook their heads.

"And by the way," said Cyril, holding the ornate key close to the Team, "if you think you're going to get this so-called 'Magic Key' by being *nice* to me, forget it."

"OK. Geez!" said Shawn.

Cyril stood back and eyed the Team for a moment. They watched him in return. His angry look unexpectedly grew into an almost sinister smile. "You're staring at me," he said. "You're wondering how I lost my eye? Why do I wear this patch?" He moved his face very close to the Team—so close his wine-infused breath nearly overwhelmed them. "Well, I'm going to show you something." He placed a couple of fingers on the bottom of the patch. "Now get ready," he said. "When I lift this patch, you'll see the most grue-some, horrible sight you've ever witnessed. You'll want to vomit. You'll have nightmares forever. *Warning:* blood and yucky stuff will likely squirt all over you, so prepare yourselves. Ready?"

"No!" said Grayson, Cassie, and Shawn together, covering their faces and backing away from the giant as much as possible. Ayeli moved with them but remained quiet.

Cyril lifted the patch.

Seconds of silence ensued as the Team kept their hands over their eyes. Finally, Shawn spread his fingers just a bit so he could see what was under Cyril's patch. "Oh!" he said in surprise, pulling his hands away from his face. "It's just another eye." To the Team, he said, "He has *two* eyes, just like normal people!"

Grayson and Cassie removed their hands to behold that the giant's previously hidden left eye was like his right.

Cyril laughed. "Krythelia hates it when I do that to people," he said, "but I enjoy it. So much fun!"

"Now look at my eyes," he said. "What do you see?"

"They look the same," said Cassie. She pointed to Cyril's right eye, the one the patch had *not* hidden. "But that one's starting to, like, wiggle."

"Exactly." He pointed at his left eye. "I wear the patch over my left eye here, which is my good eye, so my right eye gets exercised," he said. "When my left eye is covered, my right gets a workout. I have what you might call a *lazy eye*." His right eye started to twist to and fro rather furiously. The giant returned the patch, and his visible eye calmed down. "Someday, this lazy eye will stop being lazy. Both eyes will work together."

Cyril looked closely at Grayson and the hat tucked in the Team leader's belt. "Hey!" said the giant. "That's your beanie I've heard so much about. Shouldn't you be wearing it? Put it on. Let's see how it looks."

Grayson retrieved his beanie and placed it on his head.

The One-Eyed Giant laughed. "Oh my!" he said. "That's awful! Put it away. The sight of it will ruin my one good eye."

Grayson returned the beanie to his belt.

"Why do you wear it?" asked the giant.

"Orders of The Great Rumpty D," said Grayson.

"Oh yes, *him*," said the giant. "Rumpty D. I heard some not-so-great things about the despot. Never met him personally. Don't want to.

"What a horrible punishment, making you wear that tasteless adornment. I suggest you ditch it next opportunity.

"Oops! I forgot," said the giant. "There may not be another opportunity."

Cyril turned his attention to Cassie. "Pretty flower crown," he said.

"Thank you," said Cassie.

"I hate pretty," said Cyril. "Ugly is much more appealing. I'm ugly, and that makes me interesting, don't you agree? Do you think anyone would buy a book called *The Handsome Duckling*? No, of course not. It's *The Ugly Duckling* that everyone likes."

"Actually," said Cassie, "I think you're kind of cute. If you would only trim or shave that beard, you would look pretty good."

"Hmph!" grunted Cyril.

He slumped down on the floor again, his back against the cupboards. "Krythelia likes to wear those flower crown things too," he said.

"Is she pretty?" asked Shawn.

"Yes, she is. Lovely."

"Do you like it when she wears flowers?" asked Cassie.

"Yes, I do. They add to her beauty. Hard to believe that such a lovely creature could be even *more* lovely. I mean, can one improve a rose? No! Krythelia is perfect just as she is, yet when she wears those flowers with all their magnificent colors, oh! She stirs my heart even more."

"You said you hate pretty," said Shawn.

"I didn't say—hey! Stop it! You're confusing me. Mind your own business."

"I believe our Cyril is a poet at heart," said Grayson.

"Nonsense!" said Cyril. "You, Humblebee, be quiet! All of you... quiet!"

Cyril consumed more wine.

"You're sure drinking a lot of wine," said Cassie, ignoring Cyril's demand to be quiet.

"No, I'm not," said Cyril. "Wine has health benefits. Just ask Krythelia."

"Not *that much* wine," said Cassie. "Krythelia wouldn't want you drinking that much, and you know it!"

Cyril paused, then said, "You are what is called a *scold*, young lady!"

Cassie did not respond.

"Can you not see that I'm miserable?" said Cyril, his speech becoming slurred.

"There's something I should tell you," said the giant.

After another long pause, Cassie finally said, "Do tell. We are waiting with bated breath."

"I wasn't the best husband *before* the witch put the curse on me. I...I took Krythelia for granted sometimes. I said unkind things to her. I was impatient with her. I didn't show her how much I loved her enough. I wasn't as affectionate as I should have been. I was selfish. I admit it. Not all the time, mind you, just sometimes. So, this curse thing, it only made me worse. Now I'm grouchy all the time. Still, I can't blame the witch entirely, to be honest."

"You can change," said Grayson.

"I don't think so," said Cyril. "This curse, it's...hey, stop arguing with me!"

"He wasn't arguing," said Shawn. "He was just trying to be helpful."

"Well, he wasn't. And you, young man, you stop arguing too."

"I wasn't. I...never mind."

Cyril took another drink of wine, refilled the glass, and became quiet and still. His visible eye started to close—presumably along with the not-visible one.

"Would you like me to sing you a song?" asked Cassie. "That might make you feel better."

"My sister has a great voice," volunteered Shawn unwittingly.

"Go ahead," said Cyril. "Do whatever. But don't think you'll get the key. And don't think you'll make the curse go away."

"I understand," said Cassie. "This is a lullaby our daddy used to sing to us when he put us to bed." In a lovely, soft voice, she sang,

> *Go to sleep, my children*
>
> *Go to sleep, my children*
>
> *Go to sleep, my children*
>
> > *It's late into the night.*
>
> *We'll not sleep, dear Daddy*
>
> *We'll not sleep, dear Daddy*
>
> *We'll not sleep, dear Daddy*
>
> > *Until you hug us tight.*

"I know what you're up to," mumbled Cyril. "Don't you..."

He didn't finish what he had to say. He attempted to keep his uncovered eye open but was only partially successful.

Cassie continued...

> *Close your eyes, my children*
>
> *Close your eyes, my children*
>
> *Close your eyes, my children*
>
> > *The moon is soon to rise.*
>
> *Kiss us first, dear Mommy*
>
> *Kiss us first, dear Mommy*
>
> *Kiss us first, dear Mommy*
>
> > *And then we'll close our eyes.*

The giant closed his uncovered eye completely. He rolled over on his side, grumbled a bit, then fell fast asleep. Not wishing to wake him, the Team spoke in hushed, quiet voices.

"Now what do we do?" asked Cassie.

"We surely can't jump," said Grayson. The shelf on which the Team stood was at least twenty feet above the cottage floor.

In addition to a variety of decorative knick-knacks placed on the shelf, some items would prove helpful to the Key Team: a notebook, pencil, giant ball of cord, and a pair of scissors. Shawn eyed the cord—suitable for rope from his perspective while probably used as string by the giant. "This is the same rope the giant is using to hold the key," he said.

"Yes, it is," said Grayson. "Probably strong, too. And I know what you're thinking, but I don't think we can grip the rope tight enough. We'll slip and fall."

"We don't have to climb down it, like, hand over hand," said Shawn, "we can belay ourselves down."

"Belay?"

"Yeah, watch. I'll show you." Above the shelf was another shelf, supported by ornate, antique brackets formed by cast-iron into vine-like loops and swirls. Shawn pulled a length of rope from the ball and tossed its end through a circular loop of iron, leaving the cord draped over the bottom part of the opening. The junior Team member recovered the rope and threw it for a second time through the loop. The very thick "string" was now wrapped twice around the opening's base.

Shawn formed the end of the rope that had gone through the loophole into a secure harness and sat in it. The young belaying expert asked Grayson to pick up the part of the cord that had not yet gone through the bracket and was still attached to the ball. "Now pull on the rope and hold onto it," he instructed the Team leader.

"Tight," he added.

Grayson complied. Shawn felt the rope grow taut. He put his weight on the harness and lifted his feet. Grayson was able to keep Shawn in the air with minimal effort. "Now, let me down," said Shawn. Grayson carefully moved his section of the rope *up* toward the bracket. This, in turn, eased Shawn *down* onto the shelf. "Friction," he said, nodding in the direction of the rope wrapped around the bracket's component.

"Most clever, Mr. Solskin," said Grayson.

"My brother *is* quite clever," said Cassie, "I have to admit."

Ayeli meowed as if in agreement.

Shedding the harness, Shawn divulged his plan: He and Cassie would first lower Grayson to the ground, belaying him with the rope. Then Grayson, controlling the rope from below, would belay Cassie and then Shawn. Ayeli would ride with Shawn.

"I have an idea," said Cassie. She walked over to the notepad and pencil. "Let's first write a note to Cyril. I mean, like, let's let him know we don't hold a grudge or anything. He's doesn't seem all that bad at heart, does he?"

"No, he does not," said Grayson. "Good idea, Cassie." She flipped open the cover of the yard-wide notepad to reveal a blank page. She hoisted the giant pencil and, with suggestions from Shawn and Grayson, jotted a message to the giant:

> Dear Cyril,
>
> We hope you feel better. You are not as bad as you pretend to be. We like you despite yourself. We hope you and Krythelia get back together.
>
> Wishing you all the happiness.
>
> The Key Team—
>
> Cassie
>
> Shawn
>
> Grayson
>
> Ayeli

(It was Shawn who added Ayeli's name to the list.)

Cassie placed the note against the wall so Cyril would be sure to see it.

The Team refocused their attention to getting off the shelf.

"OK. Grayson, you're first," said Shawn. "Cassie and I can belay you down."

"Yeah," said Cassie, "we can do that."

"Mmmm," Grayson murmured with a complete lack of enthusiasm.

Shawn helped Grayson into the harness. The Team leader tightly gripped the harness's main rope with both hands and, with a mixture of dread and bravado, backed up toward the edge of the shelf. "I hope you realize I have faith in you," he said with a still-trembling and not convincing voice, "both of you."

"Thanks, Grayson," said Cassie. "Don't worry; you'll be fine. We have done this many times with our dad."

Together, Cassie and Shawn slowly released sections of rope, hand under hand, on their side of the bracket as Grayson stepped over the edge of the shelf and into thin air. The kids felt Grayson's weight on the rope, but the bracket's drag on it made their task easy as they slowly and carefully eased him down onto the cottage floor.

With considerable effort, Cassie and Shawn manhandled the giant's heavy scissors to trim the rope so that half reached the floor from the bracket's far side and half descended to the bottom from the near side. Grayson returned the empty harness to the shelf from his position on the floor by pulling down on the near-side half of the rope. Cassie fitted herself into the harness when it reached her. Grayson, releasing the cord little by little, gently belayed the young lady to the floor.

Grayson once again returned the harness to the shelf. It was now Shawn's turn. He stepped into the harness and held on with both hands. Ayeli jumped into his lap. "Ayeli," Shawn said, "now don't freak out. We're going to have a fun ride."

Ayeli, apparently comfortable with Shawn's assurance, purred.

Grayson belayed Shawn and a very calm Ayeli down from the shelf.

The Key Team was safely together again, with the shelf that was to have been their prison-without-bars far above them.

The quartet (three humans plus one cat) approached the giant's head cushioned by his arm resting on the floor. The Magic Key, still hanging from the small golden necklace attached to the cord wrapped around Cyril's neck, lay directly in front of the giant's face, near his mouth. Just as Grayson bent over to pick up the key, Cyril stirred and rolled over. The key did not roll with him: it now lay against the back of his neck. This was good news for Grayson because he wouldn't have to suffer the giant's foul, wine-infused breath, yet it was also bad news because it would be more challenging to secure the key, partially hidden in Cyril's black hair, without waking the behemoth. The Team leader cautiously brushed away a tuft of hair covering the key. This caused the giant to reach back and swat at what he must have assumed, in his stupor, was an insect. Grayson ducked from the slap and carefully—*very* carefully—unlatched the necklace and removed it and the key from the cord around the giant's neck. The key, about four inches in length, was made of gold with an old-fashioned long stem. Embedded in its circular, ornately designed head was what appeared to Cassie and Shawn to be a beautiful crystal, perhaps a quarter-inch thick and about the diameter of a silver dollar. The many cut facets (sides) caught the light and sparkled cheerily. Grayson looped the key chain around his neck where it joined the vial of healing nectar given to him by Hyacinth the Flower Queen.

The Team leader tiptoed back to his companions and motioned them out the door. "We'd better hurry," he whispered. "Cyril may wake soon, and I hate to think what might happen when he discovers the key is missing."

The Team crossed the meadow, waved at the unicorns, and entered the wide path down to the cove. The trees and flowers were as unfriendly as before, but the Team did not feel threatened—initially, that is.

"So, Cassie," said Grayson, "I'm old and don't eat well and have all that gristle and stuff?"

"Uh…" said Cassie. "Like I said, I had to think fast."

"Hmm."

"Saved you, didn't I?" said Cassie.

"Yes, I suppose you did."

Meanwhile, back at his cottage, the giant sensed that something was amiss, woke up groggily, and reached behind his neck for the key. Realizing that it was missing, he came fully awake in an instant. He rose, went to his front door, and shouted at the top of his lungs, "THEY STOLE MY KEY! STOP THEM! STOP THEM!"

The Key Team heard this even though they had traveled some distance down the path. Shawn picked up Ayeli, and they all began running as fast as they could. Unfortunately, the trees and plants heard the giant's commands as well. Now, rather than merely making unpleasant sounds, the disgruntled flora were determined to stop the Team before they reached the end of the trail. The trees growled and batted at the four of them with their branches. The flowers made ear-splitting, shrieking sounds and swatted at the team with their large, gray petals.

Shawn tripped and purposely turned himself as he fell so that his body hit the ground without crushing Ayeli, who promptly slid from his arms and ran slightly ahead of her friends. Cassie, running

behind Shawn, stopped and quickly helped her brother to his feet. She could easily have run ahead of him but chose not to. Grayson followed close behind the siblings. He could easily have run ahead of both but also chose not to.

A large tree branch smashed down in front of the runners but they managed to jump over it.

The giant continued to repeat his commands: "STOP THEM! STOP THEM! STOP THEM!" The trees and flowers, despite their fury and Cyril's angry orders, failed to thwart the Team from reaching the cove.

The comrades dashed onto the dock. Grayson rapidly untied one of the ropes securing *The People's Boat* while Cassie loosened the other mooring. The Team scrambled onto their craft. The dolphins, rapidly assessing the situation, took positions in their respective harnesses.

The giant appeared at the top of the cliff overlooking the cove. "YOU WON'T GET AWAY WITH THIS!" he yelled. He picked up a boulder that, even for him, was enormous—nearly the size of a compact car in Cassie and Shawn's world. He held it over his head. "DON'T YOU DARE LEAVE!" he yelled.

Cassie and Shawn, together with Ayeli, quickly took their seats on the boat's front bench while Grayson braced himself against the bow's railing. "Dolphins," he shouted, "we need to leave. NOW!"

The dolphins churned up a great deal of water and headed out to sea with the boat in tow.

"I SAID DON'T LEAVE!" shouted Cyril. Then, in a quieter voice, he added, "PLEASE?" He hesitated a moment, then hurled the boulder down toward the fleeing vessel. It smashed into the water a few yards behind the watercraft's stern with a loud *WHACK!* Although it came close to swamping the boat, the impact created a mammoth wave that served to push it farther out to sea.

"Come back!" shouted the giant, his voice now subdued and more distant.

"Aww," said Cassie. "He sounds sad. I don't think he got our note."

"Me neither," said Shawn.

"Nope," said Grayson.

Ayeli meowed and stretched, relieved to be out of danger—for the moment.

Safely out to sea, the dolphins slowed to a standstill, not knowing where to go next. Grayson directed them, "To the Island of Light People—GO!" The dolphins took off for their next destination.

Chapter 9

Light People

The dolphin-powered *People's Boat* sailed swiftly toward the Island of the *Light People*. The lunch hour was approaching, or at least it seemed that way for Cassie and Shawn. With their hunger having been magnified by the aroma of the giant's cooking, they took advantage of the wherlops and zingtons stored in the boat's cabin. After Grayson assured the kids that the fruit was safe to eat, Cassie and Shawn gathered enough courage to try the wherlops, which had a peppermint-like flavor, and the zingtons, which were more like pears, but sweeter. The youths agreed that the fruit was quite tasty.

"So, tell us about the Light People," said Shawn.

"They appear to be made of, well, *light*," said Grayson. "They glow, somewhat like candles, but much brighter. I don't think they are actually made of *light* as such; they just look that way. I have no knowledge of their composition. They're not solid, exactly, or liquid, or air."

"Maybe like Jello?" asked Cassie.

"I don't know what 'Jello' is," said Grayson, But whatever they're made of, it's unusual stuff—a bit strange, I must say.

"There are—or at least *were*—two kinds of Light People," continued Grayson, "the *White Light People* and the *Rainbow People*."

"What about the *Voids*?" asked Shawn. "The Wise Old Tree at the temple said the Void King has a Magic Key."

"True," said Grayson, "the Voids used to be Rainbow People, full of color. A long time ago, they and the White Light People lived together in harmony. They would throw parties together and dance with each other. All Light People love to dance, or at least they used to. And their kids would play together. But the Rainbow People, because they had such a variety of colors and were so pretty to look at, began to think of themselves as better than everyone else. Eventually, they stopped associating with the White Lights. They stopped dancing with them. They would no longer let their kids play with them. And they started to insult the White Lights, making the White Lights feel like they were less than *real* Light People."

"Reminds me of some people in our world," said Cassie.

"The Voids need to be taught a lesson," said Shawn.

"The Good or Evil Witch must have thought the same thing," said Grayson. "She placed a curse on the Rainbow People that caused them to lose their color and become a dark, dull gray—void of color.

"And it gets worse. Since the witch placed the key with them, the Voids have become *especially* nasty and mean. Now they're void not only of color but of almost anything good in their nature."

"Lot of good the curse did," said Shawn. "Looks to me like the Good or Evil Witch is as bad as the Voids."

Ayeli hissed disgustedly.

"Not necessarily," said Grayson.

"What do you mean, 'not necessarily'?" asked Cassie. "You're too nice, Grayson."

"That may be true, Cassie. The thing is, one can never tell *why* the witch does what she does. Her methods are mysterious."

Ayeli meowed and rubbed against Grayson's legs.

"And that's likely to be true with the Voids," continued Grayson, "even though at the moment they seem to be...um—"

"Rotten," said Shawn.

"Misguided," corrected Grayson. "One can never be sure of what is in the hearts of others or why people behave the way they do. Look at Cyril the Giant: you sensed that he was a nice man even though he seemed not to be."

"True," said Cassie.

"So perhaps we should hold off judging the Voids," said Grayson. "Let's see what happens when we meet them."

"OK...maybe," said Cassie.

"How do you know about the Light People, how the witch cursed them and all that?" asked Shawn.

"I learned of their misfortune through a Wise Old Tree," said Grayson. "The trees also taught me about holding off judgment. That's one reason they're called 'wise.'"

After a brief silence, Shawn said, "So, you think The Great Rumpty D is a good guy underneath?"

Grayson laughed. "You've got me there, Shawn. No, some people are just plain evil, and I think Rumpty D is one of them."

"Wow," said Shawn. "Coming from you, that's pretty harsh."

Grayson nodded in agreement.

After finishing a wherlop, Cassie said, "Did you know that white light is made of all colors?"

"Excuse me?" said Grayson.

"All the colors of the rainbow—they're in white light." A smile with a hint of smugness appeared on the girl's face.

"Why do you say that?"

"Because it's true." In a manner that displayed her impatience with people whose knowledge of science is lacking, she said, spacing out her words, "White … light… is… made…of…all…colors!"

Grayson cocked his head, raised an eyebrow, and gave Cassie a suspicious look.

"Look at the sparkles of light on the water," she said. "What color are they?"

"White."

"So you say. May I see the key you got from Cyril?"

Grayson undid the necklace holding the key and handed it to her. She looked through the key's crystal at the water around the boat. "Ah yes," she said, "just as I thought."

She handed the necklace back to Grayson. "Look at the sparkles through the crystal."

Grayson did as she asked.

"Now what do you see?" asked Cassie.

Grayson gasped, "Why, colors! The sparkles are all the colors of the *rainbow*! Amazing! What a wonderful discovery! Where did you learn this?"

"From a Wise Old Tree."

"Really?"

"No…from a wise old dad. Our dad. He's sort of a science geek."

"I don't know what a 'geek' is, but it must be a good thing."

"It is," said Shawn.

Ayeli meowed, jumped on top of the railing, and stared at the key.

"Ayeli wants to see too," said Shawn.

"You think so?" asked Grayson with a smile. He held the key near Ayeli's eyes. Ayeli surprised everyone by looking intently through the crystal. She meowed as if saying, 'Wow! Isn't that something?!'

"That is one amazing cat," said Cassie.

Grayson looked through the crystal once again. "You know, Miss Solskin, I think this discovery will prove to be very important to the Light People... perhaps even miraculous, I dare say!

"Incidentally," he added, "the material in the key is not just a crystal. It's a diamond."

"A diamond?" asked Cassie and Shawn together.

"Seriously?" asked Cassie. Her scientific knowledge had failed to reveal this aspect of the crystal's true nature to her, but like a genuine scientist, this did not challenge her confidence in herself.

"It must be worth a fortune," said Shawn.

"Not really," said Grayson. "It's from Gem Island. You can find all sorts of pretty stones there: diamonds, sapphires, rubies, emeralds..."

"Cool!" said Shawn. "Can we take—"

"No," said Grayson, "you cannot take them back to your world. They would vanish in seconds."

"Aww, man!" said Cassie and Shawn together.

* * *

The dolphins brought *The People's Boat* to a dock at the edge of the Island of Light People. Grayson showed Shawn and Cassie how to correctly secure the watercraft with its two ropes—one at the bow, one at the stern.

The island consisted of a mound surrounded by flat prairie-like land. Lush vegetation covered hill and ground alike with bright flowers, healthy trees, and bright green grass.

The Team took a path leading to an opening at the base of the mound. They walked through it and entered a long winding tunnel. Several yards in, they came across a steep circular stairway descending deep into the ground. The only light came from a very faint blue glow emanating from large rocks spaced at various points along the sides of the stairway. "This is spooky," said Shawn, his voice echoing off the stairway's walls.

Soon the stairway opened to a large round cavern. Two glowing beings came forward to greet the Team and bowed briefly. Their shimmering bodies could be recognized as human in form (more or less). They radiated pure, bright white light, and appeared to be fuzzy, slightly out of focus. Only their human-like eyes were sharply defined.

They were *White Lights*.

"Master Grayson!" said one. "It is good you are here. We must take you to the queen. There is no time to lose."

The escorts guided the Team to the middle of the cavern, where dozens of White Lights had formed a half-circle around a dais raised a yard above the cavern floor. A throne placed on top of the platform hosted an attractive lady.

"Her Majesty, Amanata, Queen of the White Lights," announced one of the escorts.

The queen, the escorts, and all her subjects radiated pure, bright white light. A silver crown embedded with dozens of sparkling diamonds adorned Queen Amanata's head. She wore a radiant, bright white gown.

She was sobbing, and the people around her appeared to be upset. When the queen noticed the Key Team approaching, she descended from her throne to meet them. She acknowledged the Team members, including Ayeli, with a brief smile forced through her tears. Although no one had taught Cassie and Shawn how to interact with royalty, Shawn instinctively honored the queen with a modest bow, and Cassie curtsied. They correctly sensed it was not the time to introduce themselves. The siblings seemed unaware of their growing maturity as they displayed sympathy for the queen and her subjects' distress—even though they did not know the cause.

Ayeli remained silent as well, likely out of respect for the queen's dismay.

Queen Amanata gently took both of Grayson's hands in her cotton-soft, warm ones. "Oh, Master Grayson," she said, "we were told you would come. You're here just in time. Please tell me you can help us."

"Help with—" said Grayson.

"My daughter, Luziette. She went to visit Zon, son Valdoc, the Void King. The King always allowed her entrance to the Void's cavern because Luziette has always been nice to the little fellow, ever since she babysat for him when he first came into the world. Now, without warning, the Voids have decided to hold her prisoner. I am afraid they are going to harm her. She's so naive, so trusting."

"Oh, my goodness!" said Grayson, "We'll do our best."

"I am certain Zon is not a participant in the Voids' actions," added the queen. "He's really quite sweet."

"I understand," said Grayson.

The Team, accompanied by a half-dozen White Light People, approached the small entrance to the Void chamber. Two Voids stood guard just inside the opening. As with the White Lights, they appeared to be slightly out of focus. Unlike the White Lights, hardly any light radiated from their gray, moderately translucent bodies. Their only color came from bright, glowing red eyes with tiny black dots as pupils. They stood aside to let the Team pass but refused to let the White Lights through. Due to the Voids' ability to sap energy from White Lights by mere touch, an army of Lights could not have overcome even a single guard. One of the Lights was reminded of this the hard way: when he bravely, but foolishly, attempted to force his way in, a guard lightly pressed a finger on the Light's forehead. The helpless victim's glow flickered and dimmed to a dull Void-like gray. The courageous White Light slumped to the ground, wounded but still alive.

Having just entered the cavern, the Key Team heard the painful whimper of the wounded Light and turned to see what happened. Cassie covered her mouth. Shawn clenched his teeth and placed his hands on his cheeks. Grayson scrunched his face and frowned. All three gasped.

"Shame on you!" said Cassie to the offending sentinel.

Ayeli approached the scoundrel, hissed, and swatted at him with her paw (without touching), then scampered back to her companions.

Neither guard appeared to care about Ayeli's anger or the Team's concern for the Light's suffering.

Grayson put his hands on Cassie and Shawn's shoulders. "We can't do anything for him right now," said the Team leader to the horrified youths. "We must focus on our mission."

A Void motioned the Team to the cavern's center, where many Voids were gathered around a pit about a dozen feet in diameter. Its rocky circular wall slanted a half-dozen feet down to a glowing green mist deep enough to engulf anything—or anyone—that fell in. Waves of the fog-like vapor rose up and down as if disturbed by a slight breeze.

A Void was restraining young Luziette, the White Light princess, as she struggled to break free. Her captor had allowed her to retain her bright luminescent glow. The defiant princess was about as tall as Shawn and perhaps the same age.

Like the guards at the entrance, nearly all the Voids appeared as fuzzy, gray, shadowy forms distinguished only by their piercing, incandescent red eyes. They would be barely visible in the darkness of the cavern were it not for the light cast by the pit, the princess, and one small child. The young one did not appear to be a Void: about a third as tall as the others, he had large blue human-like eyes and a body that glowed brightly with all the colors of the rainbow. "Rainbow Child," whispered Grayson to Cassie and Shawn.

Although the basic shapes of the little tyke and the Voids were human-like, they were clearly *not* human.

Upon seeing the Key Team, the colorful youngster moved close to a tall Void and wrapped his arms around one of the Void's legs, like a fearful child seeking protection by a parent.

The father gently placed a hand on his child's head. Dad wore a diamond-studded gold crown as well as a gold chain necklace around his neck. A key with a large emerald at the center of its ornate head—almost certainly a Magic Key—was attached to the necklace. "Ah, young Grayson Humblebee," he said in a deep, raspy voice, "we've been expecting you. Welcome to our modest abode. I see you've brought some friends.

"Who are you?" he said to Cassie and Shawn.

"We're with Grayson as part of the Key Team," said Cassie. She spoke politely despite her distress over the recent wounding of the White Light.

Grayson walked over to the luminescent Rainbow Child and crouched down to be at eye level. "Hello there," he said in a quiet, gentle voice. "My name is Grayson. I bet your name is Zon."

Zon shyly nodded his head.

"It's very nice to meet you, Zon. I've heard good things about you."

Zon smiled.

Grayson stood and returned to his Team.

"Key Team, eh?" said the king. "So that's what you call your-selves. Clever."

"Why did you kidnap Luziette?" asked Shawn.

The king cocked his head and smirked at Shawn as though the young Team member had asked a dumb question whose answer was obvious.

"Answer the question," snapped Cassie, her politeness fading. "Why did you kidnap—"

"You're both very rude," interrupted the king. "Do you not know I am king of the Voids?"

"We figured that," said Cassie, "and you were once the king of the Rainbow People too. But you seem to have all lost your compassion along with your color."

"Except for Zon," said Shawn. "He kept his color and I hear he is nice too."

"I'm with my brother on that," said Cassie.

To Grayson, the king said, "Your young friends show *spunk*."

"Yes, they do," agreed Grayson.

"Their kind of spunk is unbecoming," said the king.

"Please answer their question," demanded Grayson. "Why did you kidnap the princess?"

"First of all, we didn't kidnap her," said the king. "She came of her own free will to visit my son, Prince Zon, but she knows White Lights are forbidden to mingle with us since the Curse."

"But you still let her come in here," Cassie pointed out.

"To teach the Lights a lesson," said the king. They have been warned but did not think we were serious, like that Light who tried to enter our domain a moment ago. Now he's lost his radiance. Arrogant fool! They never learn. They forget their place.

"Our two peoples *must* be separate!" continued the king. "Now is the time to prove that we are serious about that—*very* serious. We intend to offer Luziette as a sacrifice in the Pit of Absolute Nothingness.

"And you've come just in time to see the fun."

"Don't you dare!" said Grayson with unusual anger. He moved toward the Void holding the Light Princess, but another Void restrained the Team leader—not with physical force so much as with a kind of electric shock that caused Grayson's muscles to freeze. Cassie and Shawn attempted to intervene in the same manner but squealed and winced in pain when they also received shocks from the shadowy figures.

The Voids' bodies did not seem to be made entirely of light; they felt, as Cassie suggested earlier, more like globs of Jello. Any Team member could easily have pushed them aside were it not for the evil beings' ability to produce an electrical charge at will.

"Members of the Key Team," said the king, "you are familiar with the Pit of Absolute Nothingness, are you not?" None of the Team answered. "No?" asked the king. "Allow me to demonstrate.

"Young lady," said the king to Cassie. "Roll a boulder into the pit, a heavy one. See what happens."

"Perhaps you could roll it yourself?" asked Cassie, suspecting a trick. She displayed no hint of fear in her voice—she was successfully hiding her apprehension.

"No can do," said the king. He held up his hands, shaped like fuzzy mittens of dim gray light. "We Voids lack the physical strength and agility of you...ah...*humans*...to move heavy objects.

"You are humans, correct?"

"Yes," rasped Cassie.

"Funny ears," said the king.

He nodded to the Void holding Cassie. The creature then released the cantankerous girl to allow her to approach one of many boulders lining the pit's edge. The transparent mist's green glow enabled the pit's rocky bottom to be readily visible. (To Cassie and Shawn, it looked similar to a small swimming pool in their world illuminated by underwater lights at night.) Unfortunately, the mist could be deadly despite its appealing beauty.

Cassie turned and glanced uneasily at the king and the Void restraining Luziette, then nudged the boulder over the pit's edge. It bounced down the incline and into the green fog. Waves of mist radiated outward from the point of impact. A blinding cloud of sparks engulfed the heavy stone and trailed it, like the tail of a comet, as it slowly sank toward the bottom of the pit. Muffled sizzling and popping sounds could be heard. Then, before the boulder hit bottom, it vanished into...

Absolutely nothing.

Gone without a trace.

A Void took hold of Cassie once more.

"Wasn't that something?" sneered the Void King. "Just think what a spectacle the princess will make. I can hardly wait."

"How can you talk like that?" asked Shawn. "I mean, you want to kill her. Why? She never did anything to you!"

Tears formed in Shawn's eyes—and Cassie's and Grayson's as well.

"Why?" asked the king. "Didn't I just tell you?'

"To teach the White Lights a lesson?" asked Shawn. "So that you can stay separate from them? That's really stupid!"

"It's not that simple," said the king. "The White Lights have become arrogant since we lost our color due to the witch's curse. They think they are better than us and seek to humiliate us by being *bright* and lit up like they are. *We* were the ones with all the colors of the rainbow, just like my Zon here.

"Isn't he awesome, by the way, with all his bright, beautiful colors?"

The Key Team members nodded in agreement.

"*We* were the beautiful ones," continued the king, "the superior ones. *We* were the *Rainbow People*, not them. They—with their bland white light—they have the nerve to look down their noses at *us*? How dare they! Now they must suffer, just as they make us suffer. Justice will be served! Isn't that right, Zon?"

The toddler released his grip on his father's leg and looked up at the king. With eyes glistening with tears, he defiantly shook his head. "No, Father, it's not right," he said in a trembling, soft voice. "Luziette is my friend. Please don't—"

While he was speaking, Zon moved away from his father to see his dad's face. Too upset to be aware of impending danger, he inadvertently backed up to the pit. Before the king or anyone else could prevent it, he slipped, tumbled down the pit's rocky embankment, and came to a stop on a ledge just above the deadly green mist's surface. He started to cry.

"Zon!" yelled the king, who moved to the pit's edge and peered over at the small Void, who was precariously close to losing his young life. "Oh no! My son!" cried the king. "Please, no!"

"Well, save him!" ordered Grayson with unusual firmness.

"I can't—we—I told you—we are not strong enough," said the king. "We can't grip the rocks, let alone pick up Zon!"

Ayeli let out a pitiful, sad, whimpering sound.

"We could save him," said Shawn.

"Oh, would you? Can you?" pleaded the king, wringing his mitten-like hands.

"I think so," said Shawn. "Maybe."

Ayeli meowed encouragingly.

Shawn glared at the lightless beings holding him and his companions. The Voids understood and released the Team.

"OK," commanded Shawn, "we'll make a chain: I'll climb down to get Zon. Cassie, you hold me. Grayson, you hold Cassie. Ayeli, let us know if any Voids do something stupid."

Ayeli flicked her tail menacingly and scowled at the Voids nearest the pit. She then focused her attention on her companions.

With the life of the king's beloved toddler on the line, the Voids were not about to do anything stupid.

Shawn stepped onto the pit's wall and eased himself down, gingerly stepping on one protruding stone after another. "Zon," he said reassuringly to the whimpering lad below, "stay still. Don't worry. We're coming to get you. Just don't move!"

Shawn, a short distance down on the slope, looked up to Cassie. The siblings grasped hands. Grayson, with one arm looped around a heavy boulder on the rim, stepped onto the slope and connected with Cassie, who cautiously took a step farther down the hill. Shawn then edged closer to Zon. With all three now holding hands on the steep wall and arms stretched taught, muscles were strained to the limit. While all made sure their feet were well planted, their knees nonetheless wobbled due to fear and stress. They would not be able to hold these positions much longer.

If any of the human Key Team members slipped, they would all tumble into the pit, and that would be the end of them.

With one foot braced on the ledge holding Zon, Shawn managed to put his free arm around the young prince. Zon, in turn, threw his arms around Shawn's neck. "Ow! Hey!" cried Shawn, feeling the electric shock of the toddler's grasp. "Let go! No! Don't let go! Just turn off the electricity!"

Zon ceased shocking his rescuer.

The Team members slowly and carefully pulled each other—and Zon—back to the top of the pit and onto safe ground. Shawn kneeled down carefully so the still-whimpering prince could safely release his hold on his rescuer. The little one scampered to the king and leaped into his father's arms.

Wide-eyed, Ayeli had anxiously been shifting weight from one side to the other as she closely monitored the drama from the pit's rim. She issued a triumphant meow when the Team was safe.

The king turned to the Void holding Luziette and said, "Release the princess."

The Void did as ordered. Luziette, now free, ran toward the cavern's exit, then stopped abruptly, turned, and ran back to Zon and the Key Team. Luziette gave young Zon a quick hug and said, "Bye, my friend, be careful now! I probably won't be back; I'll miss you!

"Bye, Key Team!" she said as she waved. "Thank you so much! Thank you! Thank you! Thank you!" To Ayeli, she added, "Bye, kitty! Thank you too!"

Ayeli meowed graciously.

Luziette then entered the main cavern and ran into the arms of her delighted mother.

Turning to the Key Team, the Void King said, "Why did you do that? You risked your lives to save one of *us*. You could have made demands. You could have insisted we release the White Light princess first, but you...just went ahead...we were so mean to you!"

"And mean to the White Lights," said Cassie.

"And the White Lights," said the king.

"Grayson told us you might not be as bad as you seem," said Shawn. "He said you're probably OK deep down. I don't know; maybe he's right."

"You may not be human," added Grayson, "but you are living beings. I am sure I speak for Cassie and Shawn—and Ayeli—when I say it is not in our hearts to let a living being perish. Even if Zon had become a Void, we would have saved him—or any of you."

Cassie and Shawn nodded in agreement. Ayeli issued a quiet meow.

The king's previous nasty attitude vanished—like the boulder in the pit but without sparks. "Grayson is exceedingly kind," the king said to Shawn, "but so are you—yes, *you*, young man—and your sister. You saved my precious son, and more than that: the three of you...you have lifted the curse. It's going away—I can feel it! We will no longer have to be so...evil!"

The king choked up. The red glow in his eyes faded and gave way to a more human-like appearance with blue irises set against white backgrounds. A tear formed at the corner of one eye and ran down his cheek. As it did, it left a trail of multi-hued colors—like those of Zon—that spread across his face and washed over his entire body. The king put his hand on the shoulder of the Void standing beside him, and that fuzzy shape soon radiated the same bright colors. In turn, the newly transformed Void embraced another who commenced glowing with bright hues and naturally colored eyes. Within seconds, all the now-bright shapes were hugging each other. Brilliant colors of the rainbow soon filled every *former* Void until they were no longer dark, menacing creatures. They lit up the cavern.

They were *Rainbow People* once again!

To Cassie and Shawn, the king said, "You both have such courage!"

"To be honest, I was scared to death," said Cassie.

"Me too," said Shawn.

"As was I," said Grayson.

Ayeli meowed as though admitting that she was afraid as well. She then licked her paws, demonstrating that her fear was a thing of the past.

"Young lady," said the king to Cassie, "I don't think I caught your name."

"Cassandra," said Cassie. "Most people call me Cassie."

"I'm Shawn," said Shawn. "Most people call me Shawn…ha-ha."

"Shawn Ha Ha?" said the king. "Curious name."

"No," said Shawn. "It's not 'Shawn Ha Ha.' I say 'ha-ha' to be funny. See, Cassie says—"

"I get it," interrupted the king. "Just 'Shawn.' You have a sense of humor."

"Thanks," said Shawn. He picked up the Team's furry companion. "Our companion here is Ailuros," he said, "but we've named her Ayeli for short. Easier to pronounce."

"Hello, Ayeli," said the Rainbow King.

Ayeli meowed politely.

"And I am Valdoc," said the king.

"We're the Key Team, remember?" said Cassie. "And The Great Rumpty D sent us to get that key."

"Well, *he* thinks he's great, anyway," she added.

"Ah yes," said King Valdoc. "I am aware of—"

"To the Key Team," interrupted one of the recently rehabilitated Rainbow People, who led the entire colorful group to shout in unison,

> *"Hip-hip-HOORAY!*
>
> *Hip-hip-HOORAY!*
>
> *Hip-hip-HOORAY!"*

Applause and more cheers followed.

The human members of the Team smiled. Ayeli waved her tail benevolently.

"Grayson, Cassie, and Shawn," said the Rainbow King, "we are deeply, *deeply* indebted to you. How can we ever repay you?"

"Well," said Cassie rather coyly, "there is the matter of—"

"Oh, yes!" said Valdoc. "That!" He removed the necklace with the Magic Key and handed it to Cassie. She then gave it to Grayson, who placed it around his neck to join the giant's key and the vial of healing nectar. He thanked the king.

"Now we must make amends to the Light people," said Valdoc.

"Good idea," said Grayson. "May we join you?"

"Of course."

"But there is something I'd like to do first," said Grayson. He withdrew his beanie from his belt and casually approached the edge of the Pit of Absolute Nothingness. The Key Team leader placed the silly-looking beanie on his head and turned to the Rainbow People. "This is my very own beanie," he said. "It's a gift from the Great Rumpty D. What do you think?"

The Rainbow People mostly responded with polite silence. "Interesting," one quietly muttered.

"Hmm," muttered Grayson. "Not fans of beauty, eh?"

He turned back toward the pit, took off his beanie, caressed and gazed at it in a fake-admiring manner, grinned, and tossed it into the toxic green roiling vapor. Unlike the boulder that before had descended toward the bottom of the pit, Grayson's beanie rose and skittered about over the mist as it generated hissing and popping sounds and became engulfed in bright white sparks. It withered in size and, like the boulder, vanished into...absolutely nothing!

Cheering and clapping erupted from the crowd of Rainbow People. They joyfully shouted words like "Yay!" and "Woo-hoo!" and "You're the man, Grayson!" Grayson turned toward them once more, placed one foot in front of the other, spread his arms outward, and smiling broadly, took a deep bow. More clapping followed.

Cassie and Shawn had enthusiastically joined the crowd, and Ayeli meowed happily.

The Key Team led the newly glowing Rainbow People toward the White Light People's cavern entrance. A few White Lights had remained near the opening, attending the wounded, still-gray Light in a hopeless attempt to revive him. On seeing the Rainbow People, they stood and backed away in fear, awe, and confusion. As the Rainbows exited their chamber, the Rainbow who was a Void just minutes ago, and who had previously wounded the Light, paused and offered a hand to his victim. He helped the Light to his feet, and as he did so, the White Light's former brilliance returned.

The once-Void-now-Rainbow-person rejoined his people.

* * *

The Rainbows formed a half-circle around the White Lights gathered with Queen Amanata. King Valdoc deposited his son with the other Rainbows and approached the dais supporting the queen and her newly freed daughter. A half-dozen White Lights blocked Valdoc's way. The queen, safe yet apprehensive, cautiously pushed Luziette behind her.

The White Light guards allowed the Key Team to advance to the queen's dais. "Your Majesty," said Grayson, "the curse is lifted. The Rainbow King is his old self."

"Oh," said the queen, "he once again thinks his Rainbow People are superior to us mere White Lights?"

"No, Your Majesty, his old, *old* self. When you all got along."

The queen looked at the Rainbow King. "Valdoc," she said, "I once held you in high regard, but you turned obnoxious and arrogant.

And that was *before* the curse. With the curse, you turned evil—pure evil."

Valdoc lowered his head.

"But I do trust Master Grayson," said the queen. "He is wise; perhaps I should listen to him."

"Thank you, Your Majesty," said Grayson. "It was the curse of the Good or Evil Witch that made the Rainbow People turn so... dark. That's not who they are deep down."

"It was not a *curse* that gave them a sense of superiority," said the queen.

Valdoc spoke up. "That is true," he said. "We cannot blame the witch for our behavior prior to the curse."

"You attempted to *annihilate* my beautiful daughter," said Amanata.

"No, Your Majesty," said Valdoc, "that is *not* true. We never *truly* intended to harm her. All my talk about sacrificing her to the pit was bluster, for show—just talk, meant to, I don't know, keep our peoples separate, perhaps. The little good that is in the Good or Evil Witch would not have permitted us to harm Luziette. To be honest, I was hoping for some excuse *not* to follow through with my threat.

"My son, Zon, provided that excuse. Not by almost falling into the pit, but by begging me not to take away his friend. He loves Luziette, you know. How could I not yield to the pleadings of a child?"

"Indeed," said the queen. "Children have such great power over us."

"Let me add," said Valdoc, "that it was not Zon's innocence alone that lifted the curse; it was the compassion of the Key Team, who put their lives at risk to save my son—and would have done so for any of us—that enabled us to be Rainbow People again."

The queen warmly smiled at Grayson and his companions. She then motioned to the Lights guarding Valdoc. "Allow him through," she said, "but not the others."

Valdoc ascended partway up the steps leading to the White Light Queen. "Your Majesty," said the king as he honored the queen with a bow. And to the princess who shyly stepped from behind her mother, he said, "Your Highness."

And to both, he said, "We are so, so sorry for what we have put you through. I cannot imagine the terror you must have felt."

Ayeli meowed as though concurring.

The former Void King turned and faced the crowd of White Light People and Rainbow People gathered together. Raising his voice so all could hear, he said, "Our behavior was appalling even *before* we became Voids. When we were Rainbow People, we had become enamored of our colors. We became haughty, full of ourselves. We thought we were—it pains me to say this—*superior*. We treated you, the White Light People, in a most dreadful way.

"Then we lost our color. We were no longer the superior ones but the *inferior* ones. The curse, for all its pain, did show us how horrible that feels."

One of the Rainbow People bent down on one knee. Another Rainbow did the same, and soon all Rainbows were on their knees, their heads bowed in deference to the king, the queen, and all the White Lights.

The Rainbow King turned again to the royals. "Your Majesty, your Highness," he said, "and White Light People gathered here, I know I speak on behalf of all Rainbow People when I—*we*—humbly ask your forgiveness and pray to return to the harmony that once existed between us."

"Thank you, King Valdoc," said the queen, "for your most sincere apology. We can forgive you, though it will take time to truly heal the wounds inflicted on us. In the meantime, you must forgive yourself also. You were under the control of the witch's curse. I accept that it is not in your hearts to harm anyone."

"You are very kind to say that, Your Majesty," said the king. "But evil *was* in our hearts."

"But Zon wasn't bad," said the princess. "He wasn't under the curse. He wanted me to live."

"True," said Cassie. "I wonder if the witch planned not to curse him so he could prevent the Voids from doing something dumb."

"Or," said Shawn, "she didn't curse him because Zon is, well—"

"Innocent," said Grayson. "The witch surely favors those who are pure of heart, like Zon, like the unicorns."

"And Luziette," added Cassie.

"And Luziette," said Grayson.

"Rainbow People," said Queen Amanata, "thank you for your gesture of humility. Please rise."

The Rainbow People rose to their feet. The White Light People applauded.

"Your Majesty?" said Shawn. "Ma'am?"

"Yes, my young friend?" answered the queen.

"Um…how did you and the other White Lights treat the Voids when they first became Voids? We hear you may not have been so kind yourselves."

"Oh dear!" said Amanata. "I was hoping that would not come up."

She hesitated a few seconds, then said, "It is true that our behavior was not the best. It is embarrassing to say this, but when the colorful lights of the Rainbow People—" She paused and turned her attention to the crowd of former Voids. "—When *your* colorful lights went dark, dear Rainbow People, we did indeed look down our noses at you. We felt it was *our* turn to be superior. We offered no sympathy, no understanding. We agreed that being separate from you was the best course."

"But Zon and I didn't want to be separate," said Luziette the Princess.

"That's right," said little Zon.

"Yes," said Amanata, "and we attempted to force you, dear Luziette and Zon, to be away from each other. What an awful thing to do!

"Rainbow People, now it is we White Lights who must ask for *your* forgiveness."

"I think I can speak for all my people," said King Valdoc, "when I say that forgiveness is offered, though there is little to forgive; your behaviors and attitudes are understandable."

"I realize there are great differences between us," said the queen, "but we must—"

"Not that much," interrupted Cassie.

"Excuse me, young lady?" said the queen.

"You're not as different as you think," said Cassie. "Master Humblebee, the key, please."

The Team leader handed Cassie the first key they had retrieved from Cyril the One-Eyed Giant. She first looked at the queen and other White Light People through the key's diamond to ensure she did not make a fool of herself. Confident of her position, she said, "Your Majesty, look through the diamond in this key at the people around you." She handed the key to the queen.

Queen Amanata held the key to her eye. She gasped, took the key away, then gazed through the jewel a second time. "That's very interesting: it makes all of us resemble, well, Rainbow People. But of course, it's a Magic Key—an elegant trick."

The queen handed the key to the Rainbow King, who also observed White Lights via the diamond. "Impressive," he said.

"It's not magic," said Cassie. "It's not a trick. It's *science*. The diamond is, like, a bunch of prisms. It's showing you what is in white light. White is not just one color; it's *all* colors. You White Light People are made of *all* the colors of the rainbow, just like the Rainbow People. You're all the same—mostly."

The White Light queen and the Rainbow king seemed skeptical.

"Your Majesties," said Cassie, "have you ever seen a rainbow? I mean, a *real* rainbow in the sky?"

The royals politely nodded. "Yes," said the queen. "But we rarely venture outside in the daytime. When we do, we can barely see each other, and that's disquieting."

"And where do you think those colors in the rainbow come from—the sun, right?"

The royals nodded again, more slowly this time, starting to understand.

"And the color of the sun is…" Cassie spread out her arms, waiting for an answer.

"White," the royals said.

"Exactly. See, sunlight, which looks white, hits those raindrops far away, and the raindrops act like little crystals that break the sunlight into the colors it's actually made of—rainbow colors. The diamond does the same thing with you: you're *all* like rainbows!"

The king and queen quietly pondered this for several seconds.

The king again addressed the entire gathering. "Your Majesty, Your Highness, White Lights, Rainbows…this young lady, Cassandra, has revealed an amazing truth. For too many years, we have seen our people as separate and different, but the truth is that we are far more alike than we thought. We are, indeed, *all* made of the same beautiful colors! We are the same, as Cassandra said! We are brothers and sisters!"

The king handed the key to Luziette so she could see the images as well. "Wow!" said the princess. She then passed the key to one of the Light People, who marveled at its revelation and gave it to another. Thus, the key found its way from being to being, all of whom looked through the diamond and experienced the fantastic vision of seeing each other as multiple hues of color.

"It is a shame we cannot keep your key," said the queen. "I know you need it."

"We don't need the diamond," said Grayson. He attempted to remove the gem out of the key but was unsuccessful.

"I appreciate your thought," said the queen. "That is so kind of you."

"You have diamonds in your crowns," said Cassie. "And each crown has a big diamond in front," she added, referring to the sparkling inch-round gems.

"Why so we do," said the queen. The queen of the White Light People and king of the Rainbow People removed their crowns, examined them, and held them so they could peer through the diamonds.

"Wonderful," said the queen.

"Marvelous," said the king.

The Rainbow King kneeled before the queen and took her hand. "Your Majesty," he said, "in the past, our two peoples held parties, dances. Should we resume that tradition?"

"Absolutely," said the queen.

"In that event, at the next ball, might I have the favor of a dance?"

"I would be delighted," said the queen.

Ayeli meowed approvingly.

With that, the Key Team bade goodbye to a cheering, mingling crowd of White Light and Rainbow People and retraced their steps through the dark tunnel to the sunlit world. Grayson did a little jig as they walked down the path to the *People's Boat*.

"Grayson," said Cassie, "you're very cheerful. I've never seen you smile like that before."

"Me neither," said Shawn.

"Well, why not?" said Grayson. "Just think: The Light People gave us a key, but we gave them so much more! We gave them back their dignity and self-respect, and that makes me happy."

Ayeli meowed as if in agreement.

When the Team reached the boat, Grayson hopped on board and persuaded Ayeli to follow. Then he said to Cassie and Shawn, "Sailors, unmoor this vessel."

"Yes, sir!" cried Cassie and Shawn together. The siblings untied the boat and confidently leaped onto its deck.

"Cassie," said Grayson, "you take the helm."

"Aye-aye, Captain," said Cassie. "Where are we going now?"

"To the Island of Youneverknows."

Without being told, the dolphins re-positioned themselves into their harnesses and maneuvered the boat to point away from the Island of Light People.

Grayson, Shawn, and Ayeli sat on the bench. Cassie braced herself with one hand on the boat's front railing. Pointing out to sea with the other hand, she shouted, "Dolphins! To the Island of Youneverknows—GO!"

The Key Team was off to its next challenge.

Chapter 10

Youneverknows

"Uh, Captain," said Shawn as the dolphins propelled *The People's Boat* toward yet another weird island.

"Yes?" said Grayson.

"Why do they call it 'The Island of Youneverknows?'"

"Well, you never know who is what on the island, or what is who, or what is what, or who is who."

"I always wondered about that," said Cassie in her mocking, not-sincere tone of voice. "Many times, I have lain awake at night, pondering the mystery of Youneverknows. Grayson, you have a wonderful way of making things simple, clear, and easy to understand. I mean, like, you never know who is what, or what is who, or what is what, or who is who. It's, like, so obvious!"

"Do I detect a note of sarcasm?" asked Grayson.

"What, from *me?*" said Cassie. "*Me?* Sarcastic? Oh no, never!"

Shawn chuckled.

Ayeli snorted.

"All right," said Grayson, with a hint of a smile. "What I mean is, things and people on the island are often changing from one form to another. A tree might actually be a person. A person might transform into a creature of some sort or just another person—stuff like that. You never know.

"So," he said, "it's called the Island of Youneverknows."

"Makes sense," said Cassie. "In our world, my little brother changes into a rat all the time."

"Really?" asked Grayson, "Shawn, do you—"

"I was just kidding," said Cassie. "He only *acts* like a rat sometimes."

Shawn issued a low-level growl.

"Cassie?" admonished Grayson with a scolding tone in his voice.

"OK, OK," said Cassie. "Sorry, little brother."

"It's OK," said Shawn. "I guess."

The Team reached the Island of Youneverknows, the island where the cave monster with the third Magic Key was said to have recently appeared. The dolphins guided their boat to a small dock jutting out from the island's shore. Without requiring instructions from Grayson, Cassie and Shawn jumped onto the dock and secured the watercraft to its moorings.

"What sailors you are!" said Grayson.

"Grayson?" asked Shawn.

"Yes?

"The cave monster is supposed to live here. Do you think it's just a Youneverknow?'

"I suspect not. Youneverknows don't hold their forms for long, usually not for more than a few hours. I understand the cave monster has been here for more than a week.

"And to my knowledge," he added, "Youneverknows never become monsters."

"Oh, great," said Cassie.

Three separate paths led from the dock into the woods near the shore: one to the right, one to the left, and one straight ahead. A signpost supporting a weathered board displayed an arrow pointing to the left. In crude hand-written letters, it read, **TO CAVE MONSTER.** The Key Team took the left path as directed, but just as they passed the sign, Shawn noticed the arrow now pointed to the *right*. "I thought it pointed that way," he said, motioning to the left.

"I concur," said Grayson.

"But how can that happen? Did it change?" asked Shawn.

"This *is* the Island of Youneverknows," said Grayson.

The Team switched directions and proceeded on the trail to the right. A few paces past the revised placard, Shawn turned back to double-check its guidance. The sign now said, with an arrow pointing upwards, **CAVE MONSTER STRAIGHT AHEAD.**

"Hey!" said Shawn. He stomped on the ground and placed his clenched fists on his hips. "Sign!" he commanded. "Make up your mind! Which way is the cave monster?"

"It's having fun with us," said Grayson.

"Do you think its direction is correct this time?" asked Cassie.

"Beats me," said Grayson.

The sign changed again: **ASK THE BEAR**, it said.

"Bear? What bear?" demanded Cassie with a hint of fear in her voice as she looked around.

Shawn strolled over to a nearby oddly shaped large boulder. "Maybe the sign was talking about this rock. It looks like a bear, sort of."

"Don't be silly," said Cassie.

"Shawn may have a point," said Grayson.

"Well, the more I look at it….perhaps," said Cassie. She was conflicted: she wished to honor her commitment never to agree with her brother, yet she also wanted *not* to disagree with Grayson.

Ayeli meowed, sniffed the rock, and cautiously touched it with her paw.

Shawn climbed on top of the boulder and stomped on it with both feet. "Nope," he said, "solid as a rock. Not a bear."

Suddenly he felt the stone shift beneath his feet. "Ohmygosh!" he shouted. "It's moving!" He looked down to see the boulder's surface change from solid granite to something like a soft, thick brown carpet.

Ayeli jumped straight up then fled behind Grayson.

A deep, gruff voice came from within the boulder, whose shape continued to change. "Hey kid," it growled, "get off! Can't you see I'm trying to get some sleep here?" The boulder—if you could call it a boulder—moved and wobbled.

Shawn, startled, nearly lost his balance. "Ohmygosh!" he screamed again. He quickly jumped off and faced the evolving being. "You…you talk. You're a talking rock!"

Cassie, equally surprised, cupped her hands over her mouth and giggled. Grayson smiled.

Ayeli meowed from the safety of Grayson's legs.

Shawn bent over the now hairy boulder and, with his hands on his knees, said, "Um…sorry, sir…I didn't mean to…" He couldn't think of anything more to say.

The boulder's hair grew longer. Parts close to the ground changed to thick, muscular arms and legs tipped with immense claws. A protruding shape changed into a bear's head. The boulder's large center became the bear's body covered with thick brown hair.

"Ohmygosh!" Shawn said. "You *are* a bear!"

The bear raised on its hind legs. "Perceptive of you to notice," it said. It towered over the Team, being at least twice as tall as Shawn. It threateningly displayed its claws, bared its sharp white teeth, and let out a deep, piercing growl. The Team backed away. Quiet whimpering sounds could be heard from Cassie and Shawn.

Ayeli gathered her courage, came out from behind Grayson, approached the bruin, and growled as best she could.

The bear looked down at Ayeli. He frowned, placed his claws in front of his mouth, and swayed side to side. "Oh, my goodness!" he said. "A fierce and ferocious cat! Oh my! Whatever shall I do? Oh, I beg you, little kitty: spare me!"

Ayeli looked up at the bear and cocked her head without saying a word. Slight smiles appeared on the faces of the human Team members.

The bear turned his attention to Grayson. Softening, he said, "Oh, it's you, Master Humblebee." Motioning toward Shawn, he said to Grayson, "You need to teach this boy some manners. He can't just go stomping on any rock he sees, willy-nilly—not on this island."

"He didn't know you were a Youneverknow," said Grayson, "He meant no harm."

The bear let out a soft growl. "Kids these days," he grumbled.

"Mr. Bear," said Cassie, "do you know which path leads to the cave monster?"

"Didn't the sign tell you?"

"It kept changing," said Shawn.

"Well, that's the problem with signs these days." said the bear, "Can't make up their minds. Indecisive, that's what they are. Pitiful.

"Who are you?" he asked, softening some more.

Despite the bear's grouching about signs and kids, his gentle voice was encouraging, and the Team felt safe enough to move closer to him.

"I'm Cassandra," said Cassie. "You can call me Cassie if you like."

"And I'm Shawn," said Shawn. "You can call me Shawn. Just plain Shawn."

"I get that your name is Shawn," said the bear. "Should I think otherwise?"

"No. It's a long story."

Grayson and Cassie smiled at this.

Shawn gently lifted Ayeli and held her so the bear could more easily see her. "This is Ayeli," he said. "We're the Key Team. We're here to—"

"I know why you're here," interrupted the bear, "to get the Magic Key from the cave monster."

Cassie and Shawn nodded.

The bear pointed at the path to the right. "The monster is that way." he said, "Not far."

"Good luck with the key thing," he added. "Even *I* am afraid of the cave monster. I wouldn't want to tangle with *him*. No sir. Did you know he's kidnapped the Merkelots' kid? Holding him prisoner."

"My word! No," said Grayson.

"Yeah. Timilier—that's the kid's name—bragged about visiting the beast from time to time. Said he wasn't afraid; said he was friends with the monster. Nobody believed the boy until some passersby saw the creature by himself just outside the cave. That's the only time he's been seen by someone other than Timilier. Now the monster won't let poor Timilier go home. I don't know why. Mean beast, that monster."

"We appreciate the information," said Grayson.

"Would you like to come with us?" asked Shawn.

"I'd love to," said the bear, "but…uh…I'm exhausted. Better get back to my nap."

"Fair enough," said Grayson. He winked at Cassie and Shawn and said, "Let us be off."

"Say hello to the Wise Old Tree along the way," said the bear as the Team prepared to resume their mission.

"We shall," said Grayson.

"It's a nice tree," added the bear. "We visit frequently. He scratches my back with his branches. Very kind."

"And he's real?" said Shawn. "I mean, like, a *real tree* and not a Youneverknow?"

The bear chuckled. "Very real, indeed. Not a Youneverknow."

Cassie, Shawn, and Grayson said goodbye to the bear and proceeded along the path to the right as the bear directed. Ayeli meowed goodbye politely and padded along behind.

After a few minutes, the Team came across a tree in the middle of a clearing by the path. Although it was unlike the trees surrounding it and quite old, none of its features suggested it might have a personality—at first. "Excuse me?" said Cassie. "Are you a Wise Old Tree?"

The tree's bark formed itself into a face. "Wisdom would dictate that I not attribute that accolade to myself," he said with a deep voice, "but some have flattered me with that description.

"And you are the Key Team," he said. "I suggest you continue on your way and help the Merkelot boy—there's something very odd about that whole situation. No time to lose. We can chat later."

"Indeed, we must proceed," said Grayson.

The human members of the Team said goodbye to the tree and followed Ayeli's lead up the trail.

Chapter 11

Cave Monster

Soon the Key Team came to a small cottage beside the path. A middle-aged man and woman who had been sitting on the porch approached the Team. Their faces conveyed sadness and worry. "Oh, Master Humblebee," said the lady. "We're so glad you're here." She looked at Cassie and Shawn. "I'm Mrs. Merkelot."

"And I am Mr. Merkelot," said the man.

"I'm Cassandra, and this is Shawn," said Cassie.

"And this is Ayeli," said Shawn. "We're here to help Grayson... Master Humblebee."

"Oh, that's nice of you," said the lady, "very brave too."

"Timilier, our son, ran away," said the man. "Now the cave monster has him."

"We heard," said Grayson. "I am so sorry."

"Timilier is a little rebellious at times, but he's a good boy," said the father. "Can you help us? I know you are here just to get the key, but can you get our son back? We know that's a lot to ask."

"We'll do our best," said Grayson.

"Are you Youneverknows?" asked Cassie to the Merkelots. "Couldn't you—"

"No, we're not," said Mrs. Merkelot. "If we were, we would surely have been able to rescue Timilier ourselves."

"Only a small number of people and things on this island are Youneverknows," said Grayson. "I don't know why that is."

"Is Timilier a Youneverknow?" asked Shawn.

"No," said Mrs. Merkelot. "At least I don't think he is. But if he is, he would choose to be the gentlest of Creatures. I Know Him."

"We understand," said Grayson."

"And if he is playing at being a monster," said Mrs. Merkelot, "he could only be one for a short time—less than a day. Those are the rules here.

"So he could not *possibly* be the cave monster," she added.

"Right," said Grayson. He motioned to Cassie and Shawn to proceed. After a few paces down the trail, he stopped and turned to the frightened parents. "We *will* get your son back," he said.

Still farther down the path, Cassie quietly whispered to Grayson, "It was risky of you to make a promise like that."

"Sorry," said Grayson. "I should have spoken to you and Shawn first. I didn't intend to make you feel obligated to help me rescue the boy. That wasn't part of the deal; in fact, you are not obligated to help me at all. I can't ask you to put your lives in danger."

"All for one and all and one for all," said Shawn, "like you said."

"All for one and all and one for all," repeated Cassie.

Grayson smiled.

Ayeli let out an approving meow—to the extent that cats can meow approvingly.

The Team soon arrived at the monster's cave, not far from the Merkelot's cottage. They entered through the cave's small entrance into a large cavern. Several burning torches hung on the cavern's rocky walls. Their flames cast an orange glow lighting up the entire room. The Team noticed a sword buried in a large boulder just inside the entrance. Only its handle—its *hilt*—and a few inches of the blade could be seen.

"Hmm," said Cassie. "A sword stuck in a big rock; that seems familiar."

Ayeli jumped to the top of the boulder and sniffed the sword's hilt.

Cassie's 'seems familiar' comment induced curiosity on Shawn and Grayson's part, but they did not have time to question her; the Team's attention soon went to a monster sitting motionless on a stone bench at the edge of the cavern. It was brooding, looking down and holding its head in its hands. At the sound of Cassie's voice, it looked up, saw the Team, and rose to greet them.

The creature stood at least a foot taller than Grayson. Its body was swollen with thick muscles and covered with dark green scales over light green skin. Its eyes were solid black with no irises or pupils. Its claws were long, black, and sharp as knives.

Beside it, propped against the bench, was a sword with a thick blade as long as Shawn was tall. The weapon appeared to be quite heavy; indeed, only a monster could handle such a weapon with ease.

A finely decorated gold key was attached to a golden necklace looped around the monster's beefy neck. A ruby the size of a quarter was mounted in the key's center. The key's ornate golden design was quite similar to the two keys previously recovered by the Team, who quickly deduced that it too was a Magic Key.

The monster smiled a malevolent, sinister smile revealing gray, half-decaying teeth with fangs like those of a wolf. "Ah, young Grayson Humblebee," it said in a deep growling voice, "I've been expecting you."

"You're holding Timilier, the boy," said Grayson. "Where is he?"

"You wish to see him?" asked the lizard-like creature.

"Yes, please," said Grayson—ever polite despite his barely suppressed anger.

"Wait here," said the monster. It lumbered to a dark passageway at the far end of the cavern and disappeared through it.

The Team heard a high-pitched, mournful voice of a young boy issuing from the other side of the passageway. "Help!" the child screamed, "Is somebody out there? Please help me. I want to go home!"

Ayeli issued a prolonged, sorrowful meow.

The monster reappeared through the entrance. "Oh, how sad," it said, "I am afraid I can't release the boy."

Ayeli growled menacingly.

"Why not?" asked Shawn.

The monster's eyes narrowed as he studied Cassie and Shawn. Cassie put an arm around her brother and pulled him close to comfort him—and herself. The siblings backed up from the ogre a bit even though they were already at a safe distance.

The beast turned to Grayson. "What are these?" it growled.

"*Children*—and friends of mine," said Grayson. Considering that he was facing a creature that could tear him to shreds, his voice sounded firm and without a hint of fear.

"And that?" asked the monster.

"A cat," said Shawn.

"What is it usually?"

"What do you mean, 'usually'?" asked Shawn. "A cat."

"Not a Youneverknow?" asked the monster.

"No, she's a *CAT*," he said defiantly.

"You can never know for sure," said the monster. "Get that: *you never know*?

"Anyway," it said, "I can't release the kid."

"Why? What did he do?" asked Cassie, matching her brother's aggressive tone.

"What did he *do*?" said the monster. "What did he *do*? He's mean to his parents—really mean. Disobeys them. Talks back. Never cleans his room despite being told to do so over and over again."

Cassie sensed something amiss with this creature and her sassy, sarcastic nature began to reassert itself. "Oh my!" she said. "Never cleans his room? That is *very serious*! No wonder he's being punished! String him up, I say!"

"You're making fun of me," said the monster.

"Me?" said Cassie. "*Me*? Make fun of a dumb monster? Oh no, not me!"

In contrast to Cassie, Grayson showed *more* fear—not for himself so much as for Cassie and Shawn should they put their lives at risk by taunting the beast. "Cassie," Grayson cautioned in a quiet voice, "be careful. Don't irritate him."

"I don't like being made fun of," growled the monster. With arms raised to the level of his shoulders and his hands curled in a way that made his sharp black claws all too apparent, it slowly, menacingly, approached Cassie and Shawn.

Cassie's fear returned. She drew Shawn closer and backed them both still farther away from the beast. In a sad, apologetic, almost tearful voice, she said, "Sorry. I didn't mean to—"

"Cave monster!" commanded Grayson. "Leave them alone."

The monster stopped, turned, and faced the Team leader.

"Release the boy," said Grayson.

"Can't," said the monster.

It fingered the Magic Key. "Don't you want this oh-so-important item you came for?"

"Release him," said Grayson, "Or—"

"Or what."

Grayson said nothing. What *could* he say to such a loathsome behemoth? He turned and glanced at the sword embedded in the boulder—as though it beckoned him.

"Oh," said the creature, "you want to fight? You grab that sword. I'll grab mine. If you win, you get the boy.

"But let me check it first," he said, "to make sure you can pull it out of the rock."

The monster approached the boulder, wrapped a claw around its hilt, and with one arm lifted the sword—and the heavy boulder with it—off the ground. The boulder did not yield the weapon. "What a pity!" said the monster. "It's stuck!"

The creature released the boulder. Surely weighing hundreds of pounds, it hit the ground with a *thud*. "Guess you'll never get the kid after all," said the monster, "and you'll never get this key, either." It walked away from the boulder, farther into its cave, and stood by the bench and its sword. "You know, Grayson, I could slice you to pieces with my sword here, but I tell you what: I'll leave it be, and we'll fight hand-to-hand, *mano-a-mano*. Then I'll just *tear* you to shreds with my bare hands."

It paused for a response and then said, "Well?"

"Oh," squealed Cassie, "I get it! I know!

"Grayson," she shouted as she released her grip on her brother, "pull the sword out of the rock."

Grayson, Shawn, and even the monster gave Cassie quizzical looks as if to say, *are you nuts?*

Ayeli, casually licking her paws, seemed not to notice. Perhaps she did not understand human language after all. Or, more likely, she *pretended* not to notice.

Cassie ran to Grayson and placed a hand on his arm. "You can do it," she said. "The monster can't pull it out, but *you* can. I *know* you can. That sword is meant for you, Grayson. Trust me."

Grayson said nothing. He slowly approached the boulder.

The monster watched in amusement with its massive arms folded across its chest and a smirk on its face.

"Do it!" ordered Cassie.

Grayson tightly grasped the sword's hilt, put his foot against the boulder, then pulled the sword out of the stone as if the solid granite rock were made of bread. With widened eyes showing shock and amazement, he gave Cassie a *you were right!* grin. The Team leader held the glistening weapon in front of him and examined the elaborate decorations extending down its blade. "*Rexgladius,*" he quietly whispered to the sword as though it were a living being. Then the teenager said to his teammates, "I know this sword."

The monster gasped. "How did you—that's not fair!" It unfolded its arms, and its smirk vanished.

Cassie returned to Shawn.

To the monster, Grayson asked, "How did you come by this sword?"

"The witch left it here," said the monster, " when she gave me the key and did the curse thing."

"Oh yes, the curse," said Grayson.

"Yeah," said the monster, "but never mind. That's none of your business."

"Fine. Let the boy go," said Grayson. "Do that, give us the key, and I'll do you no harm." He slowly walked toward the monster, showing no fear, sword at his side.

"You'll do me *no harm?*" said the monster with a smirk. "Ha! You make me laugh." It picked up its own sword. "You seem to be unaware that I am way bigger than you and many times stronger. My sword is twice the length of yours and twice as heavy. Now you must die. Sorry your little friends have to see this."

Grayson turned sideways toward the ugly brute and held his sword chest-high in a horizontal position, ready for battle. The beast raised its sword over its head and brought it down, intending to slice Grayson in half. The weapon's momentum was halted, however, by Grayson's sword. Over and over, from all angles, the monster swung and thrust at Grayson without success. The teenager blocked every swing and easily brushed aside every thrust. Every few seconds, the beast was left open, allowing Grayson an opportunity to put an end to him, but Grayson chose not to take advantage. The fighters' swords collided and generated loud metallic clanging sounds that echoed off the walls of the giant cavern. The monster was clumsy and awkward; it relied—unsuccessfully—on brute strength alone. Grayson was light on his feet, agile, and moved with the skill of an experienced swordsman.

Cassie and Shawn were, of course, fearful for their leader. They winced and gritted their teeth with every clash of the swords. But at the same time, they were astonished at Grayson's ability to keep the monster at bay. Was this young man, now fearlessly challenging a ferocious behemoth, the very same Grayson Humblebee who before had meekly submitted to insults from an egg-shaped buffoon?

Shawn picked up Ayeli and held her in his arms. The cat watched the battle with great intensity.

The monster, now wet with sweat (unusual for a reptile), nearly out of breath, and immensely frustrated, backed up from Grayson. The creature took a deep breath and with one final, desperate effort, it raised its sword above its head with both hands, issued a loud, angry growl, and charged at its opponent. Using all its remaining strength, the monster brought its weapon down with great force, a force so powerful that Grayson could not have stopped it with an ordinary sword.

But his sword was not ordinary: It sliced through his adversary's sword as if through cardboard. The monster's now-detached blade tumbled through the air and landed harmlessly on the ground. The hulking brute—dumbfounded and still holding the hilt of its once-powerful weapon—looked down at the remaining stub of a blade. It threw the handle on the ground and glared at Grayson.

Grayson casually strolled toward his opponent while holding his sword out in front of him. "It. Is. Time. To. Release. The. Boy," he demanded, poking the monster's chest between each word for added emphasis.

The creature took a step backward with each jab.

Grayson was positioned with his back to his teammates, the beast before him. The monster looked beyond the Team leader to Cassie and Shawn, still standing close to each other near the cave's entrance. It suddenly bolted around Grayson, raced to the kids, and enclosed them both with its massive left arm. It held its right hand in front of Shawn with its claws curving inward toward the trembling boy's face. "Drop the sword, Humblebee," it said, "or I'll rip the faces off your precious companions."

Ayeli, held tightly by Shawn, hissed and attempted to claw the monster's arm, but she could not pierce the beast's thick, scaly skin.

Grayson stood motionless.

"The sword," said the monster.

"Don't do it, Grayson!" yelled Cassie. "It'll kill you!"

Grayson nodded to Cassie and, with a wincing yet brave half-smile for her benefit, laid his weapon on the ground.

"Now back off," said the monster. Grayson stepped back a few paces. "More," said the foul beast. Grayson backed up farther. He stumbled on a crack in the cave's floor and fell backward onto the ground.

The monster released the kids and pushed them aside. With its chin raised in a show of arrogance, it strutted slowly toward Grayson. The Team leader was attempting to right himself.

"No!" yelled Cassie and Shawn together. Ayeli let out a piercing yowl as well.

The creature took its time, enjoying the advantage it had over its foe. It smiled in an evil, smug sort of way, ready to pounce on the helpless teenager who was bracing himself on his elbows. The creature seemed not to notice the Team leader's sword on the floor as it stepped over it and continued its slow, menacing pace.

Grayson's sword now lay between the younger Team members and the monster.

Cassie whispered a brief instruction to her brother. Shawn nodded in agreement.

With the monster intently focused on Grayson and unaware of the kids behind him, Cassie bolted forward and picked up Grayson's sword. As she did so, Shawn threw a stone that bounced off the wall on the monster's right. The beast turned toward the sound. "Hey, monster!" shouted Shawn. The monster swiveled further to its right and glared at Shawn. It did not see Cassie dash past its left and hand Grayson the sword. Now cautiously backing up toward Grayson and still facing Shawn, the behemoth had a quizzical expression on its face. It likely wondered why Shawn yelled and where Cassie had gone. Continuing to back up, it tripped on the same crack in the floor that caught Grayson. It started to fall, and as it did so, it twisted its body so that it now faced the Team leader still lying on the ground.

Grayson pointed his sword up at the tumbling beast, who fell on the sword. The blade entered its chest and pushed through its body.

The monster screamed with a pathetic, child-like, high-pitched sound. It was not the sort of cry one would expect from such a vicious being.

The ogre fell on top of Grayson.

It and Grayson both rolled over, leaving the beast on its back. Grayson got to his feet and withdrew his sword from the monster. He kneeled beside the dying creature and put his hand on its chest. Blood oozed from its mouth and the wound on its body created by Grayson's sword.

The beast stared into Grayson's eyes and attempted to speak. "Master Grayson," it said quietly with a wheezing sound. "I...I..."

"Shhh," whispered Grayson. "Don't talk." Grayson had not wished to injure the creature, but events had moved too quickly for him to consider an alternative. Now, though, he had an idea.

He removed the vial of healing nectar from the gold chain still draped around his neck. He poured a few drops on the monster's bloody chest wound. Shawn and Cassie together approached Grayson and the defeated beast. Grayson enlisted the kids' aid in rolling the monster over so he could put more drops on the exit wound on the monster's back. They returned the creature to face-up position. "Here, drink this," said Grayson sympathetically to the monster who, although it could barely do so, opened its mouth. Grayson, holding up the monster's head, enabled it to drink the remaining honey-colored contents of the vial.

"Why are you doing this?" asked the monster softly as death approached. "I meant to kill you."

"Shhh," whispered Grayson. He gently patted the monster on its shoulder.

"Yeah, Grayson," whispered Shawn. "Why *are* you helping it? I mean, like, shouldn't that healing stuff be saved for you or maybe one of us if we get in trouble?"

Grayson looked up at Shawn. "The creature is in pain. I could not live with myself if I did not try to ease its suffering." He smiled and said, "Perhaps I am not ruthless enough, as Rumpty D would suggest."

"Yeah," objected Shawn, "but—"

Shawn interrupted himself when he noticed a change coming over the monster, who began to diminish in size. The solid black color of its eyes changed to white with bright blue irises. The creature's skin on its head and arms took on a pleasing tan hue. Its claws transformed into small human-like hands. Its tough scales and skin morphed into well-cared-for clothing: jeans, a T-shirt, and sneaker-like shoes. Its yellow wolf-like fangs withdrew into its mouth to become the ordinary clean white teeth of a young human. Smooth brown hair grew from its head. Its body, massive and threatening just moments ago, was reduced to that of a lean, healthy boy about Shawn's age and height.

The monster was no longer an *it*; it was a *he*.

The gold chain with a Magic Key remained around the child's neck.

Grayson helped the *former* monster to his feet.

The boy lifted his shirt to inspect what had been a wide, horrible gash but was no more. No blood, not even a hint of a scar, was to be seen. He ran his hand over his smooth chest. "I don't feel any pain," he said in the voice of a youngster, the deep monster's tone now missing. "It's gone. I don't understand. And I'm…I'm not a monster anymore. I'm me!"

"Indeed, you are you—Timilier!" said Grayson, "and now I see why, when you were a monster, you couldn't release the boy Timilier. You *were* Timilier all along!"

"You're a Youneverknow," said Shawn.

"That is true," said Timilier.

"And you never let your parents know you are a Youneverknow?" Shawn made this more of a statement than a question. "That was not a very cool thing to do," he added.

"I...I know," said Timilier with a trembling voice and with his head lowered.

Ayeli padded up to the boy, rubbed against his legs, and purred.

"You certainly had us fooled," said Grayson.

"I'm so sorry," said Timilier, "I didn't mean to be a monster. Well, OK, I *did* want to be a monster, but just for an hour or two—not for *days*—and I sure didn't want to be that awful. I think the witch made me stay a monster when she gave me the key and left the sword stuck in the rock. I don't know what happened. I'm really not that mean, not in real life. Honest!"

"I believe you," said Grayson.

"Am I going to be punished?"

"Not by me. You're not to blame."

"But I *am* to blame. I've been so mean, even before I became a monster. I have been so cruel to my mom and dad."

"You didn't clean your room," said Cassie, smiling.

"No, worse," said Timilier, not understanding Cassie's attempt at humor. "I disobeyed them. I yelled at them. I—" Timilier choked up. "I told them I hated them—*hated* them. But that wasn't true. I *felt* like I hated them, sometimes, but I know I loved them, really. I was just angry."

"Perhaps you were a *little* monster?" asked Grayson.

"I guess."

"Hoping to be a *big* monster?"

"Well—"

"But not a *bad* monster," said Cassie.

"No."

"I have news for you, Timilier," said Grayson. "Most of us have little monsters inside. Most of us would like to be bigger, stronger, or fiercer."

"Really? But not you."

"*Especially* me. As a matter of fact, I would *love* to be a monster and stand up against a certain egg-shaped ruler in Topplesville and give him his comeuppance."

"Honest? Bring him down but not kill him, I hope."

"Not kill him. *Close*, perhaps," said Grayson with a chuckle. "But no, not kill him. Just show him what justice is like.

"Timilier," Grayson said, his voice soft and gentle, "I want you to know this: the monster that tried to kill me, the monster that threatened my companions here, that monster was not you. That monster was acting out a curse from the Good or Evil Witch. I don't know why she did such a thing, but she did. I should have a talk with her."

"If you can find her," added Shawn.

Ayeli sneezed.

"Thanks, Grayson," said Timilier, who started to cry. "But still, I've ruined everything. I told Mom and Dad to stay away from me. I was so mean. I wish I could say I'm sorry.

"You want to know something?" he continued. "I hate this messy cave. I can see why Mom and Dad hate my messy room. I wish I could just go home and clean it. I just want to be an ordinary kid—a *good* kid.

"Well, too late," he said. "I guess. My parents must really hate me now."

"Not true," said Shawn.

"They love you; I guarantee it," said Cassie. "That's what good parents do—they love you no matter what, and your parents are good. I know that; I've met them."

"Like *our* mom and dad," said Shawn. "They love us even when we're bad."

"Really?" said Timilier.

"Yeah," said Cassie. "My brother's a monster sometimes, and they still love him. I mean, like, I don't see how anybody could love him, but *they* do."

"You turn into a monster?" said Timilier to Shawn.

"No, not really," said Shawn. "Not a monster like you did. She's kidding."

"Well, I *was* a monster," said Timilier. "A *real* monster. And now my parents won't want me back."

"I can assure you, they will," said Grayson.

The boy looked at Grayson with tear-filled eyes. "Grayson?" he said. "If you see them, could you tell them I'm sorry? And could you tell them I do love them?"

"You can tell them yourself," said the Team leader, as he nodded toward the entrance to the cave where Mr. and Mrs. Merkelot had entered and were cautiously approaching.

"Mom! Dad!" yelled Timilier. He ran towards his parents then stopped halfway, not knowing what to expect. Mom and Dad smiled broadly, rushed to their son, and took him into their arms.

"Oh, Timilier," sobbed Mrs. Merkelot, "we missed you so."

The youngster's parents had arrived, unseen, just as the monster was changing back to Timilier, in time to overhear their distraught son's lament.

"You don't have to apologize," said Mr. Merkelot, "and you don't have to say you love us. We know you do."

"And the young lady is right," said Mrs. Merkelot, "we do love you, no matter what. We always have. Always will."

By this time, the eyes of Grayson, Cassie, and Shawn had become conspicuously misty.

Ayeli rubbed against Mr. and Mrs. Merkelot and meowed softly. Mr. Merkelot bent over and scratched her behind her ears. A quiet purr could be heard.

"Master Grayson," said Mr. Merkelot, "and you brave children, how can we ever…we owe you so much—"

"Oh!" Timilier suddenly blurted. He turned toward Grayson. "Don't forget this!" He removed the gold necklace and ornate key from around his neck and handed it to the Team leader.

"Thank you," said Grayson. "To be honest, I did forget about it."

Now all three of the Magic Keys were in the Key Team's possession.

The Key Team waited in the cave to allow the Merkelot family to be by themselves as they returned to their cottage.

A thick, finely embellished belt lay beside the boulder that previously held Grayson's sword. Attached to the belt was a protective case—a *sheath*—for a sword. The Team leader picked up the belt, fastened it around his waist, and slipped the blade into the sheathing. He did all this casually as if he had done it many times before.

"You're keeping the sword?" asked Shawn.

"It's his," said Cassie.

Shawn briefly wrinkled his forehead, raised his eyebrows, and puckered his lips in curiosity, not understanding Cassie's comment. He said nothing, however.

After a few minutes, the Key Team left the cave and headed back on the path leading toward their boat. Along the way, Grayson, Cassie, and Shawn had a bounce in their steps as they reflected on how they helped young Timilier regain his true self, grow up a little, and reunite with his mom and dad. Even Ayeli seemed to dance from one side of the trail to the other. Grayson held his head exceptionally high.

The Team reached the clearing occupied by the Wise Old Tree, who again reconfigured his bark into a recognizable face. "I see you've recovered the key," he said. "And Rexgladius too. Congratulations."

"Thank you," said Grayson.

"And you rescued the Merkelot boy."

"We did."

"Of course you did," said the tree.

"How did you know that?" asked Shawn.

"I know Grayson all too well," said the tree. "He would not allow an innocent child to perish."

"To say we 'rescued' him would not be entirely accurate," said Grayson. "Turns out Timilier wasn't actually in danger."

"And he wasn't all that innocent," said Cassie.

"Innocent enough," said Grayson.

"How did you know we are the Key Team?" asked Cassie. "How did you know we were coming?"

"My cousin in the temple told me."

"How could he tell you from so far away? I mean, you're both stuck in the ground."

"Low frequency vibrations. *Very* low, through our roots. Humans and most animals can't hear them, yet they are strong enough to travel through the ground and the seas over great distances."

"I think elephants and whales in our world talk to each other that way," said Cassie.

"Interesting," said the tree.

"Is that how Cyril and the Light People knew to expect us, through other trees?" asked Cassie.

"Perhaps; hard to say. I expect the witch prepared them for your arrival."

"How do you know about Rex...Rex—" asked Cassie.

"Rexgladius?" said the tree.

"Yes, Grayson's sword."

"Um," muttered the tree. "I am afraid I cannot reveal how I know about Rexgladius. State secret: I must not expose a state secret."

"Hmm, state secret," muttered Cassie in disbelief. "Yeah, right."

"Where's your axman?" asked Shawn. "Why aren't you guarded?"

"The Great Rumpty D and his Special Guards apparently do not know of my existence. A couple of guards did pass this way once, but I pretended to be a mere tree. Not especially bright, the guards."

"Mr. Tree," said Cassie, "We have some questions. Can you be honest with us?"

"How could I *not* be?"

"Well, the tree we first met near Hyacinth's garden and the tree at the temple—"

"Their lives are constantly under threat," said the tree. "Did not the first tree, in a roundabout way, let you know he was bluffing about 'true news' and the like?"

"He did, in a quite clever way too. So, tell us the truth about The Great Rumpty D."

"I have never met him personally," said the tree. "I don't get around much. But from what my fellow trees have told me, he is dishonest, cruel, incompetent, illiterate, and incredibly stupid. And yet he's very much in love—with himself."

"Wow!" said Shawn. "You don't prevair--prevair—"

"*Prevaricate*," corrected Cassie.

"Yeah," said Shawn, "You don't prevaricate; I mean like, you don't make stuff up just to stay out of trouble, do you?"

The tree simply smiled.

"So, if The Great Rumpty D is all those awful things," continued Shawn, "how did he get to be the ruler of Transmongonia? Was he elected?"

"Elected? Hardly! When the king disappeared, no one was in charge, so Rumpty was able to take over, but not by the will of the people."

"What about the Crown Prince?" asked Shawn. "Shouldn't he have become king right away?"

"Yes, he probably should have."

"He *definitely* should have," added Grayson.

"But he went into hiding," said the tree.

"Why," asked Cassie. "Do you know why?"

"I believe I do," said the tree, "but I cannot reveal that at this time. State secret, you see."

"No, I don't see," said Cassie. "Anyway, tell us more about The Great Rumpty D."

"When the king disappeared, Rumpty had just escaped from what is commonly known as Egg Island."

"I knew it!" said Shawn. "He *is* an egg!"

"Egg-like," said the tree. "The people from that island do indeed *appear* to be eggs, but they're not *real* eggs, although they have shells and are fragile like eggs."

"So, you couldn't fry them?" asked Cassie.

"Or scramble them?" asked Shawn.

"Or make an omelet with them?" asked Cassie.

"Or bake with them?" asked Shawn.

"Or make deviled eggs with them?" asked Cassie.

"How about in a Cobb salad?" continued Shawn. "I bet they—"

"Very funny, you two," said the tree. "No, none of those things.

"By the way," said the tree, "Egg Islanders prefer to be called *Ovoids*, not eggs. The word 'ovoid' describes a shape that is egg-like but is not necessarily an egg. A movement is afoot to have the island's name changed from Egg Island to Ovoid Island or Island of the Ovoids. But progress is slow; people are resistant to change."

"Oh!" said Cassie. "I know!"

What did she know? All eyes turned to her.

"Their shells are *exoskeletons*!" she said.

"Exoskeletons?" said Shawn and Grayson together.

"Yeah," said Cassie. "We have skeletons inside us to support our muscles and stuff. So do most animals like horses and monkeys and...penguins. But some creatures have their skeletons on their outside, like tortoises and beetles and crabs and insects.

"Exoskeletons," she added.

"Huh," said Shawn and Grayson together, showing awareness of their new knowledge.

"I hadn't thought of that," said the tree, "but yes...it makes sense: exoskeletons. Perhaps Ovoids are not that unusual after all.

"Smart young lady," he said.

"My sister knows lots of things like that," acknowledged Shawn,. "Science and stuff." He then shifted back to the main topic: "You said The Great Rumpty D *escaped*?"

"Yes," said the tree. "He was on trial for the attempted murder of his cousin."

"Oh. My. Gosh!" said Cassie. "Don't tell us his cousin's name was *Humpty*."

"It was, as a matter of fact. Good guess!"

"Humpty Dumpty?" asked Shawn.

"No, just plain Humpty D, like Rumpty D. Interesting you should ask."

"So, what happened?" asked Shawn.

"Humpty is the son of the king of Egg Island—"

"A prince," said Shawn.

"True. It was a warm summer evening, and Humpty—a charming young lad—was sitting on the palace wall—"

"—and he had a great fall," interrupted Cassie and Shawn together, laughing.

"No, he didn't fall, exactly. He was pushed."

"I fail to see the humor in this," said Grayson to his companions.

"Humpty," the tree continued, "is very much liked by everyone who knows him. Rumpty was quite jealous. He's *not* popular, as you can imagine. As I was saying, Prince Humpty was sitting on the palace wall, watching the setting sun, minding his own business, and Rumpty came up from behind and pushed him off—or so it is *alleged* by a tree who grew in the palace yard and saw the incident. The evidence is scant; there were no witnesses other than the tree."

"A Wise Old Tree?" asked Shawn.

"True."

"Then the Ovoid people should have believed the tree."

"And Rumpty should have been punished," added Cassie.

"I quite agree," said the tree. "Nonetheless, even someone as foul as Rumpty D deserves a fair trial. He knew he would be found guilty, of course, so he escaped.

"And by the way," said the tree, "it was not a *great* fall, just enough to severely injure Humpty. It cracked his shell."

"If he *was* an egg," said Shawn, "his insides, his yolk and stuff, would have run all over the place.

"Unless he was hard boiled," said the tree, smiling.

"Oh, yeah," said Shawn. "I hadn't thought of that."

"I am glad Humpty lived," said Cassie, barely containing a laugh. "And so, like, did all the king's horses and all the king's men put Humpty together again?"

The tree paused, raised an eyebrow, and observed the kids. He was apparently unable to understand why the youngsters were smiling. "Horses were not required, my dear," he said. "But the king's surgeons were. I understand they have done a decent job of putting Humpty…ah…together again, as you put it. He's in good care, mending quite nicely."

Cassie and Shawn could not contain themselves anymore; they laughed uncontrollably.

"Cassandra and Shawn Solskin," said Grayson with unusual sternness, "I am surprised that you take pleasure in poor Humpty's misfortune."

The kids' laughter faded—more or less. "You two are serious, aren't you, Mister Tree and Grayson," said Cassie. "I mean, like, did that really happen?"

"Yes, it really did happen," said Grayson.

Shawn and Cassie giggled. They could not help themselves.

After a silent pause, Cassie and Shawn's faces expressed a more respectful attitude. "Sorry," said Cassie. "We're not happy that Humpty got hurt. It's just that we didn't know you were serious. I mean, like, in our world, there's a 'Humpty Dumpty' poem, but it's make-believe. We have a story about a one-eyed giant, too, except his name is Cyclops, and he has only *one* eye in the middle of his forehead, and he really *does* eat people. And we have stories about unicorns and witches, but they're just stories, fairy tales, and myths. People made them up; they are not real.

"But in *your* world, *our* fairy tales and myths are *real*.

"So, talking about Humpty Dumpty like he's an actual person just seemed funny," she finished awkwardly.

"Interesting," said the tree. "Allow me to continue the *true* tale of Rumpty D:

"He managed to escape hours before the trial. He made his way to the Transmongonian mainland, but along the way, he picked up those Special Guards from Bully Island and convinced a few Transmongonians that he would do wonders for them and, with the help of the guards, he gained power."

"How can he control so many people?" asked Cassie. "I mean, like, he's just an egg."

"Great question—a question for the ages," said the tree. "I believe the answer is *fear.* Not that people fear him personally—he can't do anything by himself—they fear those who do his will, the Special Guards. It is they, with their swords, who help keep ordinary citizens in line.

"And to remind you, he's not an egg; he's merely egg-like."

"Could the guards take over Transmongonia," asked Shawn, "and rule it themselves?"

"Perhaps," said the tree. "But each guard worries that if he even *suggests* that they take charge, the others will send him to the dungeons. None of them knows who is enemy or friend, and they don't try to find out. They are all controlled by fear.

"I should add that the guards, most of them, also love having power over the people, and they don't want to lose it. Lust for power is something they share with Rumpty D."

"What about the soldiers?" asked Cassie. "They have swords. And that captain who talked to us just as we left the temple, Captain Mackenzie, he seems nice."

"Indeed, he is a good fellow," said the tree, "and in his wisdom, he knows that *because* soldiers have swords, they should not rule the country. Their job is to *protect* those who lead—nobly, *with* the will of the people, with their consent. That's important.

"The soldiers would not stoop so low as to protect Mister D," continued the tree. "His Special Guards do that. The soldiers *did* protect the king when he was in charge and did so most honorably. Rumpty D would never have had a chance while the king was on the throne."

"So true," said Grayson.

"Or if the Crown Prince took over just after the king went missing," said Shawn, "like he should have."

"Probably true as well," said Grayson.

"*Definitely* true," said the tree.

"I have a feeling the soldiers are waiting for the new king," said Cassie, "for the Crown Prince to come out of hiding and take command."

"I hope you are right," said the tree. "The captain and his soldiers will be very loyal to the new king."

"Do you know the Crown Prince?" asked Shawn.

"I believe I do," said the tree.

"You *believe* you know him?" Cassie folded her arms, squinted at the tree, and spoke as a parent might to a child caught red-handed. "You're a *Wise Old Tree*," she said. "You Wise Old Trees know everything. *Of course* you know him!"

"As I said, child, the prince is in hiding," said the tree. "If he wishes to keep his identity secret, I must respect those wishes."

Cassie growled, "Grrr! Trees!"

"Grayson, do *you* know the prince?" asked Shawn.

"Um," said Grayson. He hesitated, then said, "More or less."

"More or less? *More or less*?" said Cassie to Grayson. "You're as bad as the tree!"

"Spunky young lady," said the tree to Grayson.

"Quite," said Grayson with a smile.

"What's the prince like?" asked Shawn.

"He's OK, I suppose," said Grayson. "Timid."

"Is he afraid to be king, thinks he's not good enough like The Great Rumpty D claimed?" asked Shawn.

"He can't rule over a colony of mice?" asked Cassie in a calmer voice. "That's according to Rumpty Stinky D."

"That's a great poetic moniker," said Grayson. "But to answer your question: I think the prince could handle mice, as long as there are not too many of them…and as long as they don't have swords."

The kids giggled.

"But as far as ruling Transmongonia," continued Grayson, "the Crown Prince would have much to live up to. His father was a good king—wise, brave, honest, and kind—yet firm when he had to be. The people loved him. Their welfare was his highest priority…"

Grayson was silent for a moment, then said, "The Crown Prince would be a great disappointment to the people of Transmongonia, after so great a king."

"Or so he thinks," said the tree.

"Or so he thinks," said Grayson.

"You said you can't say *why* he's hiding," said Shawn to the tree. "Can you say *where* he's hiding? Do you know?"

"He's hiding…um…within…ah…perhaps I better not say. State secret as well."

"Oh, *Tree!*" said Cassie. "You and Grayson! The both of you. You and your state secrets! You said you would be honest with us, but you're being evasive."

"I am at least *honestly* evasive," said the tree. "I am honoring the Crown Prince's wishes."

"Hmm. That's good of you," said Cassie insincerely. "I guess. But still, there's something both of you know, and you're not telling us."

"I bet there is no 'state secret,'" said Shawn.

A long silence ensued.

Ayeli, who had been silent most of this time, moved farther up the path, stopped, turned around, and meowed.

"I believe Ayeli is once again reminding us of our duty," said Grayson.

"Or, she's helping you avoid our questions," said Cassie.

"Mister Tree?" she asked.

"Yes, my dear?"

"I have a couple of academic questions for you."

"Oh, good. I love academic questions."

"How does one address a princess…or, say, a *prince*?"

"Your Highness," said the tree.

"And, um, how does one address, oh, say, a queen…or a *king*?"

"Your Majesty," said the tree. "Why do you ask?"

"Just curious; state secret."

"Ah, I see," said the tree with a broad grin on his face. "I believe I understand."

"Well, time to go," said the young lady. "We are glad to have met you, sir."

"The pleasure has been mine," said the tree.

The Key Team bade the tree goodbye and continued down the path. No one spoke; each was caught up in their thoughts.

When they reached the trail's end near the dock and *The People's Boat*, Shawn paused near (but not *too* near) the large boulder that was also a bear. "Shhh," he whispered to Grayson and Cassie as he put his ear closer to the rock, "I think I hear it snoring."

The topmost board on the sign with the ever-changing messages now said **HAVE A NICE DAY**. Those words then reshaped themselves into **COME BACK SOON!**

A smiley face appeared on a separate board underneath.

"This sign is obviously a Youneverknow," said Shawn, "I wonder if it's, like, *alive* or something. Anyway, I think it likes us, even if it did give us the wrong directions at first." He walked over to the sign's wooden post and gently scratched it. The whole sign wiggled. "It's ticklish," said Shawn with a chuckle.

Cassie and Shawn unmoored the boat, and the Team hopped on board. The dolphins once again assumed their places and oriented the craft toward the open sea without a command to do so.

"Shawn," said Grayson, "your turn at the helm."

Grayson and Cassie sat on the bench with Ayeli in between. Shawn stood at the bow with one hand on the front railing and the other pointing in the desired direction. "Dolphins!" he shouted. "To Topplesville—GO!"

Chapter 12

Jig's Up

he *People's Boat*, under stupendous dolphin power, lurched forward. Sweet, moist salt air caressed the faces of its passengers as the craft sliced through the water.

Shawn noticed some faraway islands perched on the ocean's horizon. "Grayson?" he asked. "I see there are other islands out there. Are they also kind of like, uh, weird, like the ones we just visited?"

"I don't know if 'weird' would be the right word," said Grayson, "but all are certainly different. Each has its specialty: there's the Island of Witches and Wizards; Dinosaur Island; the Island of Pirates; the Island of Monsters (not related to the cave monster); Science Island; Volcano Island; Bully Island—the Island of Bullies where the Special Guards came from—and a few more. Perhaps you and Cassie can return sometime in the future and see for yourselves."

"That would be cool," said Cassie.

"Yes," said Grayson, "'cool' as in a good thing, not a cold temperature, right?"

"You're catching on," said Cassie.

Grayson gave Shawn several minutes to enjoy his role as captain, then motioned him to take his seat next to Cassie and Ayeli. Grayson then stood, put his back to the railing, and faced his companions. "Cassie," he said, "I am curious: How were you aware that I could pull the sword from the boulder when the cave monster—much stronger than I—could not?"

"Yeah," said Shawn.

"Grayson," said Cassie, "you really don't know how you could do that? Shawn? Both of you?"

Grayson and Shawn shook their heads.

"I mean, it's like, so obvious," she said.

Grayson again shook his head.

"The Sword in the Stone?" said Cassie. *"King Arthur? Merlin? Excalibur?"*

Grayson shrugged. He was at a loss, as was Shawn.

"Well, in our world," Cassie explained, "there are stories about this kid, see, and he's the only one who could pull a special sword out of a stone. No one else could because the sword was meant for him—just him. He was destined to be *king*."

Grayson paused, then said, "I don't see where—"

"Oh, come on!" interrupted Cassie. "The jig's up, Grayson. I'm on to you: *You* are the Crown Prince! *You* are meant to be king of Transmongonia...*Your Highness!*"

Grayson's body stiffened at the words 'Your Highness.' He paused in silence for a few seconds.

"That's quite an accusation, my friend," he finally said in a gentle tone.

"I'm not *accusing* you, Grayson," said Cassie. "It's not like you're a criminal or anything. I'm just saying you are the Crown Prince. That's a good thing."

"OK, you *believe* I'm the Crown Prince," said Grayson. "What makes you think—"

"The way you took charge, for one thing," said Cassie. "When you had to, that is: like you did with Cyril the Giant, and the Light People, and—when you confronted the cave monster—the way you fought him with your sword. That was no 'meek little Grayson Humblebee.'"

"Yeah," agreed Shawn.

"And especially pulling the sword out of the rock," said Cassie. "I mean like, *duh!*"

"When you saw the sword," said Shawn, "You recognized it. I don't think we were supposed to notice, but we did. So, where have you seen it before?"

"Not in a museum," said Cassie.

"Not in a museum," agreed Grayson.

"And," said Shawn, "you whispered something, some sort of funny word, 'rex' something. The tree said that word too."

"Rexgladius," said Grayson.

"Yeah, that's it," said Shawn. "You said it kind of weird like—not like you were talking to *us*, more like you were talking to *it*, the sword."

"As if I were meeting an old friend after a long absence, perhaps," said Grayson.

"Yeah, like that," said Shawn. "Weird."

"In a way, the sword *is* an old friend. I have known it for a very long time."

"So, like, what does it mean, Rexgladius?" asked Cassie.

"I am afraid that if I tell you," answered Grayson, "I'll have to give up all pretense."

"You mean you'll have to be *yourself?*" said Cassie with her usual sarcasm, "What a shame!"

"Rexgladius: it comes from a language that is ancient to us," said Grayson, "and perhaps in your world as well. Roughly translated, it means *sword of the king.*"

"Aha!" said Cassie as she folded her arms and bore a smug expression on her face. "It was your father's sword!"

"It was," said Grayson. "Father taught me how to use it over many happy afternoons in the palace. He encouraged me to practice, hour upon hour. He was correct when he said that I might need it someday, though he hoped not. So yes, you have found me out: I *am* the Crown Prince."

"Yay!" said Cassie and Shawn together.

"Sounds like your dad was a neat guy," said Shawn.

Grayson smiled. "He *was* a neat guy."

"And you're a neat guy too," said Cassie.

"You are kind," said Grayson.

"Why did you pretend to be in hiding?" asked Shawn. "That's not very honest; I mean, like, you're not hiding from us; you're right here."

"The truth is," said Grayson, "I *have* been hiding. Not from you, not from The Great Rumpty D or anyone else, but from *myself.* From my...*responsibilities.*"

"You don't think you'll be a perfect king," said Cassie.

"That's right."

"Not as good as your father," said Shawn.

"I'm afraid that's true."

"Well, Grayson Humblebee, sir," said Cassie, "it's time to get over that nonsense. You're a good kid, a decent kid, and you're like, a *courageous* kid. You deserve to be king."

"But I am still a *kid*...too young to—"

"Grayson!" said Cassie sharply. "Hush! You're old enough to be king. You've got all the smarts and everything—more than most adults."

"Yeah," said Shawn.

Ayeli meowed as if in agreement.

Cassie paused, then said, "I have a secret for you. Ready?"

"Let me have it."

"Your father may have been an excellent king, a great king, but he wasn't perfect."

A slight frown appeared on Grayson's face.

"I mean," continued Cassie, "Shawn and I never knew him, obviously, but I can assure you, he made mistakes, had doubts, worried. I bet he probably even believed he should not be king sometimes. I mean, like, he was *human*—well, except for the pointy-ears thing—and humans aren't perfect. So, give yourself a break."

Grayson paused for a long time while Cassie and Shawn—and Ayeli—waited in silence. The Team leader placed his hands on his hips, looked down, then looked up at the sky. He turned and faced outward toward the Transmongonian mainland that was looming closer. He seemed lost in thought for a moment, then he turned and looked at his comrades. "It was Father's wish that I succeed him," he said, "that I become king, that I rule our people to the best of my ability."

He thought some more and then said, "OK, Miss Solskin, Master Solskin, I shall honor his wish. I shall hide no more!"

Cassie and Shawn cheered and clapped their hands. "Yay!" they shouted.

Ayeli walked over to Grayson and rubbed against his legs, purring with approval.

Cassie and Shawn took a few minutes to absorb the new revelations.

"So, do we call you *Your Highness*?" asked Shawn.

Grayson smiled. "*Grayson* will do," he said.

"Yes but, what if we *want* to call you something cool?"

"I have not yet been crowned, Shawn," said Grayson, "but it is proper to address a prince as *Your Highness*. Then, when he wears the crown, when he's king, *Your Majesty*.

"Those words sound so foreign to me," he added. "I suppose I must get used to them. Except that I still may not become king."

"Why not?" asked Cassie and Shawn in unison.

"Don't forget," said the young Crown Prince, fingering the keys suspended on the gold necklaces around his neck, "these keys are to reveal the three ultimate powers necessary to be king. I am to give them *personally* to The Great Rumpty D so that the powers can be first revealed to him—to *him*. That is the witch's order; I can't go against her. The Great Rumpty D may acquire even more power than he already has. Perhaps he will have magical powers. Or most likely, he'll have the ability to make himself king and have the crown stay on his head as he so desperately wants—"

"Yuck!" interrupted Shawn.

Ayeli hissed.

"Perhaps he'll just have me thrown in the dungeons," said Grayson, "never to be seen again. Who knows?"

"Or maybe even us? Could he throw us in the dungeons?" asked Shawn.

"Not if I have a say."

"You wouldn't let him?"

"I would be furious if he attempted to put you in the dungeons. You'd be amazed at what I can do when I am angry."

"We've *been* amazed," said Cassie. "Remember the cave monster?"

"I do."

"You've got a problem, Grayson," said Cassie.

"Oh? What is that?"

"You didn't say anything would happen if Rumpty D threw *you* in the dungeons, but if he tried to throw *us* in the dungeons, you wouldn't let him. All day you've been fearless in defending us, or the Light Princess, or Timelier when you thought the monster kidnapped him. And you even spoke up—not very loud, but you spoke up—when Rumpty D said bad things about your father."

"What about your mother?" asked Shawn. "What would you have done if he insulted *her*?"

"Oh," said Grayson, "I would have—I hate to think what I would have done. I think Rumpty knew, at some level, that if he uttered one disrespectful word about Mom, he would be in big trouble—not just from me, but from all Transmongonians. *Big* trouble. Everyone loved the king, but they were *crazy* about my mother!

"So Rumpty D was smart enough," continued Grayson, "to keep his mouth shut when it came to the most beloved lady in all Transmongonia."

"So, you defended your dad a little bit," said Shawn, "and you would have come down hard on Rumpty D if he insulted your mom, but you haven't stood up for yourself."

"You need to work on that," said Cassie.

"Yeah," said Shawn.

Ayeli growled and stared intensely at Grayson as if to reinforce his friends' command.

The Team leader slowly nodded, then rocked his head from side to side. His brow wrinkled, and his lips pursed. He was clearly contemplating Cassie and Shawn's—and Ayeli's— view of him.

"There's something that makes me kind of suspicious," Cassie ventured after a long pause. "The Wise Old Tree at the temple said the witch placed a bunch of names in a hat. And of all the names, *you* were selected to be the person to retrieve the Magic Keys. I mean, like, you're the Crown Prince; you're special. You're not just any Transmongonian."

"Probably not a coincidence," said Shawn.

"Right," said Cassie, "I think the witch wanted you—just you— to be the one. I think she rigged the name-picking thing like Rumpty D said."

"Yeah," agreed Shawn.

Ayeli sneezed.

"I don't know why the witch would do that," said Grayson, "unless perhaps she wanted me to fail. Maybe she wanted to get rid of me. After all, I avoided becoming king when that was my duty. It is my fault Rumpty D was able to gain power."

Ayeli made a sound between a sneeze and a snort. The Team members looked questioningly at her for a moment, and then Cassie continued her argument.

"Oh, give me a break, Grayson Humblebee, Your Highness," said Cassie. "Enough of putting yourself down. The witch picked *you* for a good reason."

"Yeah," said Shawn.

"You told us that although her curses cause people a lot of pain," said Cassie, "everyone ends up better off. She's the Good *or* Evil Witch, remember? Maybe a little more good than evil."

Ayeli meowed and licked her paw as though bored with the conversation.

"The witch didn't want you to fail, dummy," said Cassie affectionately. "She wanted you to succeed!" Cassie paused and then added, with a little less confidence, "I bet."

"Cassandra, Shawn," said Grayson in a tone slightly less gentle than usual, "I very much appreciate your faith in me. But to remind you: these keys do not hold the ultimate powers by themselves. They only *unlock* the chest that will *reveal* those powers, and that chest is in possession of The Great Rumpty D. *He* will be given the keys, and *he* will unlock the chest. *He* will be the first to know what those powers are, and *he* will almost certainly use those powers to make himself king and do whatever he wants."

Cassie defiantly folded her arms once more. "Hmph!" she muttered.

Shawn followed his sister's lead by folding *his* arms and echoing Cassie's "Hmph!"

"Mrrowwww!" growled Ayeli as though she, too, was annoyed with Grayson's resistance to reason.

An awkward silence prevailed until the Team reached the mainland. As the dolphins guided *The People's Boat* alongside the Topplesville dock, Cassie said, "We love you, Grayson…no matter how ridiculously stubborn you are."

"Yeah," said Shawn.

"Back at you," said Grayson.

Ayeli purred.

Chapter 13

Confrontations

Cassie and Shawn jumped onto the temple dock and secured the boat. Grayson and Ayeli followed. The dolphins exited their harnesses, headed farther out into the water, and resumed their joyful, child-like play.

Glert and Smert, the Special Guards the Team encountered in Queen Hyacinth's magical garden, were waiting on the dock. They stood side-by-side, blocking the Key Team from walking onto shore. They held their bulky arms across their chests defiantly.

"Why, Misters Glert and Smert," said Grayson, "how nice to see you again."

"Oh, now would 'ja listens to that, Smert," said Glert. "'How nice to see you,' he says. Ain't Liddle Geeky Humblebum here bein' so polite?"

Smert smiled and nodded his head.

"We'll take them keys," said Glert. In a mocking fake-polite, sing-song voice, he added, "if ya don't mind."

"Sorry," said Grayson, "I do mind. I am to give these to The Great Rumpty D personally."

"Says who?" asked Glert.

"Says the witch."

"The witch ain't here. She's—."

"*Isn't* here," interrupted Shawn.

"What?" snarled Glert as he glared at Shawn.

"As I told you before," said Shawn, "you shouldn't say 'ain't.' You should say *isn't* or *is not*. 'Ain't' is not proper grammar."

Shawn finished his lesson with a smirk.

"Mind yer business, kid," said Glert. "Anyways, like I says, the witch ain't here." The guard sneered at Shawn once more, emphasizing that he, Glert, was in charge. He turned back to Grayson. "The witch is vanished," he said.

"*Has* vanished," Shawn quietly whispered in a voice barely loud enough to be heard by Glert but still detected. Another brief sneer appeared on the brute's ugly face.

The Team leader purposely ignored the verbal battle between the eleven-year-old and his obnoxious yellow-eyed opponent. "The witch may be away," said Grayson to Glert and Smert, "but I'll adhere to her order nonetheless."

"Yer ta hand over the keys to us," said Smert, "on order of his Most Magnificent and All-Powerful Great Rumpty D."

"I don't wish to argue," said Grayson. "Please stand aside."

"The keys," said Glert.

"Oh, dear me," said Grayson. He drew his sword.

The dolphins stopped their play. Motionless and with considerable apprehension, they watched Grayson and his adversaries.

"Oh, look Glert!" said Smert, "Geeky Humblebum has a sword. Ain't that cute?"

"It is," said Glert. "Where'd you get it?" he said to Grayson. "You steal it? It's too fancy for a nobody like you."

"I think I've seen it somewhere before, Glert," said Smert, with a slight hint of concern in his voice. "Can't quite recall. Anyways," he said to Grayson, "you shouldn't be playin' with swords, Liddle Humblebum. They's fer adults."

"His name is Grayson Humblebee," said Cassie. "A lot of people call him Master Grayson. Actually, you should call him Your—"

"Oh, brave little girl," interrupted Glert. "I get it: You and yer brother here got the keys while yer *Master Geeky* stayed cowering in the boat, shakin' like a leaf. Ain't that so?"

"No, it is *not* so," corrected Cassie.

"Your grammar sucks," said Shawn to the guards.

"Y'know kid, Shorn er whatever yer name is," said Smert, "yer gonna have ta watch yer manners. Yer gonna be slaves, did'ja know that?"

"Yeah," said Glert, "after we get rid of Geeky Humblebum here, yer gonna be personal slaves fer The Great Rumpty D. No goin' back home for yous."

"So, Liddle Humblebum," said Smert, "ya let these kids do yer work fer ya, eh?"

Grayson glowered.

Ayeli, sitting by his feet, hissed at the bullies.

"Now, put yer fancy sword away and give us them keys," said Smert. Each guard drew his sword.

"Hey guys," said Cassie to the guards. "You better be careful. You don't you know who you're dealing with."

Smert and Glert chuckled.

"Gentlemen," said Grayson, "sheathe your swords, and I'll let you keep them."

"You hear that?" said Smert to Glert. "*Sheathe* our swords, he says. Sheathe! Must have some real classy upbringin' this one usein' words like that." The guards broke into serious laughter. "An' get this: he'll let us keep our swords!"

"He's oh-so-kind!" laughed Glert.

Both guards laughed so hard that tears formed in their yellow eyes.

"Gentlemen," said Grayson. "This is becoming annoying. I am afraid I must insist you put away your swords and allow us to pass." He turned sideways toward the guards and held his sword in front of him in a vertical position, ready for battle. "Perhaps you would like to meet Rexgladius," he said.

"Rex who?" asked Glert.

"Rexgladius."

"Never heard of him," said Glert.

"Sounds kind of familiar," said Smert, again with a shade of caution. "Who's this Rex-whatever?"

"Rexgladius," repeated Grayson, briefly admiring his sword.

"Oh," said Glert, "he's got a name fer his sword there. Rex-glady-something. How sweet!"

"Better look away," Smert said to Cassie and Shawn. "Ya shouldn't have ta see yer friend's head get chopped off like it's gonna."

Cassie and Shawn displayed not the slightest bit of concern. "You'll be sorryyyyy," said Cassie in a pleasant singsong voice.

Smert held out his sword with an outstretched arm and pointed it toward the sky for show. He then brought it to a horizontal position, lunged at Grayson, and swung it forcefully toward the Team leader's neck. Grayson, not wanting to engage in extended swordplay, met the guard's weapon mid-swing with Rexgladius and sliced it in half. Smert's hilt-less blade spun through the air and landed in the water, safely away from the dolphins.

Now it was Glert's turn. The angry Special Guard lurched at Grayson with his sword, and the Team leader, as he did with Smert, divorced Glert's sword blade from its hilt. The blade-without-a-hilt also tumbled into the water, with the dolphins still out of harm's way.

Glert and Smert, motionless and dumbfounded, gazed downward with their yellow eyes at their former weapons' now useless hilts. The two, tall, muscular, once-fierce bullies looked like pouting children on the verge of tears.

"Told you so," said Cassie. She exhibited a proud smirk.

"Now you're busted," added Shawn, also with a smirk.

Ayeli meowed happily.

"Gentlemen," said Grayson, "if you would be ever so kind, please step to the side of the dock." Grayson motivated them with his sword. "Closer. That's it. Now turn and face the water."

The guards complied and stood on the dock's edge.

"Are yer…yer gonna kill us?" asked Smert in a trembling voice.

"To be honest," said Grayson, "I hadn't thought of that. Something to consider."

"I can't swim," said Smert.

"Me neither," said Glert.

"Not to worry," said Grayson, "the water's not too deep."

"Hey!" said Smert. "I know! That sword, it's—and you're—"

Grayson did not wait for Smert to voice his belated recognition of Rexgladius or his overdue understanding that Grayson was the Crown Prince; instead, he placed a foot on the guard's behind and pushed. Smert let go of his sword's hilt, pawed at the air with his arms, kicked wildly with his feet, and splashed into the water.

Grayson stepped behind Glert. "Wait a minute," said the guard. "Wha' did Smert wanna say?" Glert did not receive an answer but instead experienced the well-deserved into-the-water treatment. His yelps and motions duplicated those of his colleague.

The two Special Guards—now not so special—disappeared below the surface of the Transmongonian Sea but quickly bobbed back up. They were able to stand on the sandy bottom and keep their heads above water—barely. They spit out goodly portions of the salty sea, coughed, and made pitiful attempts to swim.

Cassie and Shawn laughed, clapped their hands, and cheered with delight. The dolphins let out high-pitched, gleeful dolphin laughter as they stirred up the water in joyful celebration. Ayeli also meowed in a way that might be taken as laughter—to the extent that cats can laugh.

"Don't worry," Grayson said to the guards as he motioned toward the shoreline. "You can easily make it to the beach—eventually. Don't be in a rush."

He sheathed his sword.

* * *

The Key Team left the dock, headed up the path leading to the Rumpty D Temple, and ascended the temple's entrance steps. Morfo and Flippo, the two Special Guards who had met them on their arrival, hesitantly stood in their way and partially drew their swords. Grayson began to unsheathe Rexgladius as well. Having witnessed Glert and Smert's embarrassment on the dock, the guards knew better than to challenge the Team leader. They sheathed their swords and stepped aside.

"Thank you," said Grayson. "I appreciate that."

The Team walked onto the temple's vast floor. A crowd of several hundred Transmongonian citizens had gathered in anticipation of the Team's arrival with the Magic Keys. The crowd respectfully parted for the youngsters—and their feline teammate—as they approached the Rumpty D Stage at the temple's center.

Ayeli jumped on the stage, scampered to the Wise Old Tree, climbed up its trunk, perched herself on one of its thick upper branches, and settled in to watch the spectacle that was about to unfold. Grayson, Cassie, and Shawn also ascended the stage. They approached the dais that supported Rumpty D's throne and stopped a few feet away.

"Geeky Humblethumper, you've returned," said The Great Rumpty D, looking down with contempt from high on his perch. "How did you—where are Smert and Glert?"

"They went for a swim," said Shawn.

"They're a little wet behind the ears," said Cassie.

Rumpty D pointed at the entrance guards. "Morfo! Flippo!" he shouted. "Go get Glert and Smert and take them to the dungeons. They failed their duty."

The tyrant was not aware that the two entrance guards had deferred to Rexgladius. "Sir," responded Morfo loudly from his and Flippo's position at the temple entrance, "Glert and Smert did their best to stop—"

"SILENCE!" Rumpty D shouted. "I said, take them to the dungeons!"

"Yes, sir," said Morfo meekly, like a child commanded to do a tedious chore. He and his companion ambled down to the dock, where they would have to wait for Glert and Smert to slowly wade to shore. Morfo and Flippo's conspicuously leisure pace was an unusual sign of defiance against their egg-shaped boss. Fortunately for them, the ruler lacked enough understanding to notice.

Rumpty D turned his attention to Grayson. "I see you've got the keys," he said. "I wonder how you managed that. Doesn't matter. Guards, seize him, get the keys!"

Two Special Guards approached Grayson, who drew his sword and held it in a way that should have cautioned them. (They had not witnessed the defeat of Glert and Smert.)

"Kill him," ordered Rumpty D.

The guards drew their swords and commenced an attack. The Key Team leader allowed the guards—neither an accomplished swordsman—to chop, thrust, swing, and swipe every way they could to vanquish their younger, more athletic foe.

They were spectacularly unsuccessful in their effort. The weapons' *clang-clang-clang* sounds bounced off the temple's dome and marble floor. Grayson quite successfully demonstrated that he was, in fact, very much an expert swordsman.

Although the young Crown Prince had frequent opportunities to run Rexgladius through each of his foes, he chose not to. He was also aware that if his weapon severed the guards' swords completely, the loose blades tumbling through the air might be dangerous to the spectators. Thus, he applied just enough force with Rexgladius to cut into his opponents' blades so that mere threads of steel held them to their hilts. When the guards then moved their weapons even slightly, the severed pieces of metal fell with a *clunk* to the stage floor. Grayson glared at the guards and, with a firm grip on his sword, posed as if ready for more combat. The guards, now swordless, backed off.

Grayson approached the tall dais from which The Great Rumpty D had observed the fiasco (for the guards) unfolding below. Two Special Guards posted at the dais's base stood momentarily in Grayson's way. In light of the recent demonstration of the teenager's expert swordsmanship with the magnificent Rexgladius, they wisely chose to step aside and allowed Grayson to ascend the steps leading up to Rumpty D.

Standing a yard from the ruler, the Key Team leader raised his sword and carefully positioned its razor-sharp edge an inch above the wide-eyed, trembling tyrant. Grayson could easily have dissected Rumpty, but he declined the opportunity. The young prince then rotated Rexgladius and rested its flat side on Rumpty's head. While continuing to hold it there, he turned toward the audience and loudly announced for all to hear, "Hello! For those who don't know me—or have been forced to *pretend* not to know me—my name is *not* Geeky Fumblebum. Your exalted ruler here has ascribed that name to me as one in a list of colorful insults that are, I must say, quite imaginative. That roster includes gems like *Dumblebum, Bumblethorpe, Thumblebump…*"

Some in the crowd chuckled.

"…*Thirdlewop*," he continued, "*Humbledeedum, Feemlefopper…*"

The crowd started to laugh out loud. "…and," said Grayson, "perhaps my favorite, *Deedlewhopper.*"

The crowd laughed uproariously. Grayson allowed himself a chuckle as well. Cassie and Shawn were delighted to see him have so much fun. The Great Rumpty D did not laugh. He glared.

Grayson waited for the laughter to die down.

"My name," he continued confidently, "is *Grayson Humblebee.*"

The crowd erupted in cheers and applause. They had never heard this quiet, unassuming young man speak with such authority.

Grayson removed his sword from Rumpty D's head and leaned in towards the dictator with his face inches away from Rumpty D's. Looking straight into the dictator's startled eyes, Grayson quietly yet firmly whispered to his nemesis, "My name is Grayson Humblebee, but you can call me *Your Highness.*"

Grayson removed the keys from around his neck and handed them to Rumpty D. "On orders of the witch," he said and descended from the dais.

The dictator, his trembling having subsided, had his two personal bodyguards, Borzton and Flectinin, bring him the strongbox from the base of the dais. In it was the secret to the three ultimate powers for ruling Transmongonia. The guards held the chest as Rumpty proceeded to undo the three hinged locks keeping the lid shut.

Without Rexgladius lying on his head and Grayson safely at the bottom of the dais, Rumpty regained a bit of bravado. "Well, *Your Whateverness*," he said to Grayson in a voice purposely within earshot of all in the temple, "you've had your little show. Soon the secret to the ultimate powers, the most powerful and greatest of powers, the most glorious of powers, will be revealed, and they will be *mine!*" His attention constantly shifted between Grayson and the spectators, addressing both at once. "It is *I* who shall have those powers. It is *I* who shall have the adoration of all Transmongonians—"

A slight booing could be heard from the crowd. Rumpty looked out at the onlookers and glowered.

He now defiantly addressed his audience. "It is *I*," he asserted, "who shall have more power than even the witch herself, wherever she is..."

Ayeli hissed from her spot on the Wise Old Tree.

"...and it is *I* who shall be king, not Geeky Humble-whats-his-name here," said Rumpty. He looked down and sneered at Grayson. "And the crown *will* rest happily on *my* head!"

Ayeli snorted.

A few more boos could be heard.

Ignoring the boos and with a wide grin on his face, Rumpty unlocked the chest in excited anticipation like a child opening a

Christmas present. While Borzton and Flectinin continued holding the chest, the tyrant lifted its lid. A small piece of paper—a note—could be found resting on the bottom of the otherwise empty container. Rumpty withdrew the note and examined it. His cocky grin vanished. He furrowed his brow, squinted, and contorted his mouth. His expression indicated no understanding of what was before his eyes. He peered desperately into the chest to see if something else might be in it. He ordered his bodyguards to turn the chest upside down and shake it to see if anything might fall out.

No such luck.

He handed the note to the crownkeeper. "Here, read this," he said.

The crownkeeper, with the deep, pleasant, and refined voice of an educated man, read:

> *The secret to the three ultimate powers*
> *will be revealed*
> > *not in this chest*
> > *but in the quest.*
> *And the crown shall rest*
> > *on him*
> > *who meets the test*
> > *and is shown to possess*
> *the three ultimate powers*
> > *needed to rule this kingdom*
> > *with justice*
> > *which are*
> *Courage, Compassion, and Wisdom.*

"Give it to me," demanded Rumpty D as he snatched the poem back from the crownkeeper. Amazingly, the old gentleman did not appear bothered by such rudeness; in fact, he was smiling—if ever so slightly. He was doubtless aware of the message's meaning and its likely effect on his not-very-beloved boss's future.

"What is *this?*" asked Rumpty D angrily. He held the note with two fingers at arm's length as if it were a used Kleenex. "I don't understand: 'Not in this chest, but in the quest'? What nonsense is that?" He looked over at the Wise Old Tree. "Tree?" he said.

"Well, sir," answered the tree, "a mere container cannot hold the powers you desire so strongly. Nor can one possess them by simply reading words on a piece of paper."

"What?!" demanded Rumpty D.

"No, sir," answered the tree. "The secret to a just power—and I must emphasize a *just* power—was to be revealed not by the keys themselves but in the *quest* for the keys. That's what the poem means."

"You're not making sense. Axman! Order the tree to make sense!"

The Temple Axman tasked with guarding the Wise Old Tree had placed the heavy blade of his ax on the ground. He leaned on its long, upward-pointing handle as if it were a cane. With one leg casually crossed in front of the other, he looked like he was on the verge of performing a song-and-dance routine. He yawned, turned to the tree, and said in a calm, quiet voice, "The Great Rumpty D wants you to make sense."

The axman's passive defiance infuriated Rumpty. "AXMAN!" shouted the tyrant while pounding the arms of the throne with his puny fists, "I'll not stand for this insolence. Guards! Seize the axman and take him to the dungeons!"

None of the Special Guards responded. (Perhaps they knew that to do so would incur the wrath of young Grayson Humblebee and his mighty sword.)

Rumpty D let out a growling, angry sound: "Agghhhh!"

"Sir," said the tree to Rumpty D, "do you not recall that if the Crown Prince were to come out of hiding—"

"He's still hiding," said Rumpty D. He pointed at Grayson. "This kid, this Geeky Humble whatever, *thinks* he's the Crown Prince, of all things. But he's not. He's a fake, believe me. Sad!"

Rumpty held up his index finger. "Hold on," he said. He whispered an order to Borzton and Flectinin, the Special Guards holding the chest. The ruler stealthily motioned with his eyes toward Cassie and Shawn in a way only the guards would notice. The guards descended from the dais and set the chest down.

"May I continue?" asked the tree.

"Go ahead."

"As I was saying, Mr. D, perhaps I should remind you that the witch desired that if the Crown Prince should come out of hiding, and *if* he should demonstrate those qualities necessary to rule this kingdom—with justice—then he would wear the crown. He would be king. And you, sir, would have no role to play."

Borzton and Flectinin casually approached Cassie and Shawn, standing on the main floor a short distance from the stage. Unfortunately, Grayson was too focused on the conversation between Rumpty and the tree to be aware of the guards or ponder their intent.

"Humbledeedum is not fit to be king," said Rumpty D. "Oh, he can swing that fancy sword of his around, but without it, he's nothing."

The dictator gave a slight, barely perceptible nod to Borzton and Flectinin, now positioned behind Cassie and Shawn.

Borzton put an arm around Cassie's shoulders and held her tight. Flectinin put an arm around Shawn and held him firmly as well. The guards then drew knives and held them at the throats of the young Team members. The youngsters' eyes widened in fear. They silently gritted their teeth.

"Now watch," said Rumpty D to all assembled. "This will *prove* little Humperbumper is a fake." He motioned in the direction of the kids and their captors. An expression of anger appeared on Grayson's face. He moved toward his teammates with Rexgladius in hand but stopped abruptly, realizing that moving closer would endanger his charges. "Guards," said Rumpty D, "if Humbledum tries anything, slit the brats' throats."

The crowd grew silent.

"Now put your sword down, Humperthumper," ordered Rumpty D.

Grayson slowly and regretfully laid Rexgladius on the stage floor.

"Now back away," said his tormentor.

Grayson reluctantly stepped back from Rexgladius.

The Great Rumpty D looked out at the crowd with the smug expression of one who regards himself as superior and spoke to the gathering in a loud voice. "This...this *teenager* may act like somebody important or whatever," he said, "and he seems oh-so-brave with his sword, but without his sword, he's nothing but a sniveling, runny-nose coward. Now watch him quiver and shake. 'Oh please, oh Great Rumpty D,' he'll say, 'please don't hurt me, please? I'll do anything you want. Please, pretty please?' he'll say. Now watch him grovel at my feet. Just watch!"

During the dictator's rant, Grayson became aware that Captain Mackenzie, who had wished luck to his Team earlier in the day, was positioning himself behind Borzton, the guard holding Cassie. The Captain's lieutenant was similarly positioning himself behind Shawn's guard, Flectinin. Both guards, sensing the military men behind them and aware that sharp sword tips were none-too-gently poking their backs, correctly figured out that it would *not* make sense at this moment to remain loyal to Rumpty D or follow his orders.

Rumpty pointed to another guard standing near Grayson. "Xerloch," he said, "take your sword and run this, this Geeky Humple-whatever through. Finish him. Kill him!"

"My name," said Grayson, "is Grayson Humblebee." He exhibited not the slightest sign of the fear he actually felt.

Xerloch unsheathed his sword and stepped toward the prince, who defiantly stood his ground and calmly faced his would-be assassin. The guard hesitated. He looked at Rumpty D, at Grayson, at Cassie and Shawn and their former captors, and finally back at Rumpty D. "Sir," he said to Rumpty D, "this young man is not a coward. He is brave."

"He's faking it," said Rumpty D. "Kill him!"

"Sir," said Xerloch, "while it is true that I am from the Island of Bullies and we are a mean bunch, I choose not to murder this lad who is, without a weapon, brave enough to stand against me. Most of us bullies do not kill people, though there may be exceptions in this temple." He gave Borzton and Flectinin, still holding Cassie and Shawn, a nasty look. "And most—certainly those with honor—do not harm children," he added.

The two guards lowered their eyes as if ashamed.

"Do as you're ordered!" screamed Rumpty D to the defiant Xerloch. "KILL HIM! KILL HIM! KILL HIM!"

The guard sheathed his sword.

Grayson gave his would-be assasin a smile and a nod of appreciation. "Xerloch," said Grayson, "Transmongonians will remember you with gratitude."

With his sword pressed against Borzton, Captain Mackenzie slowly and silently separated the thug from his knife and sword. The lieutenant did the same with Flectinin. Shawn glared at his captor. "Jerk!" he said. The guard scowled.

"What is this?!" demanded Rumpty D. "Guards! Do your duty!" ordered Rumpty. "This is mutiny! I will have you sent to the dungeons!

"Or hanged!" He added.

Grayson unhurriedly picked up his sword and sheathed it.

The Great Rumpty D, in his anger, had not noticed that the crownkeeper was no longer attempting to keep the disobedient crown on the dictator's head but was standing a couple paces behind the throne, quietly cradling the crown in his arms. The crown was now still.

"Look," said The Great Rumpty D to the Wise Old Tree, "the witch said the three powers I should demonstrate consisted of something or other. What were they?"

"The powers the *future king* should demonstrate," corrected the Wise Old Tree. "That doesn't necessarily mean you."

"Of course it does!"

"The three powers," said the tree, "are courage, compassion, and wisdom."

"Oh!" said Rumpty D. "Those things. Easy! That's what I already have. That's me all over. Way more than this so-called 'Crown Prince' here, believe me. What was the first thing?"

"Courage"

"Yeah, courage. No one's braver than me. Look at all the dangerous enemies I had thrown in the dungeons."

"*Enemies*, sir?"

"Yeah. Dissenters, enemies of the state. Dangerous people. Bad hombres. Very bad."

"The only people you have imprisoned are those who *dared* to disagree with you."

"They challenged me! In public! Frightening, but I courageously stood up to them."

"You had your Special Guards stand up to them. That is not courage."

"Is so!" said Rumpty D. "What was the other thing? Com-some-thing."

"Compassion."

"That's it! Compassion. Yeah, I am compassionate, *so* compassionate. Example: who allows the prisoners to have bread and water every day? Every day! Geeky Humbledum here? No! Me! *I* do! And look, I give the prisoners a doughnut once *every week*. Talk about compassion!"

"I am quite certain that's not the sort of compassion the witch had in mind, sir," said the tree.

"I *am* compassionate," said Rumpty D. "Why do you think the people here love me so much?"

Someone in the crowd chuckled. Rumpty D glared at the gathering, unable to spot the source.

"When you say Transmongonians love you, sir," said the tree, "many do, but I believe you are greatly exaggerating the degree of their affection. Perhaps you should listen—"

"SILENCE!" shouted Rumpty D. "I don't like your tone, Tree. You're at risk of being chopped down when this is over."

The tree was challenging The Great Rumpty D in an unusually bold manner. Aware of the danger in which he might be placing himself, the tree frequently glanced at the axman to be assured he was not stepping over the line. The axman—never a threat—kept his weapon lowered and smiled to himself with each of the tree's confrontational comments.

"What's the other thing?" asked Rumpty D.

"Wisdom."

"Oh, right: wisdom. I am *so* wise. Yes, wise. Uh...I know! Who had the temple's name changed from *Temple of the People*—boring—to a more beautiful name, *Rumpty D Temple*. Beautiful! And not only that, I allow the Wise Old Trees to tell the magnificent citizens of Transmongonia about all the fantastic things I have done. No holding back! Wonderful! Fantastic! Wise! Wise! Wise!"

"Sir," said the tree, "let me enlighten you: Intolerance of dissent is not courage. Keeping prisoners barely alive is not compassion. Vanity (naming a temple after yourself) is not wisdom. If you permit, sir—or even if you do *not* permit—you are not even close to having those qualities necessary to be king; you are unfit. And in fact, you shouldn't be ruling this land at all."

"Axman!" shouted Rumpty D. "Chop that insolent tree down. He's not a Wise Old Tree! He's a Stupid Old Tree! Stupid! Stupid! Stupid!"

The Temple Axman stood erect and proud by the tree and raised his weapon with both hands to a horizontal position as if saluting The Great Rumpty D.

The tyrant did interpret the axman's gesture as a salute—an indication of loyalty, perhaps, before the guard was to bring the Wise Old Tree to an unhappy end. "Good man!" said Rumpty. "Bravo!"

Cassie and Shawn expected the worst: "No!" they screamed.

With a smile on his face, the axman winked at the kids and released his weapon from his hands. It fell to the ground. *Thud!*

Many in the crowd cheered, while a small number booed.

The axman leaned against the smiling tree, who gently laid a branch on the shoulder of his new best friend.

"AGGHHHH!" screamed The Great Rumpty D, enormously angry and frustrated. He pounded the arms of his throne with clenched fists. If his feet had been long enough, he would have stamped them on the floor, but he had to make do by kicking them wildly in the air like a two-year-old throwing a temper tantrum. The Special Guards around him patiently watched in silence. Most frowned, one or two smiled, and many shook their heads in disbelief. Grayson shook his head as well, displaying a slight smile as he placed his hands on his hips.

Cassie and Shawn chuckled.

Grayson approached the axman and quietly asked, "What is your name?"

"Vorian, sir," whispered the axman.

"We will not forget your courage," said Grayson.

Rumpty D finally calmed down.

Suddenly, an idea occurred to the egg-shaped ruler: He scanned the crowd, which had grown significantly. "People of Topplesville," he shouted in an insincere, fawning voice. "Wonderful people of Topplesville! I just realized—this is all *fake!* This so-called Crown Prince here—Geeky Thumple whatever—does anyone know for sure he's the Crown Prince? I mean, *really?*

"Yes, he handed me some pretty keys, but they were useless, did diddly squat. They turned up a so-called poem that revealed zilch. Do you think the little good-for-nothing got them from the One-Eyed Giant and the others by himself? No! He had his little friends here get them. What did he do while they were doing *his* job? He hid! Stayed behind in his boat, shaking and quaking. It's all rigged! Fake! And by the way, where is the so-called witch? Probably hiding as well. Went back to the Island of Witches and Wizards. Hooked up with a wizard or something, afraid we'll find out her curses don't work. Yeah! She's a fake too! So look, *nobody* saw Geeky Humber whatever and his little friends get the keys, did they? No! No witnesses! Of course, the brats here—Crissy and whatever—they'll say Humbledum was oh-so-brave. They'll say anything. They're in love with the guy. Besides, they just wanna go home, believe me. Sad!

"I'll say this for Humperdump: he's sure got a lot of people fooled, like most of you folks—you're so nice—fooled the Special Guards too, the soldiers, the trees. And those poor kids. Fooled 'em all. Very smooth, he is. Well, I say throw him in the dungeons! Lock him up!"

Someone in the crowd shouted, "Lock him up!"

Others began to chant, "Lock him up! Lock him up!"

Within seconds, more—but still a small minority—joined the chorus:

"Lock him up!"

"Lock him up!"

"Lock him up!"

The chanting, loud as it was, was suddenly interrupted by a much louder, growling, high-pitched **MEOWWWWW!** emanating from a certain cat perched high on a branch of the Wise Old Tree. The crowd fell silent. All eyes turned toward the cute, furry creature with black-and-white markings and emerald green eyes. All wondered how an ordinary *cat* could issue such a piercingly loud screech that echoed throughout the temple.

Ayeli the Cat suddenly puffed up like a balloon. While retaining her black and white coloring, she morphed into a taller shape that no one could recognize. Then, within seconds, she transformed into a person that *everyone* recognized!

The crowd gasped.

"Ohmygosh!" squealed Cassie. "It's the witch! Ayeli was the witch—the Good or Evil Witch—all along!"

Black silhouettes of leaves and flowers against a white background decorated the witch's tall, broad-brimmed and pointed hat. Her long blouse supported abstract swirling black and white shapes that echoed nearly identical shapes covering Ayeli the cat. Patterns of small white flowers adorned a wide black belt wrapped around the witch's waist. She wore flowing loose-fitting black slacks that could be mistaken for a skirt. The contrasting black and white tones were appropriate for a witch with a 'good or evil' reputation, but her physical appearance was the opposite of what one would expect for a witch: She did not possess decaying, cracked teeth or the green, wrinkled, wart-covered skin of an old hag. Instead, she was a beautiful young woman with a smooth coffee-and-cream complexion like that of Hyacinth the Flower Queen. Long shiny black hair flowed over her shoulders. Her eyes retained Ayeli's emerald color and appeal, but they were now human-like, no longer those of a feline.

The witch looked down and smiled at the remaining Team members then left her place on the tree and soared midair over the crowd, wand in hand, smiling at all the citizens and soldiers on the main floor. She floated over the stage and greeted nearly all, including the guards, with the same smile.

She did not, however, smile at The Great Rumpty D.

She glided to the Key Team. Her pleasant manner put all three members at ease. With her warm, gentle hands, she held those of the Crown Prince. "Prince Grayson," she said in a soft voice. Grayson smiled and bowed his head. Next, she took Cassie's hands into hers. "Cassie," she said.

"Ayeli? Witch? Miss Witch?" asked Cassie.

"Perhaps you would like to call me Serina," answered the witch. "That's my given name."

Finally, she held Shawn's hands with the same grace. "Shawn," she said.

"You've got some explaining to do," said Shawn bluntly.

"Indeed, I do," said Serina. "Not only to the three of you but to all assembled here." She paused a moment, then said, "Perhaps we can chat later, but for now, I must speak to the people. If you'll excuse me…"

She floated above the stage, slightly above eye-level with Rumpty D and a yard away from him. Looking upon the gathering crowd and motioning at the dumbfounded dictator, she said in a loud, clear voice, "Citizens of Transmongonia, I realize some of you regard this *being* as a great leader, and you are entitled to your opinion. But most of you know that you have been ruled for too long by this egg-shaped tyrant who likes to call himself The Great Rumpty D."

In a quiet aside, she said, "I hate to compare him to an egg; that seems so disrespectful to eggs."

Many in the crowd laughed.

Returning to her louder voice, she said, "Powerful as he is, his ambition has been to gain even *more* power and become king. But, as our friend the Royal Crown-Keeper will attest, the crown itself has been most uncooperative in fulfilling Rumpty D's wish. It seems the crown—a rather independent thing—does not want to rest on the head of a ruthless ignorant thug, and it refuses to do so. I must say, I am impressed!"

Some in the crowd clapped, and others shouted, "Hooray for the crown!"

Rumpty D sat still throughout the witch's address. Sullen, tight-lipped, arms folded across his chest, he quietly smoldered with suppressed anger.

"Most of you," continued Serina the Witch, "know Grayson Humblebee here as a quiet, timid young man. And you like him—of course you do. He is a *nice* young man. But up until now, his identity has been 'hidden.'" (The witch held up her fingers as air quotes, indicating that Grayson's secret is not so secret.) "Contrary to what Rumpty D would like you to believe—has *forced* you to believe— Grayson is, in fact, the *Crown Prince*."

"Yay!" shouted someone in the crowd.

"And he is," said Serina, "the true heir to the throne."

A few more yays.

"But let me be clear," said the witch, "Grayson could not *rightfully* wear the crown until he possessed the necessary qualities to do so—as stated so clearly in the poem dismissed by our current ruler. Let us be honest: Young Grayson has not come across as the kingly sort in the past. He has allowed Rumpty D and others to bully him. While the young prince may always have been compassionate and wise, those aspects of his nature have not been easy to see. Before his parents went missing months ago and Rumpty D came to power, Grayson never took advantage of his position, never held himself above anyone, never acted like a prince. That humility was admirable in a way, but when it became necessary for him to be king—to be *kingly*—he attempted to mask his true identity. Grayson 'went into hiding,' fearful that he could not live up to his father's magnificent qualities, afraid that he would be discovered as a *fraud*—wholly incompetent to be king.

"And the Ovoid imposter who currently sits on the throne, *hoping* to be king, magnified poor Grayson's insecurities with one insult after another. Made him wear that silly hat and dull clothes. Worse, the ruler and his thugs forced *you*, my friends, to go along with his cruelty by making you pretend not to recognize Grayson as Crown Prince. Those who disobeyed Rumpty's decree, those who chose to acknowledge the truth, now reside in the dungeons, as you well know.

"Transmongonians, you must not feel guilt for participating in Rumpty D's charade. With swords of the Special Guards at your throats and the threat of imprisonment, you had little choice.

"And we cannot judge Master Grayson harshly for failing to assert himself as the rightful heir to the throne. Grayson is young. He cannot be blamed for being unaware of his true potential."

The crowd muttered a sympathetic "Aww."

"Now," continued Serina, "I had long suspected that our young prince did possess royal traits, but I could not be certain. So, I arranged a test, whereby he would be sent on a dangerous mission, along with two people from the other world, to recover the Magic Keys. Posing as a harmless cat along for the ride, I could easily judge whether or not Grayson measured up—"

"I knew it!" interrupted Rumpty D, finally having the nerve to challenge the witch. "The test *was* rigged! I knew it! I knew it! I knew it!"

"Depends on what you mean by rigged," said Serina. "Recall that you selected a piece of folded paper—one of many in a hat—and Grayson's name happened to be on that single piece?"

"Yeah, so?" asked a scowling Rumpty D.

"I never claimed there were *different* names in the hat," answered Serina. "Surprise! It turns out *every piece* had Grayson's name!

"Well, perhaps I did fudge—just a smidgen," she said. "I am known as the Good or *Evil* Witch, after all. The plan had to be reasonably secret. I do apologize for that. Now, if you will allow me to get back to the main discussion, Mr. D."

Rumpty D returned to pouting.

Serina went on, "In the manner that Grayson related to his youthful companions, confronted the One-Eyed Giant, challenged the Voids, and exposed the cave monster, I saw in Grayson great courage, gentle compassion, and profound wisdom.

"Here is an example of his character: Just minutes ago, you witnessed him laying down his sword to prevent the younger Team members from being harmed. He did so, believing he would almost certainly perish, yet he was willing to sacrifice his own life for those of his precious friends. I saw him do the same thing when the cave monster gave him an identical, awful choice—surrender his sword *and his life*—or watch the children die. Without hesitation, he laid down his sword and bravely prepared for the end.

"My heart swelled," she said, "when I witnessed Grayson give his entire vial of healing nectar to the dying beast and *comfort* a creature who had just threatened to tear the young prince to shreds. He did that with the same uncommon compassion and gentleness he demonstrated to all throughout the quest.

"Would The Great Rumpty D have done this for anyone?" she asked.

"No!" shouted a few in the crowd.

"Does The Great Rumpty D even *care* for anyone?"

"No!" shouted a few more.

"Does he care for you?"

"No!" shouted most.

"My friends," said Serina, "Grayson has convinced me that he is fit—more than fit—to be king of Transmongonia!"

The crowd clapped and cheered—including those who had previously chanted 'Lock him up.'

"The question is," asked Serina, "does *Grayson* know he is fit? His quest for the Magic Keys was much more than a test—and this is so important—I wanted Grayson to discover that *he* had those great qualities within him of which he was not aware.

"Oh, my goodness!" said the witch, interrupting her train of thought. "We have a visitor!"

Chapter 14

Comeuppance

Serina pointed toward a giant pulling a massive rowboat onto the beach next to the Topplesville dock. The crowd turned to see what attracted Serina's attention. People near the edge of the temple who could see the giant gasped in fear.

"Soldiers!" shouted Captain Mackenzie. "Ready the cannons!"

Soldiers rushed to a half-dozen cannons positioned on the dockside of the temple. They hurriedly primed the weapons with packs of powder and cannonballs and swiveled the artillery in the direction of the giant. Additional soldiers took positions beside temple columns and aimed their muskets at the intruder who had yet to finish beaching his boat. With his back to the temple, he was unaware of preparations to quickly end his existence.

Civilians in the crowd retreated to the side of the temple opposite the weaponry.

"Prepare to fire!" shouted Captain Mackenzie.

Waving their arms in the air, Cassie and Shawn ran to the captain. "DON'T SHOOT! DON'T SHOOT!" they pleaded.

"Steady…" shouted the captain to his men.

Grayson bounded up the dais supporting the throne and stood by Rumpty D. "HOLD YOUR FIRE!" he shouted. "The giant means no harm. I know him. His name is Cyril!"

"I know him too," shouted someone in the crowd. "Cyril is a good giant!"

"No, he isn't!" shouted Rumpty D. "Kill him! KILL THE GIANT! KILL—"

Grayson pressed his hand over Rumpty's mouth, silencing the tyrant's outburst.

A Special Guard ascended halfway up the dais to intervene on Rumpty's behalf but thought better of it when, it is assumed, he considered Grayson's abilities with a sword. With shoulders slumped, the would-be-rescuer-of-tyrants backed down.

Captain Mackenzie briefly turned toward Grayson, acknowledged his command, then turned back to his troops. "Gentlemen," he ordered, "hold your fire! Disarm your weapons and stand down. We have no quarrel with this giant." The soldiers set aside their muskets and returned their cannons to their previous, non-threatening positions.

Sounds of relief could be heard throughout the crowd. They moved to the temple's seaward side to observe the new visitor.

Cyril finished beaching his humongous boat. He walked up the beach and crossed the lawn to the temple. Recognizing that the cannons had been pointing at him and, noting the general look of apprehension among the citizens, soldiers, and even the Special Guards, he held up two fingers in the universal peace sign and said, in his friendliest voice, "Don't worry, folks. I am not going to hurt anyone. I just want to see Master Grayson and his young friends." He stopped at the edge of the temple; he was too large to walk onto its floor. Many people near him moved a safe distance away.

Cassie and Shawn were left alone on the temple's edge to face the giant. Cyril looked at them, smiled, and nodded his head. The young Team members responded to him with relieved grins. A soft "Awww" could be heard from Transmongonians in the crowd who could see the exchange. They were impressed that these youngsters from another world were not afraid of the giant.

Grayson removed his hand from Rumpty D's mouth and looked at it with an *Ew, yuk!* expression then wiped the tyrant's slimy saliva on his pant leg. He gave his nemesis a look that said, in effect, *Stay still, don't say a word*. Rumpty D did start to say something but, noticing that Grayson's hand had come to rest on the hilt of Rex-gladius, the ruler held his tongue. Grayson descended from the dais, hopped off the stage, and joined his teammates and Cyril.

"Grayson, Cassie, Shawn," said Cyril with his deep rich voice, "it's good to see you again."

Serina the Witch floated over to join the group. "Witch," said Cyril, "I can't say I am delighted to see you, but greetings nonethe-less."

"Thank you for that," said Serina. "I think."

Cyril was wearing a fresh change of clothes, was clean-shaven, and looked quite handsome. But that was not his most obvious change of appearance: "Cyril," said Cassie, "where's your eye patch?"

"I left it at home," said Cyril. "I don't need it anymore. My eyes work together now."

"That's great!" said Cassie.

"How are you?" Shawn asked the giant.

"Wonderful!" said Cyril. "I am on my way to see Krythelia and our families in Giantistan—the continent, not the Island. I think she'll have me back now that I am my old self again."

"You can count on it," said Serina.

"I wanted to stop by first and apologize for being so rude to the Key Team," said the giant.

"You weren't so bad," said Shawn.

"You think so?" said Cyril. "Glad I wasn't as brutal as I could have been. And I wanted you to know I didn't intend to hit you with that rock when you were going out to sea. The truth is, I didn't want to see you leave. I knew I would miss you."

"Awww," said Cassie and Shawn together.

"So, like," said Cassie, "how did your eyes get fixed?"

"Interesting you should ask. They started working when the curse was lifted."

"So, the witch put a curse on you just like the Voids and the cave monster?" asked Cassie as she gave the witch a nasty look.

"That's what made you so grumpy?" asked Shawn.

"I don't know about the other folks, but yes. The Good or Evil Witch here put a curse on me that made me act even more mean-tempered than I was—so mean-tempered that no one would be likely to be nice to me. But it was set up so that, if someone *was* nice to me, the curse would be lifted."

"If someone showed you *compassion*," said Serina.

"Yes." Addressing the Key Team, Cyril said, "Despite all my nastiness, you three wrote that kind note. You wished me well. Amazing!"

"The note was Cassie's idea," said Grayson, never wanting to take too much credit for himself.

"That may be true," said Cyril, "but, Grayson my friend, you agreed and put your name to it, even though I threatened to chop you to pieces. When I saw the note after you left, I felt the affection you and your friends expressed, and the curse went away. Just like *that*. Poof!"

"We are so glad," said Grayson.

"So, I wish to thank you," said Cyril.

"For what?" asked Grayson. "We didn't—"

"For making the curse go away!"

"Oh," said Grayson, "well, you're welcome."

"But it wasn't just the three of you," said Cyril, "there was a fourth: Ayeli, the cat. Where is she? I was mean to her as well—*very* mean. I hope she is OK."

"Oh, she's *definitely* OK," said Cassie. "Turns out Ayeli the Cat was not a cat, but the Good or Evil Witch *pretending* to be a cat. She came along for the ride to see how Grayson behaved."

"Serina, the witch?" said the giant. He looked at Serina. "*This* Serina? Seriously?"

"Seriously," said Serina.

"My goodness!" said Cyril.

"Or evilness!" he added.

"You know," he said to Serina, "The curse you put on me produced a lot of pain. I'm a little angry with you about that. But I suppose I owe you some thanks too, in a roundabout way. Maybe. I mean, while I always loved my wife, having the curse made me realize, even more, how vitally important she is to me. So, I guess I can thank you for that."

The witch acknowledged Cyril with a nod and a smile.

"I should add," said Cyril, "that color came back to the plants and flowers by the path on my island. And they are much more agreeable."

"Oh, by the way," added Cyril, "four Special Guards are outside, sitting on the beach by the dock. Two of them are very wet. None appears to be happy."

"Yes," said Grayson. "Morfo and Flippo were sent to retrieve Glert and Smert, who apparently slipped off the dock. And no, I suspect they are not happy. Perhaps they are contemplating their role in life. I suggest we let them be. No need to humiliate them further."

* * *

The witch rose, hovered over the large crowd in the temple, and addressed them: "You heard from the giant himself how Grayson— and these lovely children—lifted Cyril's curse by merely being nice to him despite Cyril's bad manners. A curse on the nasty Voids was also to be lifted in the unlikely event someone showed them compassion. Without hesitation, Grayson and his young companions risked their lives to save the life of King Valdoc's toddler despite the king's evil intent to sacrifice the Light princess. The compassion of these three—not to mention their courage—helped the Voids regain their rainbow colors and reconnect with the White Light People.

Shouts of "Yay!" and "Well done!" and "Nice work!" were issued from the crowd.

"Finally," continued Serina, "I put a curse on a Youneverknow lad that transformed him into a mean and brutal monster who suffered a near-fatal blow while fighting Grayson. And what did Grayson do? He gave his entire vial of healing nectar to a creature who had threatened to tear him to shreds. The nectar healed the creature's wound, and the monster changed back to the healthy boy he was all along. Grayson may assume it was the nectar that did this. He is *partially* correct: The nectar did heal the wound, but it was Grayson's kindness—his compassion and love for another creature—that lifted the cave monster's curse."

Shawn patted Grayson on his back.

Many in the crowd cheered and clapped.

"You see," said the witch, "Grayson has more than adequately met my test. He has—"

"What about wisdom?" interrupted Cassie. "You said wisdom was necessary. I think he's wise, but what do you think?"

The Great Rumpty D, who had purposely been ignored for some time, chimed in: "Yeah," he said, "what about wisdom? Klinker Thumper has never said anything wise in his life!"

The witch continued ignoring Rumpty and floated down near Cassie. "Well, Cassie," she said, "compassion *is* wisdom. But indeed, Grayson demonstrated his wisdom more than once on the quest, as when he suggested that you hold off on judging the Voids because one never knows what is in another's heart. Or when he understood that violence was not in Timilier's true nature and forgave him despite the boy's having been a monster only minutes before. Or, Cassie and Shawn, when he suggested you both would someday stop hating each other and be friends. *That* is wisdom."

"So true." agreed Cyril the giant.

"No, it's not!" snapped Rumpty. "Anyone can say sappy nonsense like that. Only I...uh—"

A cold, silent stare from Serina cut the dictator's claim short.

The Good or Evil Witch then floated once more above the crowd. She asked Grayson to return to the stage and stand on the third step of the dais, well above the heads of the Special Guards. A pouting Rumpty D remained perched on top. Serina addressed the Crown Prince in a way all could hear: "Grayson, Your Highness, in your quest for the Magic Keys, you proved to me that you have all the traits necessary to be king—traits in abundance, I must say. But, more importantly, I believe you have discovered within yourself qualities of strength you did not know you had, that you have gained enough confidence to take your place on the throne and govern the people of Transmongonia. Is that so?

"I do feel more confident, yes," said Grayson. "But I am humbled as well."

"And are you ready to accept your responsibilities as king?"

"I am."

Serina spoke to all assembled. "People of Transmongonia: before His Highness, Grayson, can wear the crown, you, the citizens, must consent to his rule. Do you so approve?"

A citizen shouted, "Hooray for His Highness!"

Another yelled, "Hip, hip, hooray!"

And the whole crowd echoed:

> "Hip, hip, hooray!
> Hip, hip, hooray!
> Hip, hip, hooray!"

And then the crowd of citizens, including Captain Mackenzie's soldiers, erupted in loud cheers and clapping that lasted for several minutes. Cassie and Shawn joined them. So did the Wise Old Tree's axman, whose happiness set him apart from the other *unhappy* Special Guards. The Great Rumpty D was especially distraught. His grumbling and complaining could not be heard above the people's jubilant noise, which added to his agitation.

Cyril the Giant restrained himself from shouting and clapping as loud as he wished since doing so would send disruptive shock waves throughout the temple.

The Wise Old Tree, still with a branch on his axman's shoulder and being elderly and serene, simply smiled with satisfaction.

The crownkeeper permitted himself to deviate from his usually dignified manner and did a little jig.

When the noise finally died down, Serina motioned toward the egg-shaped tyrant still sitting alone on the throne, then turned to Grayson and said, "Your Highness, I believe there is official business that needs your attention."

"There is indeed," said Grayson. He once again hopped onto the stage and bounded up the steps to the top of the dais supporting the throne and Rumpty D. The Crown Prince looked out upon the crowd and said, "Transmongonians, there is something you should know about your current ruler's past. Mister Tree?"

The Wise Old Tree, in a voice unusually loud for a tree, addressed the crowd. "That creature," he said, pointing a branch at a scowling Rumpty D, "who thinks of himself as The Great Rumpty D, did not merely emigrate from Egg Island, the island he claims to know nothing about. Instead, he *escaped* from that island because he was awaiting trial for the attempted murder of his cousin, Humpty D."

All in the crowd gasped.

Cassie and Shawn looked at each other and giggled. They still could not be serious about something that had the makings of a nursery rhyme. Grayson ignored their momentary lack of respect. The tree, with his keen hearing, did hear them but did not mind. He was, after all, a *wise* old tree.

"Young Humpty D," continued the tree, "is a *prince*, son of the king of Egg Island. A fine young man, beloved by all who know him—with the exception, as you might guess, of Rumpty D, who was tormented with profound envy of Humpty's status and the affection he received. Rumpty's jealousy—the pain of it—finally drove him to attempt to end his cousin's life.

"But he failed, fled the Island of Ovoids, and seized an opportunity to rule Transmongonia. It was here he believed he could not only be the supreme leader of your homeland; he could become *king*. Yes, the wish for more power drives him, although there is not much more to be gained. And yes, he was motivated by the assumption that the royal crown would rest obediently on his head, although that is doubtful. But what drives him above all else is his belief that, as king, he will *tower* over Humpty, a mere prince who will have to bow to *him*. And, he believes he will not only be admired but *loved* by all whom he governs.

"*That* has been his greatest desire.

"And his greatest delusion."

The crowd became quiet.

"And now," said the tree, "His Highness, Master Grayson Humblebee, has emerged to spoil Rumpty D's cherished dream. It is no wonder Mister D has devoted so much effort these past months into keeping our brave Crown Prince from ascending to the throne as he so richly deserves."

* * *

Grayson, who continued to stand beside Rumpty, spoke to the captain: "Captain Mackenzie, in my recently acknowledged position as Crown Prince of Transmongonia, I am requesting that you place this...this pitiful tyrant under arrest. He is to be held until he can be returned to Egg Island, or I should say, *the Island of Ovoids*, where his trial will resume and where his guilt or innocence will be fairly determined. Afterward, we will ask the good people of that island to send him back to us, where he will stand trial for any number of abuses against the citizens of Transmongonia."

The captain had two men ascend the stairs to the throne and attempt to pick up The Great Rumpty D. They had an awkward time of it. (Human-sized, egg-shaped beings are not easy to handle.)

"Use his pillow," shouted Shawn.

"Excellent idea," said the captain, who sent a third man to assist with the removal. Holding onto the corner tassels of Rumpty D's plump pillow, the first two soldiers lifted the pillow with Rumpty D on it as the third soldier steadied the prisoner to keep him from tumbling to the floor.

Not that anyone would have minded.

As the soldiers gingerly carried Rumpty D down the dais stairs, the deposed ruler complained bitterly. "Hey!" he shouted. "You can't do this! *I* am the one meant to be king. Not Geeky Humper-whatever. No! Me! I alone possess those powers granted by the Magic Keys. Passion and courage and stuff! Me! Special Guards! Do something!"

Rumpty's guards did nothing. In the presence of Captain McKenzie's highly skilled soldiers, there was nothing they *could* do.

"Your Highness," said Cyril the Giant to Grayson, "as it happens, I will be sailing—well, rowing actually—near Egg Island on my way to Giantistan. I would be happy to transport Mister D to his people. I have room in my craft."

"That will be most appreciated," said Grayson.

"Soldiers," said the Crown Prince, "perhaps you could place Mister D with his pillow near our friend, Cyril the Giant—the *two*-eyed giant, I'd like to add."

"Hooray for Cyril!" someone shouted.

Temple Soldiers transported Rumpty D down from his position atop the dais onto the temple floor and headed toward the grand building's exit. As they did this, the angry despot vainly attempted to strike and kick his escorts and ranted at those he regarded as enemies.

"You'll be sorry, Humperdump," he yelled to Grayson. "You just wait!

"And you, witch! What a fake you are! What a scam! This whole thing's a scam, believe me. Sad!

"And you, you brats—Casser and Shant or whatever—you'll be sorry too."

The soldiers carefully put the pillow, with the *former* ruler still on top, next to Cyril on the grass outside, near the temple's edge. Then, to keep Rumpty from rolling over, they gently tilted him so that he lay with his back on the pillow, facing up.

The now Not-So-Great Rumpty D flailed at the air with his arms and legs like a trapped beetle.

Cyril leaned over and quietly said to the wannabe king, "Be good now, and don't say a word. Remember, you are just the right size for my breakfast omelet." The giant looked at the people watching him, smiled, and winked. Rumpty folded his arms across his chest (such as it was), crossed his legs, and pouted.

"Cyril," said Serina, "you're staying for the coronation?"

"Coronation? Why yes, that would be such an honor!"

"Grayson, Your Highness," said Shawn, "the Wise Old Tree by the Garden said Rumpty D had put dissenters—people who disagreed with him—in the dungeons. What about *them*?"

"Good point, my young friend," said Grayson, who turned to the Temple Soldiers' leader. "Captain," he said, "there are prisoners in the dungeons who should not be there. Before we proceed with the coronation, could you have your soldiers release them?"

"That would be my pleasure," said the captain. A couple of his soldiers moved to a trap door on the temple floor, not far from the stage. The soldiers opened it and descended the stairs leading to the dungeons. Within a short time they emerged, followed by a dozen bedraggled Transmongonians. The prisoners' clothes were worn and they had obviously not been given enough to eat. The men among the dissenters had grown beards. Although the overhead dome shaded the temple's interior, the light was much brighter than in the underground cells, and it made the prisoners squint and cover their eyes. The freed captives appeared a little confused, but they were all smiling. The citizens on the main floor greeted them joyfully with smiles, handshakes, laughter, cheers, and hugs. Some were old friends. Some were family.

Xerloch, the guard who refused Rumpty D's order to slay Grayson, ascended the dais. "Your Highness," he quietly said, "what will become of us, the Special Guards?"

"Your fate is not for me to decide," said Grayson. "That will be the role of the Citizens' Council. My guess is that all of you will be held accountable in some manner but not held in the dungeons—which I plan to have sealed shut and closed forever. Let me say to you, Xerloch, that it was courageous and noble of you to defy Rumpty D's order to run me through with your sword. It took special courage to do so in front of the other guards who might have thought less of you. I shall certainly ask for leniency on your behalf. I imagine that after you and the other guards have been punished in accordance with our law, you will be returned to Bully Island."

Xerloch bowed. "I understand," he said.

Grayson turned to the Temple Axman and spoke in a loud voice so that all could hear. "Vorian," he said, "you have failed miserably in your duty as the Temple Axman for the Special Guards."

Vorian lowered his head.

Cassie, Shawn, and several in the crowd issued a deep-throated "Aww" out of sympathy for the axman and disappointment with Grayson's apparent harshness.

"Not only did you refuse to chop down the Wise Old Tree as ordered by your ruler," continued Grayson, "you *befriended* the tree! Furthermore, you *insulted* The Great Rumpty D by faking a salute then dropping your weapon. I should add that you have even smiled and waved at my companions—yes, I saw you—in defiance of your role to be an intimidating wielder of your ax. By your actions, you have demonstrated that you are in no way a bully, nor were you ever qualified to be a Special Guard, let alone an Axman for the Special Guards.

"Because of your attitude, many or perhaps most of the Special Guards here will revile you and most likely bully you—severely—should you return to Bully Island."

One could hear grumbling and quiet boos rising from the otherwise silent onlookers.

"It is also your contrary attitude," said Grayson with an unexpected smile and pausing a few seconds for effect, "that endears you to us Transmongonians. Therefore, when I am king, I shall decree that there be *no* punishment for you whatsoever and that, if you wish, you be allowed to remain here on the Transmongonian mainland in peace."

Vorian raised his head and beamed. Now understanding the meaning of Grayson's words, the crowd cheered and applauded, as did Cassie and Shawn.

While the freed prisoners connected with other Transmongonians, Shawn signaled to Serina that he wanted to speak to her. She floated over to him. "Explaining to do?" she asked.

"Yeah," said Shawn. "You seem like a nice lady, so why are you so cruel? I mean, like, you made Cyril and the Rainbow People and the kid, Timilier, suffer so much. Why didn't you just make them happy and have them give the keys to Grayson?"

"That is an excellent question, Shawn. If it were possible to make all the people in Transmongonia happy all the time—and all in your world as well—I would do that. But I can't. I'm just a witch, and my power is limited. I am obligated to obey the rules of the universe, and those rules say that if there is to be happiness, there must also be sadness and pain.

"Yes," she continued, "Cyril and the Voids and Timilier suffered from my curses, but they came out stronger and more at peace as a result. You heard Cyril talk about his renewed affection for his wife. You saw the Light People reunite after being apart for so long. And you witnessed how Timilier realized that he truly loves his mom and dad—"

"And they love him," said Shawn.

"Yes," said Serina, "they love him."

"I still don't like what you did."

"I know, dear."

"Are you going to say I'll understand someday?" asked Shawn. "That's what Mom and Dad would say."

"I'll spare you that. You must tire of hearing it."

"Yeah," agreed Shawn.

"Still," said Serina, "your mom and dad did a great job of raising two fine children."

"Thank you," said Cassie and Shawn together.

Chapter 15

Coronation

Serina smiled and floated back to the dais with Grayson standing beside the empty throne. "Transmongonians," she said to all, "it is time for—"

Serina's speech was interrupted by a familiar *clickity-clack-clickity-clack* of unicorn hooves on the temple's marble floor. The small herd appeared, followed by the almost-out-of-breath Spenerton, the unicorn wrangler. Cassie, as could be expected, jumped up and down, clapped her hands, and squealed with delight. Cassie was only a bit more enthusiastic than Shawn, who was also excited to see the beautiful creatures.

"Oh, my goodness!" said Spenerton when he saw Grayson on top of the dais. "It's you, Grayson, I mean, Your Highness and, oh my goodness—" He saw Serina as well and said, "You're...you're the Good or Evil, I mean...um!"

Spenerton became aware of the empty throne beside Grayson. "Some people were running all over the village," he said, "and shouting…and, oh my gosh! So it's true: The Great Rumpty D has been—he's gone! And it's true, sir, Your Highness, you're going to be—oh my goodness!"

Grayson smiled, as did Serina. They were charmed by the unicorn wrangler's awkward excitement.

"Sir, Your Highness," said the wrangler, "and Miss Witch, I am so sorry the unicorns barged in like this. I couldn't keep them inside the corral. I think they wanted to be part of this, this big moment in our history. They're so excited! I'll get them back to the corral at once."

"No-no," said Grayson. "Allow them to stay. I will be very much honored by their presence."

"Yay!" shouted Cassie.

"And your presence as well, Spenerton."

"Oh, thank you, Grayson, I mean, sir, Your Highness."

The unicorns mingled with the crowd. They tossed their heads and whinnied and snorted in delight from the loving attention shown by Transmongonians, soldiers, and (of course) Cassie and Shawn. Even Serina, in an un-witch-like gesture, floated down to the unicorns and petted them. Most of the Special Guards showed—or pretended to show—no interest in the creatures. Finally, Spenerton herded his charges together and positioned them an appropriate distance from the stage. There they remained, respectful and quiet, for the ceremony to come.

Serina floated back to be by Grayson atop the dais. The Good or Evil Witch addressed the crowd once again. "Transmongonians, as I was saying before this delightful interruption, it is time for the coronation. To officiate the ceremony, I shall summon a lady more qualified than I." She waved her hand midair in front of her. A beautiful, sparkling swirl of violet and white mist appeared then evaporated, leaving Hyacinth the Flower Queen in its place.

The crowd cheered and clapped. Hyacinth smiled and bowed. She acknowledged Cassie and Shawn, who grinned with delight.

"It is such a pleasure to see you," said Queen Hyacinth to all. "Dumlock, the axman who was guarding the Wise Old Tree by my garden, is on his way here. He has left his ax behind.

"Shall we begin?" she said.

"If you will first permit me," said Serina the Witch. She hovered in front of Grayson and waved her wand up and down in front of him. Suddenly His Highness was wearing a magnificent bright red velvet cloak with a snow-white collar and gold trimmings. A fine shirt, pants, and shoes composed of the finest materials replaced his peasant clothing. He was now dressed as a king should be.

The crowd oohed and aahed with approval.

"You may proceed," said Serina to Queen Hyacinth.

"Thank you, dear sister," said the Flower Queen. Then to Grayson, she said, "Your Highness?" She motioned him to take his seat on the throne. She signaled to the crownkeeper, who, crown in hand, approached Grayson and stood behind him. "Master Grayson Humblebee," said Hyacinth, loud enough for all to hear, "you have shown yourself to possess the three most important qualities in a leader: courage, compassion, and wisdom. Now you are about to assume a most responsible and noble position. Will you, as king, rule this kingdom honorably, with equality, justice, and mercy for all?"

"I will," said Grayson.

"And will you obey the laws of this land as faithfully as would any citizen?"

"I will."

"And will you be willing to sacrifice your personal welfare for that of the people?"

"I will."

Hyacinth nodded to the crownkeeper. Then, smiling and with an air of integrity befitting his position, the gentleman slowly and gently placed the crown on Grayson's head. The crownkeeper removed his hands and stepped back. The bejeweled adornment remained still and calm on the king-to-be, apparently content with its new host.

"Sir," said Hyacinth to Grayson, "you have the right to take on a name of your choosing. What say you?"

"Perhaps I should first check with my advisers," said Grayson. He looked at Cassie and Shawn.

"I still like *Grayson*," said Cassie.

"Me too," said Shawn.

"Well then," said Grayson, "I shall retain my name of Grayson but will add Edwin as my middle name to honor my noble father and our great king."

"Then, by the power vested in me," said Hyacinth, "I hereby designate you, Grayson Edwin Humblebee, King Grayson the First, Ruler of Transmongonia and All Its Dominions."

The crowd broke out in thunderous applause and cheering. Someone shouted, "Long live the king!" Another Transmongonian did the same. Soon the whole assembly was chanting:

> *"Long live the king!*
> *Long live the king!*
> *Long live the king!"*

Cassie and Shawn chanted with them, then clapped their hands and jumped up and down for joy.

His Majesty, King Grayson, stood and addressed the crowd. "Ladies and gentlemen," he said, "boys and girls, citizens of Transmongonia…" He looked at Cassie and Shawn and smiled Warmly, "…and special guests."

Both Cassie and Shawn blushed and returned the smile.

"As my first official act," he continued, "I would like to perform the Ceremony of Knighthood." He withdrew Rexgladius from its sheath.

The crownkeeper—now the official *Royal Crownkeeper*—displayed a broad grin as he withdrew a long red satin pillow from a small compartment on the floor behind the throne. He laid it at the feet of the king. Grayson looked at his admiring companions and smiled. "Cassie and Shawn," he said, "please come forward." With a bit of apprehension, the young Key Team members ascended the dais steps to the throne and stood before the king.

"Please kneel," said Grayson.

The children kneeled side by side on the pillow. They looked at their beloved Team leader, smiled, and bowed their heads. "Your *Majesty*," said each. Cassie and Shawn briefly looked at each other and held hands.

The king held Rexgladius vertically in front of him. He first spoke to Cassie. "Mistress Cassandra," he said, "on this day, you, together with your brother, demonstrated compassion, courage, and wisdom—more than could reasonably have been asked of you—and in so doing helped to reveal truths that have benefited all of Transmongonia." His Majesty gently touched Cassie's left shoulder with the flat of Rexgladius's blade, then her right shoulder, then the top of her head. "For this, I dub thee Dame Cassandra Solskin, Knight of the Realm."

The king turned to Shawn. "Master Shawn," he said, "on this day, you, together with your sister, have demonstrated compassion, courage, and wisdom—more than could reasonably have been asked of you—and in so doing helped to reveal truths that have benefited all of Transmongonia." He gently touched Shawn's left shoulder with Rexgladius's blade, then his right shoulder, then the top of his head. "For this, I dub thee Sir Shawn Solskin, Knight of the Realm."

During the ceremony, Cyril the Giant wiped away tears. Tears welled in the eyes of nearly all Transmongonians present as well—citizens and soldiers alike. Drops of pitch appeared in the eyes of the Wise Old Tree.

Most of the Special Guards preferred to scowl. Still, there were exceptions: Xerloch, the Special Guard who refused to kill Grayson, could be seen dabbing his eyes and Vorian, the Temple Axman who became chums with his Wise Old Tree, shed tears profusely without embarrassment.

Rumpty D, still involuntarily lying on his back on his pillow just outside the temple—and still guarded by Cyril—rolled his eyes but remained silent.

Cassie and Shawn stood and released each other's hands. They curtsied and bowed, respectively, before His Majesty King Grayson. Then they turned, beaming, and faced the crowd. Grayson stepped between them, took their hands, and raised their arms together like politicians in our world do when celebrating an electoral victory.

The crowd, having been silent throughout the ceremony, once again erupted in loud and enthusiastic cheers, applause, and laughter.

As whoops and shouts from the crowd in the temple subsided and more people in Topplesville became aware of the good news, bells in the town hall and churches began to chime, and the distant roar of people cheering throughout the village could be heard.

* * *

Cassie, Shawn, and King Grayson the First descended from the dais. Serina the Witch and her sister, Queen Hyacinth, floated down alongside them and mingled with the crowd.

The late-day sun was sinking toward the horizon. Its rays reached under the temple dome and bathed all in a bright orange glow. "Grayson, sir, Your Majesty," said Shawn, aware of the late hour, "I think it is time for us to go home."

"My brother is right," said Cassie.

"Let's say goodbye to the Wise Old Tree first," said Shawn.

Cassie and Shawn walked over to the tree. As they did so, the remaining members of the crowd respectfully parted and bowed. Cassie and Shawn nodded in return. The Wise Old Tree smiled as the children approached. "Thanks, Tree," said Cassie, "for telling everybody about the Magic Keys and the ultimate powers and all that stuff."

"And for standing up to Rumpty D like you did," said Shawn. "That was awesome."

Cassie and Shawn each wrapped their arms around the tree—as much as possible, that is. He hugged them back—as much as a tree *can* hug.

"And thank you," said the tree, "for all you have done. I know the other trees feel the same. And by the way, give my regards to the cottonwood in your backyard."

Cassie and Shawn were taken aback. They did not quite believe the Wise Old Tree would know *their* tree but smiled and nodded in acknowledgment nonetheless. "Will do," said Cassie.

The children looked apprehensively at Vorian. The *former* axman gave them a reassuring grin. He then held out his arms, inviting a hug. And sure enough, Cassie and Shawn accepted his invitation and embraced the tall, bald, muscular, yellow-eyed, never-was-a-bully.

Serina floated to Vorian and kissed him on his cheek, causing a bright red blush to appear on the former axman's face. As the blush faded, the chalk-white coloring of his body transformed into a more human light tan. The Good or Evil Witch then briefly pressed the warm palm of her hand against Vorian's creepy yellow eyes. After she withdrew her hand, Vorian blinked his tear-filled eyes several times, and with each blink, the yellow hue gave way to expressive brown irises surrounded by a normal white color. The appearance of Vorian thus became that of a *human being*—albeit a very tall, bald, and muscular human being.

With pointy ears.

As could be expected, Cassie, Shawn, and several Transmongonians who witnessed this miracle clapped and cheered.

The children rejoined Grayson, Serina, and Hyacinth. The five of them walked to the temple's edge and descended the steps to the lawn. Cyril the Giant was waiting.

A few Transmongonians descended from the temple floor and joined their heroes.

The Great Rumpty D—or rather, the *former* Great Rumpty D— could be seen still lying with his back on his pillow, continually rocking side to side, beetle-like, in an unsuccessful attempt to sit up, and grunting with each effort. Occasionally he would glance, or rather scowl, at those who had just bested him. As if to rub salt into Rumpty's wound, a citizen approached the former dictator, bent over him, and growled: "Grrrr!"

Transmongonians no longer feared the tyrant.

"Serina," said Grayson, "it is time for the children to return home."

"I know," she said. "But first, there is something I'd like to present for your viewing pleasure," She floated up to the side of the temple's dome where the words **RUMPTY D TEMPLE** were inscribed. Then, she floated around the entire circumference of the rotunda and, with her wand, restored the engraving to its former name: **TEMPLE OF THE PEOPLE**.

The small gathering of citizens outside who could see this transformation cheered. Serina returned to the lawn with the soon-to-be-disbanded Key Team and the others.

"Miss Witch, Serina, I have a request," said Shawn.

"Yes, dear."

"Could you like, uh, send us back a little in time before we broke our dad's flowerpot?"

"We're going to be in big trouble," added Cassie.

"I am afraid I cannot do that," said Serina. "I would love to help you, but 'rules of the universe,' remember?"

"Aww," moaned Cassie and Shawn together.

"Just be truthful and admit your mistake to your father," said the witch. "I am sure you will be fine."

"OK," agreed Cassie and Shawn without much enthusiasm.

Serina waved her wand. A whirlwind of particles, accompanied by the beautiful wind-chime-like sounds, formed themselves into a doorway—the same doorway through which Cassie and Shawn had entered this world.

The kids walked up to the giant. "Cyril," said Cassie, "I am so glad to have met you."

"Yeah," agreed Shawn. "Good luck with Krythelia and all that."

Cyril the Giant crouched down and offered his hand. Using his thumb and index finger, he gently squeezed Cassie and Shawn's hands as if holding flower petals. "You have brightened my life," he said.

"And you have sure made a big change in ours," said Shawn.

The siblings walked over to the sullen Rumpty D. "Mister D," said Cassie as she looked down at him, "it's been, well, interesting. Can't say it's been a pleasure."

"Hmph!" grunted Rumpty D.

"You need a serious attitude adjustment," said Shawn.

Cyril lifted the former dictator, together with the tyrant's pillow, and commenced carrying him to his rowboat. Cyril was careful as he did this, but Rumpty D showed no gratitude and instead resumed his rant: "They've rigged that trial that's gonna be in Egg Island!" he screamed. "Fake! It's all rumors, fake rumors! I wasn't even there. Besides, the little creep—Humpty or whatever—had it coming! If I did do it, which I did not, it was an accident! Everybody on Egg Island hates me, they're jealous of me, and they're out to get me because I'm so smart, a genius."

The sound of Rumpty's grouching faded with each of the giant's steps away from the Key Team and the temple.

Cassie addressed Serina the Witch. "Miss Witch... Serina... Ayeli," she said, "I'm not sure I liked how you did it, but thanks for helping Grayson realize he could be king."

"Oh, I merely set the stage," said Serina. "Much of the young prince's new confidence was *your* doing, dear—you, Shawn, and Grayson himself." Cassie threw her arms around Serina, as did her brother.

The kids turned to Hyacinth. "Miss Hyacinth, uh, Your Majesty," said Cassie as she reached up and touched the colorful wreath of flowers still perched on her head, "thanks for everything, especially my flower crown."

"Yeah," said Shawn. "It's really pretty."

"That it is," said Grayson, who had been mostly silent.

Cassie curtsied, and Shawn bowed to Hyacinth.

Grayson—His Majesty—opened the magic door. Through it, Cassie and Shawn could see their backyard where their adventure had all started. His Majesty the King stood by the door, waiting for the kids to exit. Both siblings threw their arms around him and gave him a long, tight hug. "Oh," said Cassie, "Your Majesty, Sir—"

"Just call me Grayson. After all, we are pals. The title is not necessary."

"Grayson," said Cassie, "we are so proud of you. We are so glad you found yourself…and that you got to be king…and you got rid of that awful egg and—we love you, Grayson," said Cassie.

"Yeah," said Shawn.

"And I love you too," said the king. "Both of you."

Tears appeared in the eyes of all four members of the Key Team: Grayson, Cassie, Shawn, and the former Ayeli, now Serina the Good or Evil Witch.

"I'll remember you always," said Grayson, "with great fondness. Thank you so, so much for helping me find my way."

Chapter 16

A New Threat

Cassie and Shawn reluctantly released the embrace of their beloved companion, then bravely waved and smiled at their Transmongonian friends. Smiles and waves met them in return. The siblings walked through the portal to their world then turned back for one last look. Grayson forced a smile that did not adequately hide his bittersweet sorrow. He waved a final goodbye and quietly closed the door.

As it had earlier, the mysterious doorway separated into large chunks of wood that disintegrated into thousands of tiny bits that became swirling dust. Finally, the remains of the opening to the weird, wondrous, topsy-turvy world of Transmongonia vanished completely. The accompanying sound of wind chimes faded to silence.

As Serina the Witch had promised, Cassie and Shawn were returned to their world at the same time they left, with the sun holding the same position in the midmorning sky. As far as the youngsters were concerned, they entered Grayson's world hours earlier, but only seconds had passed in Boulder.

They walked onto the patio. Cassie felt a movement on her head and touched her flower crown. A slight crackling noise could be heard. Within seconds, the crown's petals, leaves, and stems—lovely and fresh moments ago—dried out, separated, floated away, and disappeared into thin air.

"Aww!" said the young adventurer, unhappy she could not keep a souvenir of her and Shawn's exhilarating and scary experience even though the siblings understood that the rules of their world were different than those of Grayson's.

Their dad's scattered flowers, dirt, broken pot, and shattered pedestal were as they had left them on the patio. Cassie said, "We better get this cleaned—uh-oh!"

They heard their father drive into the garage and close the garage door.

"We're busted," said Shawn.

Despite having courageously faced a host of dangers in Transmongonia, the former Key Team members now froze in fear of a possible new threat: *an angry parent!*

Through the kitchen window that opened onto the patio, Cassie and Shawn could see Mr. Solskin as he set bags of groceries on the kitchen counter. Then—terror!—they saw him look at them, pause, and move away from the window. Within seconds, he was on the patio, surveying the wreckage.

"What is this?" he asked with a hint of anger in his voice.

"That's a pedestal," said Shawn, "or it *was* a pedestal."

"Those are pieces of the pot you made," said Cassie.

"Flowers," said Shawn, pointing at the flowers scattered across the patio.

"Dirt," said Cassie.

"Very observant," said Dad. "I mean, what happened?"

"It's my fault," said Shawn. "I tried to scare Cassie with my basketball. I thought it would be funny."

"I didn't think it was funny," said Cassie. "I grabbed the ball and threatened him. He backed up against the pedestal, and it fell over."

"It fell over all by itself?" said Dad.

"I knocked it over," said Shawn.

"But I pushed him into it," said Cassie. "It was my fault. Sorry, Dad."

"Yeah," said Shawn. "Sorry."

Mr. Solskin cocked his head. "Excuse me?" he said, "Who are *you*? And what have you done with my children?"

"I'm Cassandra," said Cassie, her forehead winkled and teeth gritted with puzzlement. "You usually call me Cassie."

"I'm Shawn," said Shawn, equally apprehensive. "You usually call me Shawn."

"Oh, really?" said Mr. Solskin. "You do seem familiar, except that *my* children would blame each other for this mess. They'd be at each other's throats! But I didn't hear you blame each other; in fact, I think I heard you each take responsibility for your actions. This makes me very suspicious."

The kids half-smiled.

"Very funny, Dad," said Cassie.

"Yeah," said Shawn.

"So, like, we're busted?" asked Shawn ruefully.

"Grounded?" asked Cassie, the wrinkles in her forehead signaling worry.

"You certainly *should* be grounded," said Mr. Solskin.

With their shoulders slumped, Cassie and Shawn grimaced and lowered their heads.

"However, there *are* mitigating circumstances," said their father.

The kids looked up at him.

"You took responsibility for your actions," he said. "And—remarkably—you didn't blame each other—amazing! First time in the history of the world!" He paused a few seconds for effect, then said, "Because you demonstrated such maturity, I am suspending your sentence…this one time."

"Yay!" shouted Cassie and Shawn together.

The manner in which their father spoke reminded Cassie and Shawn of Grayson's sophisticated and gentle way with words.

* * *

Mr. Solskin returned to the house. Cassie and Shawn removed the evidence of their earlier mishap with a broom, dustpan, and a wastebasket.

"Do you think we should tell Dad about Grayson and Transmongonia?" asked Shawn.

"No," said Cassie, "he will never believe us."

Shawn looked at the giant cottonwood. "Remember how the Wise Old Tree in the temple said to say hello to this cottonwood? Do you think this tree is *wise*? Do you think it and the Wise Old Tree *really* talk to each other?"

"I Don't know," said Cassie. "Let's find out…

"Hey, tree," she said. "Hi…hello? Can you understand us? The Wise Old Tree from Transmongonia—the one at the temple—sends greetings."

They waited, but the tree did nothing, said nothing.

"Oh well," said Cassie.

"Tree," said Shawn, looking up at his basketball still perched in the branches high above, "can you give me my ball back?"

Again, the tree said nothing, did nothing.

"Worth a try," said Shawn.

They turned from the tree. The siblings heard a sound like a gentle wind coming from the tree's leaves and branches.

Yet, they could not feel a hint of a breeze.

They turned back toward the cottonwood. Its leaves rustled—ever so slightly. Its upper branches swayed—just a little bit. The kids looked up to see Shawn's beloved ball roll off the quivering limbs, tumble down from branch to branch, and end its journey in Shawn's outstretched arms.

"Ohmygosh!" said Cassie.

Shawn stood with his ball, silent for a moment, then said, "Cool! Thanks!"

The tree said nothing, did nothing.

The kids took a moment to consider what they had just witnessed. "Do you think, like, the tree really heard me?" asked Shawn.

"Uh, maybe," said Cassie. "Or maybe there was just a breeze that made the basketball come down."

"Guess we'll never know," said Shawn.

Chapter 17

Epilogue

Cassie and Shawn rested in the shade of the giant cottonwood, their backs against the tree's mighty trunk. As the bright Boulder sun slowly made its way across the clear blue sky, the sister and brother contemplated the day's magnificent adventure.

"Do you think Grayson will invite us back?" asked Shawn.

"I hope so," said Cassie. "I'd like to see some of those other islands."

"Yeah," said Shawn. "But let's stay away from the Island of Bullies."

"Agreed."

The siblings remained still for several minutes.

"Grayson said he was upset to see us fight," said Shawn.

"I know."

"He said we'd be best of friends someday."

"I know."

"He said we might even be *fond* of each other."

"That's a stretch," said Cassie.

"So, do you think we'll at least *like* each other someday?" asked Shawn.

Cassie contemplated the idea for a few seconds. "What do you think?"

"Nah," said Shawn.

Cassie smiled.

They remained under the tree for several more minutes in pleasant silence.

"I had a thought," said Shawn. "Grayson was sent to our world to find two people 'brave enough and smart enough' to help him recover the Magic Keys. Surely there are people in Transmongonia who could have done what we did."

"You would think so," agreed Cassie. "But maybe not."

"What if our job was not just to help Grayson get the keys," continued Shawn, "but to help *him* realize he had all those nice qualities. Maybe only *we* could do that. Maybe there's something special about us. So, maybe Serina the Witch sent him to get us—just us—even if Grayson didn't know that was her plan."

"Hmm," muttered Cassie.

"There's more," said Shawn. "Maybe Serina planned to have Grayson help *us* too. I mean, we really didn't like each other before he showed up, and he helped us see each other as—"

"Cool," interrupted Cassie.

"Yeah. Cool."

"Remember when the magic door first appeared," said Shawn, "and I saw Ayeli, the cat? She looked at me like she was inviting me to step through the door, and I followed her—almost like she had me in a spell."

"Maybe it *was* a spell," said Cassie. "Ayeli was a witch, after all."

"Yeah," said Shawn. "And then you followed. So maybe we were *meant* to go to Transmongonia and help Grayson, and he was meant to help us."

"Good point, little brother," said Cassie.

"That sneaky witch!" she added.

She gave Shawn a gentle bump with her fist on his shoulder. He returned the gesture with equal softness.

* * *

Shawn Solskin returned to the front of the house to continue his basketball practice. Cassandra Solskin returned to the patio table to resume creating art, but she hesitated before sitting down and walked around the house to the driveway in front. She asked her younger brother if she could join him.

"You bet," he said.

The two shot hoops until it was time for lunch. Cassandra, being older and more experienced, was able to give Shawn some pointers.

They did not become best friends that day, but they were no longer mortal enemies either.

And that felt right.

—END —

Acknowledgments

I owe special thanks to:

- Professional copyeditors Maureen Bernas and Jennifer Lien, whose creative input made this book a much, *much* richer work than it otherwise would have been. *Extra special thanks* is owed to Ms. Bernas, whose devotion to this project has been, despite minimal compensation, extraordinary!

- Jennifer Conder, Associate Director of the Denver Publishing Institute. DPI is a post-graduate department at the University of Denver devoted to training students for the world of publishing. (https://liberalarts.du.edu/publishing) Ms. Conder led me to the happy discovery of Mses. Bernas and Lien

- Middle-grade "copyeditor" Grace Rabinowitz, as well as middle-graders Michael Gerber, Kristi & Lena Gitkind, Sylvie Jones, Elle Pitts, and Thomas Russell. These young people, with their exceptional intelligence, insight, and creativity polished this work even further

- My adult kids, Cimarron and Shane, for continually pushing me to unleash my talent.

- My big brother Don, who has encouraged, protected and supported me since we were kids.

- Peg Finucane for continuing encouragement and support.

I owe a debt of gratitude as well to Judith Mohling, high school teacher Patricia Bartlett, and many others.

— *Spencer Nelson*

Text for this book first written with Microsoft Word, then finished with Adobe InDesign. Illustrations are by the author, prepared with Adobe Illustrator, Photoshop, and InDesign.

About the Author

Spencer loved engaging in creative endeavors since he was a toddler. His skill in generating paintings, drawings, and photographs brought recognition throughout all K-12 grades. As a teenager, he received awards in city and state-wide art competitions. He spent hours drawing fantasy art and producing comic strips — some in 3D! In high school, he wrote a short science fiction story solely for the fun of it.

Love of the movies drew him to study filmmaking at the University of Southern California. He subsequently made award-winning TV commercials, business films, and training films for a dozen years.

In the early 2000s, after too much time inventing machines for industry, he turned his attention to his true calling: art and writing. Collectors and clients now display his paintings and commissioned artwork in living rooms throughout the country. Recognizing a universal interest in weird creatures among the young and not-so-young, he wrote and illustrated an art instruction book, *How to Draw Monsters and Aliens* (see next page).

He fabricated bedtime stories decades ago for son Shane and daughter Cimarron when they were youngsters. Among his imaginings was the kernel of an idea that became *Quest for the Magic Keys*. The story has since expanded and changed mightily.

With a daughter's unrestrained admiration, Cimarron has been relentless in pushing her father to finish the book. Although Dad worked on the piece off and on for years, he finally set aside his notorious ability to procrastinate and became obsessed with completing *Magic Keys*. Finally, after revising umpteen drafts, he honored his daughter's wish.

The author's favorite pastimes include movie-watching, road trips, hiking, sharing board games with his family, and swing dancing. He currently lives near Boulder in Broomfield, Colorado.

Made in United States
North Haven, CT
06 September 2022

23742432R00141